And when I thi[...] children shivering [...] about old, gray ho[...] have somehow had Evil implanted in them, and about crying in empty rooms, about cold spots, warm spots, hot spots, hounds out of hell, men who hang themselves again and again and again.

And it's all true.

I *know* that it's all true.

But there's a shitload more going on over there, over on the Other Side, than any of us can imagine. And some of it's very interesting, very entertaining, but some of it smells bad—some of it stinks, in fact—and if you tried to put your finger on it, if you tried to pin it down and say, *yes, definitely, this is what it's all about, this is what Death is all about; sit back now, I'll tell you,* my God, they'd swarm all over you like angry bees, the dead would, like angry bees.

T. M. WRIGHT
A Manhattan Ghost Story

GOLLANCZ HORROR

First published in Gollancz paperbacks 1990
by Victor Gollancz Ltd
14 Henrietta Street, London WC2E 8QJ

British Library Cataloguing in Publication Data
Wright, T. M.
    Manhattan ghost story.
    I. Title
    823'.914[F]

    ISBN 0-575-04684-8

Printed and bound in Great Britain
by Cox & Wyman Ltd, Reading

DEDICATION

For Dorian
and for Phil Zaleski

BOOK ONE

CHAPTER ONE

When I think of a ghost story, I think about children shivering around a campfire while an aging man with a long, austere face summons up—in resonant, wonderfully spectral tones—the way the misdeeds of the dead will soon be visited upon the living, and I think about old, gray houses that have somehow had Evil implanted in them, and I think about rocking chairs that rock all on their own, and about crying in empty rooms, about cold spots, warm spots, hot spots, hounds out of hell, men who hang themselves in attics, and in cellars, again and again and again.

And it's all true.

I *know* that it's all true.

But there's a whole lot more going on over there, on the Other Side, than any of us can imagine. And some of it's very interesting, very entertaining, but some of it smells bad—some of it stinks, in fact—and if you tried to put your finger on it, if you tried to pin it down and say, *Yes, definitively, this is what it's all about, this is what Death is all about; sit back now, I'll tell you*, my God, they'd swarm all over you like angry bees, the dead would, like angry bees.

I came to New York, six months ago, on the Amtrak out of Bangor, Maine. I didn't need to take the train, I could easily have afforded to fly, but the hard truth is that I'm scared of flying, and trains are romantic, after all. And I have long been a romantic.

On the way down, I sat next to a woman in her early thirties who was wearing a very abbreviated miniskirt. Miniskirts were just then on the tail end of their comeback, and since this woman had long and well-muscled legs, with a lovely, soft, even color to them, and since her miniskirt had hiked up considerably around her thighs, the trip was very enjoyable.

No, it wasn't.

There was no woman in a miniskirt. That's just a tacky, sexist fantasy I like to indulge in. It has variations. The woman is wearing no underwear; the woman *is* wearing underwear, but it's see-through; the woman can't keep her hands off me—nice fantasies that push the truth away, if just temporarily.

When I got on in Bangor, the car was three-quarters full, and I entertained the idea that I'd get to ride all the way to New York—a full twelve-hour journey—with both seats to myself. In Lewiston,

Maine, however, five people got on—a handsome older woman in a tweed suit; a teen-age girl who was doing a lot of giggling; a fortyish man with thinning dark hair who was wearing a gray, pin-striped suit, carrying a briefcase, and trying hard to look important; a fat, middle-aged woman who breathed heavily and coughed every few seconds; and a young guy with a backpack and trendy mustache.

Guess who decided to sit next to me?

Listen, I've got a story to tell. You like spooky stories? Well, this is *very* spooky, about things that crawl and things that slither and things that go bump in the night.

Ever been to Manhattan? I have. I live here, and I want to tell you that there's more going on than meets the eye. Lots more.

Because Manhattan is, in reality, two cities—twin cities, sort of—and in one of those cities people move from place to place in search of a number of things (in search of employment, in search of food, in search of a place to sleep, or someone to sleep *with*, or a good show, a building to jump out of, shoes to buy), and in the other city people do pretty much the same kinds of things, only they do them for very different reasons.

And if you get stuck in that other city, that other Manhattan, you find yourself getting awfully desperate and mean-spirited, the way some people are affected by too much heat or the crying of small children.

And you get scared, too. Scared enough to give up even going to the bathroom, because you're not sure what you might find in there.

My name is Abner W. Cray and I'm thirty-three years old. I'm tall; I have sandy blonde hair, and before I came to Manhattan, I was a few pounds overweight. I've been told that my eyes are my most expressive feature, which is a nice thing to have said but which is true, I think, of most people.

I have been staying in Room 432 of the Emerson Hotel, on East 115th Street. It's early June as I write, and I've been here for four months.

Room 432 of the Emerson Hotel is small, and nasty. It's painted blue and gold; the bottom half is blue, the top half gold. The paint is nearly as old as the hotel, probably. When traffic is heavy on East 115th Street, the building vibrates sympathetically and the paint flecks off here and there, especially on the wall that faces the street, where there is some kind of moisture problem.

The floor has a large, threadbare, red oriental rug on it—from Woolworth's, I imagine, circa 1960—and there is a wrought-iron, floor-standing lamp, no shade, alongside a green, one-drawer writing desk near the door. The bed is wrought-iron as well, the mattress lumpy and soft. A Gideon Bible rests on a little, dark wood nightstand close by.

I'm a photographer—I've been a photographer since I was old enough to pick up a camera and aim it and press the shutter release—and I came to New York to do a big, coffee-table photo book about Manhattan. But I fell in love, instead. And I got stuck here.

Listen, at times it is imperative that we grab hold of things that are real, things that have mass and weight, things that can cut, things that are mechanical, soulless, gauche, and temporary.

And we need such things when we feel certain that we're going to be caught up, suddenly—or are already caught up—in something exquisite, and eternal. Like death. Or love. Or both.

And we need such things because they help confirm that we are, ourselves, soulless, gauche, and temporary. Sure it's a lie. I *know* it's a lie, but it's how most of us make it from one day to the next.

CHAPTER TWO

January 2nd—Heading Out of Lewiston, Maine

The fat woman who coughed too much asked for the window seat and I gave it to her. I had images of her coughing herself to death there, as Dustin Hoffman had in *Midnight Cowboy*. But she didn't. A half-hour into the ride she said hello and told me her name was Barbara W. Barber. "And you are?" she went on.

I told her my name.

"You don't have a nickname?" she said. "With a name like Abner you really should have a nickname."

"My mother used to call me Abe," I told her. "I don't know why—I don't think I look like an Abe."

She coughed deep in her chest, almost down in her belly, so her whole body got involved in it, and because she tried to keep her mouth closed at the same time, drops of spittle arched from her lips and landed everywhere around her.

"Are you okay, Mrs. Barber?" I asked.

She continued coughing for a few seconds, then held her hand up and dabbed at her mouth with a white lace handkerchief that she withdrew from the breast pocket of her dress. "Your mother is dead, isn't she, Mr. Cray?"

I said nothing for a few moments. I had always prided myself on being able to read people and situations. I liked to believe that I had all the bases covered and that no one could tell me something I didn't know or come across with an insight I didn't believe them capable of. But it occurred to me, at that moment, that this fat, middle-aged woman with the unlikely name was reading *me*, and it made me very uncomfortable.

"Yes," I said at last, and I conjured up a strong tone of annoyance. "My mother is dead. She died three years ago."

Barbara W. Barber turned her head to look at me. She had small, gray-green eyes, a round, puffy face, and her hair, what was left of it—because it was thinning badly—looked greasy and stiff. She coughed again, briefly and silently, then told me, "I'm a medium, Mr. Cray. I know"—another cough—"I know," she repeated, "many, many things—more things, I believe, than I *should* know." She drew closer to me; her voice became a conspiratorial whisper. "More things," she said again, "than I *want* to know."

I remember that I believed her at once. I don't know why. In retrospect, I imagine it was probably the gritty and earnest way she had about her. And I don't think I believed *what* she was saying as much as I believed that *she* believed it.

She continued, her voice changing to a low, nervous gurgle, "And sometimes, Mr. Cray, it scares the hell out of me. Because I *see*, too. And I hear. And I feel."

I felt suddenly as if I were in the grips of a religious fanatic. "Yes," I said, "of course you do."

And she said, ignoring me, "I like it, sometimes. I like it quite a lot, sometimes." She was trying to speak sensually, and it wasn't working—she sounded like a bullfrog. "Sometimes it feels very, very good, Mr. Cray. You really can't imagine how good it feels."

I glanced about for another seat. She noticed. "You don't want to sit with me, Mr. Cray? Do I make you nervous?"

"No," I lied.

"Of course I do." Another cough, then another. Her hands went to the sides of her huge breasts and squeezed hard, as if she were trying to push out whatever was in her lungs. She cursed then, low and violently, and several people nearby glanced around at her, annoyed. I smiled at them, as if in apology. Mrs. Barber went on, "I make everyone nervous, Mr. Cray."

I said nothing. I was still smiling apologetically.

"I made my father nervous; I made my mother nervous; I made my husband so nervous he left me for someone else, for another *man*, for Christ's sake!" And yet again, a series of low, nearly silent coughs erupted from her. Finally, she quieted; her hands went to her breasts again, and she caressed them—she was clearly enjoying herself.

"Jesus!" I whispered, and looked away.

"I make you nervous, too, don't I, Mr. Cray? Good, I'm glad."

I pretended not to hear her.

"Do you want to know something?" she asked.

I still pretended not to hear her. She repeated, "Do you want to know something?" She paused very briefly, then continued, "I see *everything*. Really, I do. I see *everything*. I don't want to; it's not *my* fault, but I do. I know, for instance, that your mother committed suicide."

"Shut up," I whispered.

"She wrote a little note that said: 'This isn't what I wanted, Frank. This isn't what I wanted at all.' And then she shot herself in the head. That was a very masculine thing for her to do—only men shoot themselves in the head, you know. Women slit their wrists."

"Please shut up," I said.

"I can't *help* it, Mr. Cray. I see what I see, and what am I supposed to do with it? Am I supposed to let it fester inside me?"

I closed my eyes. I said nothing.

"Frank was your father, wasn't he?" she asked.

Still I said nothing.

"And he's dead, too, isn't he?"

I opened my eyes, looked to my left, away from her.

She said, "*There's* your mother, Mr. Cray." I turned my head back; she was nodding at the aisle. "She's there, Mr. Cray. Look at her; say hello."

I looked. The aisle was empty. I looked straight ahead, focused on the NO SMOKING sign at the head of the car.

Barbara W. Barber continued, "Your mother is naked, Mr. Cray. But do you want to know *what* she is, precisely? She's a face and a pair of breasts and a pubic V, that's all. Because that's what she always supposed, in life, that mothers *were*. And she so wanted to please. She always so wanted to please!"

"You obscene bitch!" I whispered.

She coughed again, this time very high in her throat.

"You fat, obscene, miserable bitch!" An old woman in the seat ahead of me craned her head around and stared hard. I turned my head slightly to face Barbara W. Barber. I must have closed my eyes for a moment, because, if I'd seen her coming, I would have backed away. I felt her lips on mine, and they were very warm and moist and enjoyable, so I didn't back away. I responded, if only for a moment, until I realized what was happening, and a grunt of surprise and revulsion escaped from me, broke into our kiss, and forced us apart.

A small, pleased smile appeared on her lips. She

said, "Give it time, Mr. Cray. Three months, four. It's like a cancer."

I touched my lips with my fingers, very lightly. I said, "I don't understand."

"*Share* it with me, Mr. Cray," she said. "Please. *Share* it with me." Then she turned her head, made a little hole in the frost on the window with her short, chubby fingers, and looked out at the Maine countryside. I got up and found another seat.

When we arrived at Grand Central, I glanced back and saw her stand, push her way out, and head for the 42nd Street exit, one bag in hand—it looked like a carpetbag—and a huge, gray wool coat thrown over her arm. She moved much faster than I thought a woman her size could move, and every few seconds she turned her head with great agitation this way and that, as if she were looking at something.

And, of course, she was.

CHAPTER THREE

My father and I were shaving together when he died. He liked it when we shaved together—it appealed to his sense of masculinity. I think that throughout my childhood, and into my early adolescence, he looked forward to the day when I'd start shaving, and we shaved together as often as possible up until his death. It was one of the few traditionally masculine things we shared. We did not hunt or fish or go bowling together. He belonged to the Bangor Rotary Club, but I was never invited.

It was a year or so after my mother's suicide that he died. He was dressed in crisp, white boxer shorts and a sleeveless T-shirt, and he was looking forward to breakfast.

"I feel hungry this morning, Abner," he said in the middle of shaving. He took a long, slow swipe with his razor at his night's growth of beard, grinned a small, anticipatory grin, and repeated, "I feel very hungry this morning, Abner. How about you?—Do you feel hungry?"

"Uh-huh," I said. "French toast sounds good."

"Yes," he said. "French toast."

He was still grinning, but it was no longer a grin of anticipation; it was more a kind of nostalgic grin, as if he were remembering something pleasant—an almost sexual grin.

"Dad?" I said.

He stopped grinning, put the razor down on the back of the sink, studied himself a few moments in the mirror—he was a ruggedly handsome, dark-haired man, with deep-set, searching green eyes—and then he turned his head, looked at me, put his hand on my shoulder.

"Dad?" I said. "What's wrong?"

His grin reappeared.

"Dad?" I repeated. "Please—tell me what's wrong."

His hand tightened on my shoulder, his grin became a quivering, lopsided smile.

"Dad," I said again, "what the hell is wrong?"

"Well, Abner," he answered, and his voice was slow and casual, "everything, of course." And his quivering, lopsided smile froze on his face.

I started to speak, to ask him what he meant, and I saw something pass across him, something like a fog, something, I swear, that took the light from his eyes, and I knew that at that moment, as he stood with his arm outstretched and his hand gripping my shoulder, he had died.

We could have stood together like that, in the bathroom, for several minutes, I'm not sure. It probably wasn't several minutes. It was probably a few seconds—logic says it could only have been a few seconds. But at last he collapsed, and I tugged him into the living room and laid him on the couch and made telephone calls to all the right people. I did not attempt mouth-to-mouth resuscitation or chest massage. I wiped the rest of the shaving cream from his face, folded his hands on his belly, straightened his legs, and told him I was sorry he was dead.

Then I sat in his chair—a large and sturdy leather wing-backed chair—and waited for the right people to arrive. When they did, I heard some speculation between them that my father had died of a stroke or a heart-attack, and I said, stupidly, that maybe he thought it was *time* to die, which got merely an "Uh-huh" and a "Why don't you relax, okay?" Then they took my father away.

The funeral, a week later—at a big and venerable cemetery just outside Bangor—was a predictably dreary affair. My older brother Ike was there, full of sage advice and good fellowship. He said he was going to try and join the Peace Corps—"If they'll have a ne'er-do-well like me, Abner."

"Sure they will," I said.

And my Aunt Jocelyn was there—my mother's

sister; she always liked my father—and her husband Paul, too, and several of my father's fellow Rotarians.

I lingered at the graveside when the service was finished. My brother wanted to linger with me, but I told him I'd rather be alone, which he accepted readily.

I said nothing further to my father as I stood by his graveside. I started to. The words *Bye, Dad* came to me but never made it past the mental planning stages. What I was trying to do, I think, was to look past the coffin lid at what resided inside and try to relate that, somehow, to what my father had been. And I thought that what was in there, in that coffin, was still pretty whole, still recognizable as the creature who was my father, but that, soon enough, it would change—the skin would fall away, the hair recede, the lips part and decay to reveal the rictus grin.

He was dead. I would never see him or speak to him again. All I had as my memory of him. And though that was profoundly sad, there was also something secure in it, something wonderfully secure, and comfortable.

I read a statistic once that there are more people alive at this moment than have lived and died in all of history. If that's true, then someday this world is going to be very, very crowded indeed.

CHAPTER FOUR

I had a friend in Bangor who had a nice, dirty-blonde beard and a round, gentle face, and whenever he went into a laundry near his home, the proprietors—two aged Chinese men named Lu and Yang—smiled at him when he came through the doorway and shouted, "Hey, Jesus Christ, how are you doing?" My friend told me that story quite a lot, and I always enjoyed it; it tickled me.

His name was Sam Fearey. He was two years older than I, chunky, with a splash of freckles across the bridge of his nose. He looked like one of the Campbell's Soup kids grown up and a few pounds lighter.

In 1966 he got drafted and was sent off to Vietnam. I received a half-dozen dreary, rambling letters from him about what a "shitty place" Vietnam was and about what a "shitty war" we were waging there, and in 1967 he was reported as missing in action. He was never found, and rumor has it to this day that he's still alive in some tiny North Vietnamese village. I hope not. He deserves to go on to better things.

We hung around together for several years before he was drafted, and we did something once that was pretty lousy—we broke into a mausoleum.

What did we know? We just wanted to have a little fun.

We talked about it for quite a while first. We discussed it calmly and rationally, and we came to the conclusion that no one would know the difference and no one would care—least of all, the people who had been put into the mausoleum.

It was nearing Halloween, so we put it off until then—we had to do the thing up right, of course.

We didn't plan to *do* anything in the mausoleum. We didn't plan to write on the walls or tip a casket over or leave perverse little notes everywhere, as had been done by other kids in Bangor, a couple of years earlier, at a different mausoleum. We weren't *sick*, for God's sake; we were just curious.

It was Sam's idea to bring the candles, and Sam's idea to bring the cat's skull and the Ouija Board. And his idea, too, to try a little "psychic communication."

Jesus, we were just planning to have a little fun on Halloween. Everyone had fun on Halloween. Some kids put bags full of dog shit on people's porches; other kids left toilet paper everywhere (in retrospect, we certainly did have a toilet fixation), and those were really crummy things to do. Breaking into a mausoleum, lighting a few candles, and scaring yourself silly was stupid, sure—but who was it going to harm?

The mausoleum we chose belonged to the Hammett family, who went back a long, long way in Bangor. They lived in a huge, stone house just outside the city limits, on several hundred wooded acres, and as a family they had been dying off with clock-like regularity for quite some time.

The most recent addition to the Hammett mausoleum that October of 1965 was a pleasant old man named Joseph A. Hammett. He liked to fish in a public fishing pond west of Bangor, and he always had a kind word for everyone. He was put into the mausoleum toward the end of September, so Sam figured that by Halloween he'd be "nice and ripe," which made me cringe, but also intrigued the hell out of me.

The mausoleum is in a private, fenced area of Bangor's Memorial Park. There are several ways to get to it—either through the park itself (which, for a fifteen-year-old kid on a Halloween night, can be a very numbing experience) or from Route 23A, a four-lane highway several hundred yards north of the park. After considerable discussion—during which Sam called me a wimp at least a hundred times—we agreed that Route 23A would be the best route to take. The only real problem with it was the unavoidable climb up a steep and erosion-rutted hill, which, after a heavy rain, was treacherous, at best.

As luck would have it, that Halloween night it was raining, and as the two of us stood at the bottom of the hill looking up—the roof and upper walls of the mausoleum were reflecting the headlights of cars on Route 23A—I said, "Jees, Sam, I don't know about this."

He chuckled. It was his duty to chuckle at the scared kid; it was supposed to make the scared kid feel more secure. It didn't. "What the hell could happen to us, Abner?" he said. "Tell me what could happen."

I pointed stiffly at the hill. "I could get hurt pretty bad up there, Sam, *that's* what could happen."

"How? By sliding down a hill? C'mon, Abner!"

We started up the hill a couple of minutes later.

We made it to the top, of course, though with a great deal of effort, and only after we'd both gotten ourselves filthy as hell and burned on an unexpected growth of stinging nettle halfway to the top (plants that had been put there, Sam suggested, by the Hammets themselves as a way of keeping people away from their "dead relations").

But when we got to the top and stood in the rain fifty feet from the mausoleum, I had to admit that the climb was more than worth the effort and the pain.

"Look at that, Abner," Sam whispered in awe. "Just like outa *The Fall of the House of Usher* or something, right?"

"Right," I agreed.

"You seen that, haven't ya?"

"Seen what?" I asked.

He wasn't listening. He started for the mausoleum—the cat's skull, the Ouija Board, and six new, white candles in a black plastic bag that he held tightly under his right arm. He also had a number of Mallo Cups in the bag. Sam was addicted to Mallo Cups. He ate no other candy. "Mallo Cups are the best, Abner," he told me time and time again. He had, in fact, a constant, weak chocolate/marshmallow smell about him.

I followed him to the mausoleum. I had a pair of pliers and two screwdrivers—a large Phillips head and a larger slotted screwdriver—in my coat pocket. Our strategy was to unscrew one of the windows and climb in; we felt certain that the door was going to be locked. But the windows—two of them; one high on the north wall, one high on the east wall—had been screwed in from the inside. And the door was indeed locked.

"Jesus," Sam breathed. He was leaning against the east wall, rain dripping into his eyes, the glare of car headlights on Route 23A hitting him every few seconds. I stood next to him and said "Jesus," too.

"Goddamnit!" he said.

"Goddamnit!" I said.

"We'll have to break in, Abner."

I said nothing.

"I didn't come all the way up that fucking hill for nothing. We're going to have to break in."

"How?" I whispered.

"We'll jimmy the padlock."

"How?" I whispered again.

"With the screwdrivers," he said.

"They're my father's screwdrivers, Sam. What if they break?"

"They won't break."

"Yeah, I know—but what if they do?"

"Wimp," he said.

We were working at the padlock seconds later. And, thanks to several decades worth of rust, we were inside the mausoleum within minutes.

The first thing I said was, "I don't want to be here, Sam." It smelled bad; it smelled of damp wood.

Sam chuckled again, but it was quick and unconvincing, and there was a slight tremor to it. "Sure you don't, Abner," he said.

"Why are we here, Sam? There's nothin' here!" There were six vaults, three on the east wall, three on the west wall. Each vault had a heavy, dark metal door in front of it and a small metal plaque beneath with the name, birth date and date of death of the person within. We read each one—"Langley Hammet: October 12, 1873–October 15, 1951" . . . "Ariel Hammet: November 22, 1952–June 12, 1953." ("Boy," I said, "That's sad." "Happens," Sam said.) "Garner John Hammet: June 1, 1918–September 12, 1947"—until we got to "Joseph William Hammet," the last vault toward the rear of the mausoleum on the west wall. Sam stopped, knocked slightly on the vault door, and said, "Evening, Joe. All we wanta do is talk, okay?"

Then he went to the center of the concrete floor,

crossed his legs Indian-style, opened the plastic bag, took six candles out. "Got any matches, Abner?" he asked.

"No," I answered.

He cursed under his breath.

I said, "I thought *you* were supposed to bring the matches, Sam."

"I did. They're all wet."

The headlights of cars on Route 23A filtered through the grimy window on the north wall and played dully on the ceiling of the mausoleum.

"Fuck it!" Sam said.

"Fuck what, Sam?"

"Fuck the candles. We don't need them." He stuffed them back into the plastic bag, withdrew the skull of the cat, put it down in front of him, and said to it, "Hi, Flora." It had once been his cat. He'd raised her from a kitten and called her Flora in honor of a girlfriend who'd moved from Bangor to Albany a year before and whom he missed terribly.

I nodded at Flora's skull. "That's kinda sick, you know," I said.

Sam nodded. "Maybe a little. I'll tell ya, it kind of made *me* sick cleaning her off—" He stopped suddenly, put his hand up. "Quiet!" he said.

"What's wrong, Sam—"

"Quiet! I hear something." He nodded to indicate the rear of the mausoleum. "I hear something, Abner," he repeated. There was a small tremor in his voice. I strained to see his face in the darkness. I saw it. He was grinning ever so slightly. I was grinning, too.

"What do you hear, Sam?"

"A voice. Damn it, I hear a *voice*!" he whispered.

"What kind of voice?" I whispered.

"An old man's voice."

"What's it saying?"

"I don't know; I'm not sure." He paused.

"*I* don't hear anything, Sam," I said.

"It's saying something about cats, Abner."

"About cats?"

"Uh-huh. It's saying, 'Get out of here, get out of here; I'm allergic to cats—they make me itch!' " And he broke into a fit of hysterical, infectious laughter that lasted at least five minutes.

And when we had both stopped laughing, I discovered a book of matches deep in my jacket pocket, beneath a rip in the lining, and I handed them to Sam. He took the candles out, lit one, let the wax drip liberally on six evenly spaced spots around Flora's skull, and set each candle in the wax. Then we got down to business.

The dead were such fine entertainment, then.

CHAPTER FIVE

January 6

I had an appointment in Manhattan with Serena Hitchcock, a senior editor for one of the city's largest publishers. She wanted to talk to me about doing a coffee-table photo book dealing with New York's parks and tourist attractions. The possibility of doing such a book was why I'd come to New York in the first place. I had done similar work before, for magazines like *Yankee* and *Americana*, though never a full-length book, and I enjoyed it. It paid well, and it didn't demand too much creativity, which—I'm the first to admit—is not my strong suit. I'm very good with a camera; I have a fair idea of what the public will and will not like, and when I was working, I almost always delivered on schedule. But I think, after all, that I was to photography what fast-food restaurants are to eating—I was slick and quick, but I had about as much substance as a snowflake. I knew that no one would ever give me a one-man show or do an "Abner Cray Retrospective." I knew that I would never set the world on fire. And that was okay, because I didn't *want* to set the world on fire. I think that I wanted no more out of my life than to be reasonably comfortable and healthy, never to go hungry, and never to suffer too much pain, and to find pleasure where I could find it. That's only what most people want, I think. So I wasn't asking too much.

I'd never met Serena Hitchcock. We'd talked on the phone quite a few times, though, about photography and New York and books, so I had a clear mental image of her. I saw her as tall, fortyish, and thin, with the kind of smart and calculating sexuality that, I was convinced, only tall, fortyish, and thin women can possess (another tacky sexist fantasy). But when I finally did meet her, she was none of those things. She was short, a little chubby ("pleasingly plump" used to be the phrase), had shoulder-length brown hair, gray eyes, and a pleasant but basically unappealing face, like a Tupperware lady. She was wearing a brown pants suit and had stuck a tiny red rose into her lapel. She'd come out to the lobby to meet me, and as she lead me back to her office, she walked briskly several feet ahead and nodded at some of the departments we passed through—"This is the art department, Abner." . . . "These are the copyeditors' desks, Abner.''—and I said "I see" or "Very interesting," which she didn't acknowledge. And when we got to her office, I saw that it was a only a cubicle that fronted West 44th Street, twenty stories below. There were some book covers on the walls, a utilitarian-looking, gray metal desk in the center of the room—snapshots of two chunky, flat-faced kids on it—and a much used, black-cloth-on-metal secretarial chair behind it. The office said very loudly that Serena Hitchcock was small potatoes indeed.

She went around to the back of her desk, sat in her secretarial chair, told me to sit down on a flimsy-looking, armless chair in back of me. I pulled the chair closer to the desk and sat in it.

She said, "Crummy, huh?"

I smiled. "I don't understand."

"This office—" she nodded—"it's pretty crummy, don't you think?"

"It's small," I said, and smiled again.

"It's temporary," she said. "We're renovating our old offices."

"Oh. Looks are deceiving."

"Sorry," she said, and smiled confusedly.

"Looks," I repeated, "are deceiving."

Her smile altered slightly. "Yes," she said, "they are."

I had a briefcase on my lap, with some samples of my work in it. I opened it, took out some color shots I'd taken in the Adirondack Mountains two summers before, handed them across the desk. She glanced at them, handed them back. "I've seen your work, Abner. That's why you're here."

"Oh," I said, and put the photographs away, the briefcase on the floor.

"We want a big book, Abner," she said. She took the tiny red rose from her lapel, began fingering it as she talked, her gaze going to it occasionally. "We're not going to be using a lot of text, a few lines per photograph—most people don't read anyway—and I'd like you to do a good amount of black and white. I think you're pretty good at black and white, Abner."

"Thanks." I knew it was just something for her to say. I didn't believe I was any better working in black and white than in color.

She went on, "And I'd like something a little off-key, too."

It took me by surprise. "Off-key? I don't understand."

She looked at the rose; I saw her smile and guessed that she was somehow amused. "No," she said, and looked up at me. Her smile faded. "You probably don't understand." She pushed herself to her feet, went to the window that overlooked West 44th Street, and stood at it with her back to me. "I don't even care if the people who buy this book notice it, Abner." Her tone had become low and meditative. "This 'off-key' thing, I mean." She turned her head briefly and grinned a quick, sad grin. She turned back, continued, "They don't even have to notice. Maybe your angles could be slightly off, or the colors not quite right, and the people—we need lots of people in this book, Abner; it's what Manhattan is all about—and the people," she repeated, paused, glanced around again, "should be . . . just people—like you and me. Just people." She turned back to the window. "Christ, I'm not making any sense at all, am I?"

It was a good question, but I had no idea how to answer it; I said nothing.

"Do you like this city, Abner?" she asked, her back still turned.

I answered truthfully, "No, Serena, not very much. It's a good place to do business, but . . . May I call you Serena?"

She ignored the question. "I despise this city! I live here; I work here—and I despise it." She nodded to indicate the street. "My brother was killed out there three weeks ago, Abner. Some cretin put a knife into his heart and he died in a couple minutes. Right on West 44th Street, in front of a dozen people. There was no motive; no money was taken. Someone decided to put a blade into him, and that was that." She shook her head quickly, as if in anger and disbelief.

"Serena," I began, "I'm sorry, I . . ." I had no idea what to say. "Right out there on West 44th Street, huh? My God, that's awful . . ."

She waved backward at me in agitation. "No, Abner, I'm sorry; forget it. Please. Forget it. I loved him—I loved my brother; we were close, we were always very close. I'm sorry. I didn't want to burden

you." She turned around, stood behind her desk
chair with her hands on the top of it. "Give us a big,
pretty book, Abner. Make all your angles perfect and
all your colors true. Give us something that will draw
the tourists here." A short pause, then, "Tell the big
lie, Abner."

"Sure, whatever you say, Serena. May I call you
Serena?"

She sat in her chair. "Your contracts will be ready
within the week, Abner. We'll talk again, then. Thanks
for coming in."

I stood. "Thank *you*," I said, and I left.

I was on the twentieth floor. I got into the elevator,
pressed the button marked "L," for Lobby, and
waited. The doors didn't close. I stuck my head out,
looked right and left, saw that the receptionist was
talking on the phone. I pressed the button marked
"Close Door" and heard, from down the hallway,
toward the receptionist: "Hold that, please." I pressed
the button marked "Open Door." "Hold that please,"
I heard again. I stuck my head out and looked toward
the source of the voice. I saw a man ten feet away.
He was in his mid-forties, was wearing a threadbare
gray suit and carrying a brown attache case in his
right hand. I caught his eye. "Do you mean me?" I
said, because he was standing very still, with his left
arm raised and his finger pointed. He looked to be in
the middle of a stride. I heard this, from the
receptionist: "I'm sorry, sir?"

I stepped way back into the elevator; my heels hit the rear wall. I was embarrassed. I heard again: "Hold that, please."

The elevator doors closed.

CHAPTER SIX

A week after I got to Manhattan I moved out of my hotel on East 32nd Street and into an apartment owned by a man named Art DeGraff. It was a very large apartment in a big, well-kept townhouse on East 79th Street, and since, Art told me, he was vacationing in Europe until May, I could use it for as long as I needed. Besides, he went on, he'd prefer not leaving it empty and I could have it for less than half of what I'd pay at a hotel, which I thought was a generous offer.

Art and I went back a long way together. We grew up on the same street in Bangor—Leslie Street—where he was shorter than I, but wiry. He had a thin, pink face, then, and coal-black hair that was continually in disarray, quick, intelligent green eyes, and a nose that, for several years after the onset of puberty, was too large for his face. Eventually, his face matured around it; it stopped being the brunt of bad jokes, and he grew into a kind of lighthearted, if slightly swaggering self-confidence that was vaguely macho, but which, by itself, lots of otherwise intelligent women found attractive.

We went to the same high school in Bangor. South Bangor High School. We had many of the same teachers, got into the same kinds of trouble (he had, in fact, promised to go with Sam Fearey and me that Halloween night in 1965, but pleaded sickness at the last moment), went off to the same college—Brockport University, in upstate New York—and dated pretty much the same girls, one after the other. We generally thought of ourselves as the best of friends, until one spring day in 1968 when he told me he was sleeping with my cousin Stacy. I slapped him. I felt foolish because of it, and I wanted to apologize at once. But I slapped him again instead—and with the side of my fist rather than my open hand, which knocked him down and broke one of my knuckles at the same time.

He lay on his back on the sidewalk just outside the science building for at least a minute, sighing again and again. I stayed quiet because I was angry with him and angry with myself, and because I was incredibly embarrassed. And at last he propped himself up on his elbows and said, "My God, Abner—"

I pointed stiffly at him, my finger trembling. "Stay away from her, Art! Stay the fuck away from her!" And I stalked off.

You understand, of course, that I'd been sleeping with Stacy, too. And I'd been assured, by Stacy herself—whom I trusted without question—that there was no one else in her life and never would be. And that's why his revelation came as such a blow to me and why I reacted the way I did.

It killed our friendship for several years, until the summer of 1972, when he called to tell me that he and Stacy were getting married. Four years can heal lots of wounds, especially if they're simply wounds to one's pride, and I told myself that I was happy for him. "That's great," I said. "Am I invited to the wedding?"

"Of course you are, Abner. You can be the best man if you'd like."

I said okay, and two months later I was the best man at my former best friend's wedding to Stacy Horn, my cousin and former lover, whom I still lusted after. The wedding took place in Holton, Maine, during a thunderstorm, and the reception under a tent in the back yard of Stacy's parents' home, a mile outside Holton. Half the tent fell over in the storm, but it was hastily reerected, and we all toughed it out for awhile—or pretended to. There was courageous laughter everywhere, and there were sneezes galore, and Stacy's grandfather, who was then approaching ninety, had to be taken inside. Eventually, the storm got the best of the rest of us, and we went inside, too, and had some wedding cake and toasted Art and Stacy in very traditional ways. All in all, that wedding was a pretty miserable affair. In retrospect, I enjoyed the hell out of it.

After that, Art and Abner and Stacy became something of an item. Art had come into some money after the death of an uncle and he wasn't averse to lavishing it on the three of us when I visited New York, and for several years we were friends again.

He and Stacy were divorced in 1977. Stacy went back to Maine to live with her parents, and Art began to sulk over the whole thing: "Jesus, Abner," he said to me shortly after the divorce, "I didn't know; I didn't *know*!"

"Know what?" I asked.

"Myself, Abner. I didn't know myself."

I saw both Stacy and Art after that, from time to time—Stacy at her house in Maine, with her parents hovering about (her father once said to me, "She's your *cousin*, Abner," to which I could say nothing; so he wandered off, mumbling to himself), and Art at his apartment on East 79th Street in Manhattan. But he and I had been out of touch with each other for nearly a year when I called to ask if I could share his apartment with him for a couple of weeks. And that's when he told me was going to vacation in Europe and that I could have the apartment all to myself.

I moved in on January 12th.

It's when I met Phyllis Pellaprat.

She was seated at Art's dining room table, playing Yahtzee. She was in her early twenties, black, with smooth, shoulder-length hair, an exquisite oval face, and large, expressive eyes, and although she was seated, I could tell that she was very tall, probably over six feet, I guessed, and that she probably exercised quite a bit.

She was dressed in blue jeans and a cream-colored halter-top tied in a knot at the front. I hadn't seen a woman in a halter-top since the early seventies, and I'd forgotten what a treat it was. She wore no shoes or socks, and she had her right leg bent, her ankle tucked under the bottom of her left thigh on the chair. She toed the carpet as we talked.

"Hi, I got three Yahtzees so far," were her first words to me. She had no accent, and her voice was high-pitched, but very pleasant, fluid, and sensual. "You want to play?" She smiled. It was a wonderfully open and appealing gesture.

I set my bags down just inside the front door. "I'm sorry," I said, "but you're going to have to tell me who you are."

"I'm Phyllis," she answered, and rolled the dice. "Fours, dammit!" she mumbled, and jotted something down on her tally sheet.

"Phyllis?" I said. "Phyllis who?"

She answered, rolling the dice again. "Pellaprat. Phyllis Pellaprat. Who are you? Are you Abner What's-his-Name? Abner Doubleday?"

"No," I said. "Abner *Cray*."

"What kind of a name is that?" she said, and tilted her head slightly to one side, as Barbara W. Barber had, though on this woman it was far more fetching. "You should have a nickname. Do you have a nickname?'' Again she rolled the dice, checked them, looked disappointed.

''No,'' I answered, and I became aware that my voice had risen slightly, in anger. ''I don't have a nickname,'' I went on, lowering my voice, ''and I'm going to have to ask you what in the hell you're doing here?! Art told me the apartment would be empty.''

''Art? Who's Art?''

''Art DeGraff. He *owns* this place!''

Her brow wrinkled, as if she were in thought. She grinned playfully. ''Sure,'' she said, ''I'm a friend of Art's. I'm his girlfriend.''

''No, I don't think so—''

''What's the matter? You prejudiced or something, Abner Doubleday?''

''My name is *not* Abner Doubleday! And no, I'm not prejudiced; I'm *angry*!'' I was gesticulating wildly now; I had come forward, so I was standing near her at the table, just to her right, and at the same time that I was yelling and gesticulating, I was positioning myself for a better look down her halter-top. I was having pretty good luck; the view was tremendous, and it was tempering my anger. ''Art told me, Miss Pellaprat, that the apartment would be empty. And it's not empty, is it? *You're* here!''

She looked quickly up at me, caught me jockeying for position, grinned, looked back at the table, threw the dice, checked them. ''Oh?'' she said. ''You don't like that idea?''

''It's not a matter,'' I answered, ''of what I like or

don't like, it's a matter of . . . ethics; it's a matter of
. . . of . . ." I was stuck, and I felt foolish.

"Of what, Abner Doubleday?" She threw the dice
again; they came up all sixes. She was very pleased.
"That's four Yahtzees in one game, Abner Doubleday!
Count 'em; four!" She put a checkmark in the appropriate box on her score sheet.

I glanced about. "Where's your coat?"

"Don't have one," she answered.

There was a closet near the front entrance. I went
to it, looked inside. Except for someone's gray
sweater— which was clearly too large for Phyllis and
which, I guessed, must have been Art's, and a black
umbrella leaning up in a far corner, it was empty. I
looked over at Phyllis, saw that she was looking at
me. I said to her, "Just please tell me who you are
and what exactly you're doing in this apartment."

"I told you—I'm Art's girlfriend. What's the matter?
He never told you about me? He's told everyone
else. You don't believe me, go on in there and check
over the fireplace." She nodded toward the living
room, to her right.

"The fireplace?" I said.

"Yeah. You'll see. In there." She nodded again.

"Maybe I should just phone the police," I said. It
was a bluff, but it must have sounded pretty convincing because she pushed herself to her feet, suddenly
angry. My original guess that she was probably over
six feet tall was correct; I am six foot two, and she
stood nearly as tall as I. "Oh, horseshit!" she
whispered, and went into the living room, so she was

out of my range of vision for a moment, and came back with a small, wood-framed photograph. "Here!"

I took the photograph, studied it. It showed Art and her, side-by-side, arms around each other's waists, on the bow of a boat. To their left, in the background, I could just make out the Manhattan skyline, and I guessed that they were somewhere in Long Island Sound. Art was dressed in a pair of white, snug-fitting trunks, no shirt, and Phyllis was dressed in a very brief white bikini. I studied the photograph for quite some time. At last, she snatched it away from me.

"Okay, dipshit," she said, "are you satisfied, or do you still want to call the cops?"

"No," I said. "I'm sorry. But Art really didn't say a thing about you."

"And he never said anything about you, either," she cut in. "Just 'Keep an eye out for Abner Doubleday.' "

I decided not to correct her. I went back to where I'd put my bags, picked them up, and asked, "Where are you going to sleep, Phyllis?"

She was playing Yahtzee again. The snapshot was face-down on the table. She threw the dice. "There's only one bedroom, Abner." She grinned.

"Uh-huh," I said, and a half-dozen wonderful fantasies danced in front of me. With effort, I shooed them away. "That's right," I said, "only one. So I guess you'll be using the couch, right?"

She looked up at me, scowled. "You're all heart, Abner Doubleday. A real gentleman."

"*I'm* paying for this place, damnit!"

She jotted something down on her score sheet. "We'll sleep together, Abner," she said casually. "Or don't you want to sleep with me?"

I fought back an anticipatory grin. "That's really not the point, is it—"

"You don't like black girls?"

"And that's not the point either."

"You're a real asshole, Abner. You should be grateful I'm willing to sleep with you."

"Oh, good Christ, I'm going to go and unpack!" I was genuinely angry now.

She inclined her head to the left, toward the living room. "Through there, my man." She chuckled. "Down the hallway, past the bathroom. Better lock the door."

"I know where it is," I snapped, and left the room to go to the bedroom. All the way there I could hear her chuckling softly.

I took a good long time unpacking, not that I had much to unpack—just a few shirts, some underwear, socks, three pairs of pants, some toiletries. And my camera gear, of course, which was in a padded, aluminum case that I stuck, for safety's sake, way back on a top shelf in one of Art's two walk-in closets.

I took a good long time unpacking because I had let the fantasies slip back; one of them was moving deliciously about in my head, and I was praying that it would come true. In it, Phyllis surprised me in the bedroom while I was unpacking, slipped her hands around my waist, from behind, lowered them, fondled me a bit, and whispered wildly erotic things in my ear. And when I turned to face her, I saw that she was naked and smiling and making comments about what a "big man" I was and that maybe I could help her out with a "little problem" she had.

At the same time that I was praying for this fantasy to come true, I was also hoping that it wouldn't. Because how was I to know how *clean* she was? Maybe she had herpes—everyone else did. Maybe she had something worse—gonorrhea, syphilis.

But she didn't surprise me, and when I left the room and went back to the dining room forty-five minutes later, I found a note:

Dear Abner Doubleday,

Had to go out for a while. Sorry. Don't worry about locking the door, I've a key of my own. Just leave a blanket and a pillow for me on the couch. I promise not to disturb your beauty sleep.

Thanks, my man,
Phyllis P.

"Shit!" I whispered.

I was near the corner of East 67th Street and Fifth Avenue an hour later. I had just bought some film at a photographic supplies store on East 65th, and I was heading back to Art's apartment. Traffic was very heavy because it was the rush hour, and a couple inches of snow had fallen during the afternoon, so people were having trouble navigating through it.

On the other side of the street and a block ahead, a man was walking north, away from me, with what looked like a bag of groceries on one arm. He was walking fast, with his head down, and he was only one of several hundred people within that block, but he walked with a tiny, hitching limp that made his left shoulder drop an inch or so with every step and made his head, as if to compensate, nod to the right an equal distance.

I had seen only one person walk that way. Art DeGraff. He'd all but shattered his knee in an automobile accident ten years earlier, and the knee had never healed properly.

I didn't believe that the man I was seeing was Art DeGraff. I believed that I was seeing a coincidence. I believed that a man Art's height and build had experienced the same kind of misfortune that Art had, perhaps also in an automobile accident. But I quickened my pace and went after him nonetheless.

I was able to keep him in sight only to the corner of Fifth Avenue and East 84th Street. He maneuvered through the Manhattan pedestrian traffic with ease; I did not—I was too polite: "Pardon me." . . . "I'm sorry." . . . "Excuse me." So I lost him.

When I got back to the townhouse, I went to the elevator, pressed the "UP" button, and waited. The elevator was one of those old, art-deco elevators that wheeze and clank a lot, and I heard it wheezing and clanking four stories above, as if getting up the energy to come and get me. I stuck my hands into my coat pockets, expecting a long wait. I heard a door open and close to my right. I looked. The long, dark green hallway was empty. I took my hands out of my pockets, saw that the elevator was on its way down, muttered a soft curse at it. The elevator stopped two floors up. I cursed again, turned, started for the stairway to my left.

"Going up, sir?"

I stopped, looked back. I saw the face of an incredibly aged man sticking into the hallway from the elevator. A smile was on the face—the kind of smile one associates with people who want very much to be of service. The smile dissipated; the mouth moved; I heard again: "Going up, sir?"

I came back, stepped into the elevator. The old man—who was wearing a regulation elevator operator's suit, black and purple and well-starched, and who was holding an elevator operator's cap in his left hand—parked himself stiffly in a corner, near the controls. "Step to the rear, please," he said.

I stepped to the rear.

"Floor, please?" he said.

I told him the fourth floor; he pressed the correct button, and the car started up, wheezing and clanking. I told the old man that I hadn't seen him earlier, when I'd arrived at the building.

"That's because I just got here," he said.

"Oh," I said.

"I'm doing what I've always done."

"Oh," I said again.

"I don't need to get paid for it. I'm doing what is familiar and comfortable. I enjoy doing it. Fourth floor, sir." The doors opened. I got out, turned.

"Thank you," I said.

"My pleasure, sir," he said. The doors closed.

I have learned this, too: I have learned that the living are not very different from the dead. And I have learned that you often have to have a very good eye indeed to tell the difference.

CHAPTER SEVEN

I thought that I was going to enjoy living in Art's apartment. I liked his tastes (I always had). Everything was well-made, and functional, and there were lots of earth colors, which appealed to me. Several feet in front of the white marble fireplace stood a huge, tar-black, smooth leather couch with a rounded back and rounded, overstuffed arms. Behind the couch, and arranged rather loosely in the large room, were several chairs—a wing-backed with rust stripes on a brown background and, facing it, near a window that overlooked East 79th Street, a dark rust, armless chair. A straight-backed, dark wood chair stood near a tall cherry secretary which housed Art's stereo equipment and TV. He had hung several prints—one of Picasso's *Boy with Dove* and another, a stylized picture of an old church with too many harsh right angles and dark colors that, I think, was supposed to be reminiscent of Andrew Wyeth, but it was too nasty and depressing for that. The walls were dark beige and looked as if they had been recently painted because they were very clean.

That first night in the apartment, I stocked the refrigerator (except for a pint of very sour sour cream, a half-full jar of Marie's Thousand Island Dressing, and an aluminum-foil-wrapped clove of garlic, it was empty when I arrived), called Manhattan Cable TV and arranged for a temporary installation (it surprised me that Art didn't have cable; he was an inveterate movie fan) went over my contracts for the big photo book, and, finally, settled down to wait for Phyllis Pellaprat to reappear.

At just past seven, Art called.

"Abner? Hi." He sounded a little down.

"Art?" I was surprised to hear from him. "Where are you calling from?"

"I'm in Nice—"

"Jesus," I interrupted, "it must be nice." And I chuckled.

"Sorry?" he said.

"I said it must be nice, Art."

"Oh. Yes. It is." A brief pause. I felt foolish. He went on. "Is everything okay there, Abner?"

"Sure, Art. Everything's fine."

"Just before I left, I was having some trouble with the heat."

"No, Art, the heat's fine, nice and toasty. By the

way, I'm having cable TV hooked up, temporarily. Is that okay?''

"Cable TV?''

"Manhattan Cable. Just temporarily. I'll tell them to cancel it if you—''

"No,'' he cut in, "that's fine, Abner. No problem.'' A brief pause; then, his voice lower, "Abner?''

"Yes, Art?''

"Have you spoken with Stacy lately?'' He sounded troubled. "In the last month-and-a-half, I mean.''

"No,'' I answered. "I haven't seen her since Thanksgiving. We had dinner together, at her parent's house. Why?''

"No reason. Just wondering. I miss her, I guess.''

"Sure you do, Art.''

"I made quite a few mistakes with her, didn't I, Abner?''

"I don't know, Art. We never talked about it very much.''

"But circumstances . . . change people, Abner. Circumstances change people.''

"Circumstances, Art?''

"Sure. Things happen. You know. Things happen and you get a chance to think. About life, I mean.''

"Yes, I understand that, Art.'' It was a lie. "Why don't you call her?''

"Stacy? You mean call Stacy?''

"Uh-huh. Why not?''

"No, Abner. I don't think so. I'd like to; God, I'd really like to, Abner, but it's too soon.''

"Too soon? I don't understand.''

"Well, you know." He seemed very ill-at-ease now. "You know, Abner—I mean, after your father died, and after your mother . . . died, you had to have time to . . . time to readjust, didn't you?"

"I guess so. Sure. But I still don't understand what that has to do with you and Stacy."

"Not very much. Not directly, at least. Nothing at all, really. It's just the parallel, I think—you get hold of something. . . something comes into your life . . ." A brief pause. "Something comes into your life, Abner, and it's very, very beautiful; it's exquisite, you understand; it's something that you've always wanted, something you've always dreamed of . . ." He stopped. I think I heard him sniffle. He went on, "You get hold of it; you hold onto it, and for a while everything's really great. And then one morning you wake up and you realize that you don't have it anymore, that it's been taken away from you, that someone's taken it away from you, some stranger has taken it away from you . . ." Another short pause. "This wonderful, wonderful thing you had hold of, Abner, has been taken away from you." He stopped again. When he continued, his voice had changed, had become stronger. "Anyway, I'm sorry, Abner. I don't want to tie you up; I can't talk too long—"

"You're not tying me up, Art."

"It's already been a couple of minutes, hasn't it?"

"I guess so—"

"You're a friend, Abner. You've always been a friend, isn't that right?"

"Sure I have. Sure. I still am." A short pause. "You sound a little strange, Art? What's wrong?"

"Wrong?" he said. "I don't know, Abner. Circumstances are wrong, I guess. Can you understand that?"

"No, Art. I can't."

Silence.

"Art?" I coaxed. "Are you there?"

After a moment he came back on the line. "Yes, I'm here, Abner. Enjoy the apartment, okay? Enjoy the Cable TV. Enjoy *yourself*, Abner."

"Yes," I said, "I will. Thanks."

"Good," he said, and hung up.

I had wanted to tell him about Phyllis, of course, and I was sorry that I hadn't had the chance to. Then it occurred to me that it was probably better that I hadn't. After all, how was I going to tell him that his girlfriend and I were going to share his apartment? What was I going to say?—"Hey, Art, when I got here Phyllis was here and she kind of . . . well, what I mean is . . ." I could see myself getting stupidly tongue-tied and not knowing how in the hell to get myself out of it. In all likelihood, though, Phyllis and Art were on the outs; otherwise, he wouldn't have gotten so worked up about Stacy. That seemed logical enough. And it made me feel better about having Phyllis around.

CHAPTER EIGHT

At a little past eight that first night in Art's apartment, I went out again. I took two cameras with me—a battered, old Nikon F and an equally battered Hasselblad—a tripod, and several rolls of very fast black and white slide film. I was remembering what Serena Hitchcock had said about doing something off-key. I knew it was all related to her brother's murder, which I thought at the time was very sad, very hard to take, and I knew she hadn't been speaking as an editor, a professional, but I thought it was a good idea anyway. Night shots in black and white are often by nature off-key, and my plan was to take some shots with the shutter open for several seconds, to suggest the movements of traffic and pedestrians against the static backdrop of the buildings themselves. Something atmospheric. Something off-key.

From the corner of East 79th Street and Fifth
Avenue I turned south, so I was heading toward
midtown Manhattan. I stayed on the east side of the
Avenue, across the street from the Park, because
there was more light, and because I had never had
trouble believing the horror stories I'd heard about
Central Park at night.

I could see occasional random movement beyond
the tall, wrought-iron fence, the hard spray of car
headlights on the trees lining East Drive, and the
erratic, quick glint of something small and bright in
the Park, as if fireflies were loose inside it.

I was dressed in jeans and a wool-lined denim
jacket; it wasn't enough (the temperature was in the
upper twenties), but anything bulkier would have
restricted the free movement of my hands and arms
(if the opportunity for a good candid shot suddenly
presented itself) and would also have made it harder
for me to run (if some down-on-his-luck New Yorker
decided to grab one of my cameras). I thought I had
most of the bases covered.

Fifth Avenue early that cold January evening was a
loud and brittle place to be. The traffic was thick and
jarring and smelly, and the sidewalks were cluttered
with the kind of people that only a city like Manhattan can produce—people who are quick-moving and
purposeful and independent, people who could easily
have sprung up from the streets and sidewalks.

I was near East 62nd Street, a couple of blocks
from Central Park South, when I saw a young man
walking toward me. He was dressed only in a ragged

T-shirt, jeans, and sandals—no coat, no gloves, no hat. I smiled. I have always enjoyed New York's crazies; they're easy to talk to, and they usually love being photographed. I swung my Nikon up and aimed it at this particular crazy. I had a 43-86mm zoom on the Nikon; I focused, took a few shots, and reached into my camera bag for a faster lens. That's when the guy saw me. He was about half a block away. He slowed, looked quizzically at me, and stopped walking when he was a couple of yards off. I saw that there was something imprinted on his T-shirt: "War is not healthy for children or other living things." I thought how quaint that was.

The guy nodded at the Nikon. "What you doin' with that thing, man?" he asked. He had a big, square head, a short and ragged reddish-brown beard and mustache, and his eyes suggested strongly that he'd gone without eating for some time. His voice cracked often, and it was a soft, high tenor, so I had trouble hearing him above the noises of traffic.

"I'm a photographer," I told him. It was my stock answer in such situations, and it usually was explanation enough. Few people want to get in the way of someone's work.

"Yeah?" he said. He seemed very ill-at-ease. "Photographer for who?"

"For myself," I answered. I was smiling blandly; I was certain that I looked friendly, sincere, harmless. "I'm doing a book."

"A book? Shit, ain't we all doin' a book?"

"Sorry?"

"Ain't we all doin' a book?" he repeated. "Ain't we all doin' a book."

"No," I said; I was a little offended. "Not all of us." I nodded at the Nikon. "If you don't want me to take your picture—"

"You working for the government, man?"

"No. I'm working for myself, as I said. I'm doing a book."

"Ain't we all?" he said.

"No," I said.

"Ain't we *all* doin' a book? Ain't we *all* doin' a book?"

He was beginning to make me nervous.

"Aren't you cold dressed like that?" I asked him.

He nodded at the Nikon again. "What you doin' with that thing, man?"

"I'm a photographer."

"Yeah," he said. "Photographer for who? You working for the government?"

"No, I'm working for myself." I realized that we'd been over that territory already. "But, as I said, if you don't want me taking your picture—"

"Photographer for who?" he said.

I didn't answer. I put the fast lens and the Nikon in my camera bag.

There are several kinds of crazies in New York City. There are the cute crazies, like the guy who dresses up in a bunny costume and skates down Broadway, and the pathetic crazies, like the ones who hang around at Grand Central and like the old men feeding pigeons and the old women who spend

much of their time at the New York Library, and
there are the malevolent crazies, like the big, power-
fully built man wielding a baseball bat who used to
prowl the East Village dressed only in white jockey
shorts. And there are the certifiable crazies, the ones
who have no business at all being outside the walls of
Bellevue. This guy, I judged, was one of those, and I
didn't want to have too much more to do with him.

I smiled at him again, nervously this time. "Okay,"
I said, "catch ya later," and turned to go back the
way I'd come.

"Ain't we *all* doin' a book?" I heard. "Ain't we
all doin' a book?"

I glanced around at him. He was leaning against a
building now, his eyes lowered and his big head
twitching to the left in time with that phrase: "Ain't
we *all* (twitch) doin' a book. Ain't we *all* (twitch)
doin' a book?"

"No," I said.

"Ain't we *all* (twitch) doin' a book? Ain't we *all*
(twitch) doin' a book?"

I watched him for a few moments longer. He'd
apparently forgotten about me. He reminded me precisely of a wind-up toy that's gotten itself stuck
against a wall.

I hurried back to the apartment, made myself a
grilled cheese sandwich and tomato soup, watched
something X-rated on cable TV, and went to bed at a
little after 10:00, which is early for me. The cold air
makes me tired. It has always made me tired.

CHAPTER NINE

Phyllis came back to the apartment at about 2:00 that morning. I heard her come in; she was singing softly. I couldn't hear the words clearly, but it sounded like a nursery rhyme, and since I had been only on the edges of sleep all night, hoping she'd come back, it woke me.

I called to her from the bedroom: "Phyllis?"

She went on singing.

"Phyllis?" I called again, and added, "Is that you?"

"Yes," she called back, "it's me." And she continued singing.

I'd left the bedroom door open, and I stared now at the doorway—very dark and monolithic at the center of the cream-colored walls—and waited for her to appear in it. I waited a full five minutes. Then I called once more: "Phyllis?"

She still was singing. She did not answer me.

"Phyllis, are you going to sleep on the couch?"

She went on singing. Her voice sounded a little raspy, as if she were coming down with a cold.

"Did you lock the door behind you, Phyllis?" I called.

I still had my eyes on the doorway; she appeared very quickly in it, as if she had been there all the while, and I was simply not seeing her. "Jesus!" I breathed. "You scared me!" I could not see her well in the darkness, but I could tell that she was wearing only a bra and panties.

"I didn't *mean* to scare you, Abner." Her voice was low, and that slight raspiness gave it a kind of gritty sensuality. "I don't *want* to scare you, Abner."

"It's all right," I said. "Did you lock the door behind you?"

"The door's locked."

I reached to my right to turn on the bedside lamp.

"No," she said, and there was urgency in her voice. "No, Abner, the dark is better. Don't you like the dark?"

"Yes," I said, and settled back. "Art called."

"Art?"

"Uh-huh. At about eight o'clock. He was checking to see if everything was okay here. I didn't mention you; I didn't think it would be . . . politic."

She didn't acknowledge that. She started singing again. I could hear the words now: *Hush little baby, don't say a word, Mama's gonna buy you a mocking-*

bird . . . And I liked the way she sang it. "Do you think it would have been politic, Phyllis?"

She still didn't acknowledge me. She took her hands from the edges of the doorway, let her arms hang loosely at her sides, stepped into the room a few feet, stopped. She continued singing. I asked her, then, "Where are you going to sleep, Phyllis? Are you going to sleep here? With me?" She stepped further into the room; she was in pale light coming in through the window. She reached behind herself, unfastened her bra, slipped out of it, let it fall. She came forward, stopped at the side of the bed. I could see her very clearly now. I reached up, cupped her breasts in my hands. I told her her breasts were lovely; I used the word *lovely*. It was a word that seemed to please her; she smiled slightly.

She slipped her panties off, swung her leg over so that she was straddling me. I kept my hands on her breasts; my thumbs diddled with her nipples; I felt her nipples erect. She was still singing, very low and deep in her throat. The raspiness was gone.

"I like the way you sing, Phyllis."

She leaned over; her mouth was close to mine. She smelled of damp wood. "You like *what*, Abner?"

"You, Phyllis." The odor of damp wood grew stronger, more offensive. "All of you."

"Of course you do," she whispered.

I turned my head away slightly.

"Is something *wrong*, Abner?"

I felt myself slip into her. "No," I whispered, and added, my voice suddenly very husky and very pleased, "Hell, no!"

AFTERGLOW

"Want to play Yahtzee with me, Abner?" She had thrown one of Art's robes over herself and was walking just ahead of me, toward the dining room.

"I think I want to sleep," I answered.

She chuckled. "Of course you do, Abner."

"That was quite a workout."

She stopped. She was still in front of me, her head turned away; she said, "Want to do it again?" and she sounded eager, which gave me a little boost.

"I can't," I told her. "I wish I could; I really wish I could, but I can't."

She turned her head slightly, so I could see her profile. She grinned. "All wrung out, Abner?"

"Something like that."

"Shot your wad?"

"That's right. Shot my wad. Sorry."

"Couldn't get it up with a rope, huh?"

"I don't know. In a little while, in an hour or two, maybe."

She turned her head farther, glanced down, nodded.

I glanced down. I was wearing blue bikini briefs, and they weren't doing much to cover my erection. I grinned, surprised. Phyllis grinned. She looked up at my face; "Hold that, please," she whispered.

"Sorry," I said. I felt my erection begin to fade.

"Hold that, please," she repeated. A quick laugh

erupted from her. And then another, and another. She turned away, went into the dining room. Her laughter now was continuous, and loud. I stayed put. I listened to her laughter continue. I remember thinking that it was like listening to a bad laugh track being played over and over again.

It could have continued for a couple of hours, although logic says it could only have been a minute or two. But I remember watching the darkness fade beyond the window; I remember hearing my clock radio switch on; I remember hearing someone in the apartment above get up and use the toilet. And I remember hearing her laughter over all of it. Even after I knew that she'd gone.

At the Hammet Mausoleum, Halloween, 1965

When the candles were lit and the cat's skull properly placed—between us; we were seated Indian-style in the center of the mausoleum floor, the plastic bag of Mallo Cups beside Sam—and after our fit of hysterical laughter was done, I said, "You think there'd be any spooks here anyway, Sam?"

And he said, "They don't like to be called spooks, Abner. It's disrespectful." A small, lopsided grin came and went quickly on his lips. "The proper word is *spirits*. *Spirits*, Abner, okay?"

I fidgeted; the concrete floor was hard and cold and my cheeks were going to sleep. "That sounds like bullshit, Sam." It was the first time I'd said anything like that to him, and it made me instantly uncomfortable.

"It's not," he said. One of the candles went out. There were six of them, all arranged in a circle around the cat's skull. Sam relit the candle very quickly, shook the match out, tossed it to one side, whispered, "Demon's breath did that, Abner."

And I protested, "I'm not a little kid, Sam—I'm almost as old as you—and I don't believe in demons."

"Then why are you here?"

"I believe in *spooks*—I believe in spirits."

"Do you?" he asked. "Do you really?"

I thought about that, and at last I answered, "I don't know for sure. I guess not. I don't know." And the same candle went out. I nodded at it. "What is that anyway, Sam?—Is that some kind of trick candle or something?"

"No," he said.

I smiled. "You're fulla shit, Sam. Admit it."

"Maybe," he answered. He took the box of kitchen matches out of his pocket, lit one, touched it to the candle. "Demon's breath," he whispered.

"Shit!" I said aloud.

"Demon's breath did that." He was still whispering; I could barely hear him. "*My* breath did that."

"What're you—still trying to scare me, Sam? It won't work."

"*My* breath," he said again. He grinned. "Gotta have some nourishment." He reached into the plastic bag, withdrew two Mallo Cups, unwrapped them, tossed the wrappers aside, popped one, then quickly the other of the Mallo Cups into his mouth. He touched the bag. "Want some, Abner?"

"No, thanks."

"Good stuff, Abner."

"Not here, Sam."

"Oh," he said, and glanced about. "Sure."

CHAPTER TEN

In Manhattan: January 14th, 1983

I showered; I shaved. Then, at 8:30, I went out to breakfast at a little Greek restaurant near Lexington Avenue and East 75th Street. It was small; the tables were small, the chairs straight-backed and uncomfortable—but the eggs were cooked in real butter, and the whole wheat bread was *real* whole wheat, the fresh-squeezed orange juice real fresh-squeezed, and the service was excellent. There are ten thousand places like it in Manhattan.

And when I was just about finished and was pushing some remnants of egg yolk across my plate with a piece of toast, a good-sized cockroach scooted across the top of the table and disappeared around the underside. I leaned over, looked under the table, saw that the cockroach had stopped several inches from the edge of the table and was sniffing around with its little antennae. I straightened, lifted my knee reflexively into the spot where the roach was, heard the roach crack, heard it hit the grimy tile floor. After a moment I looked at where I supposed it had fallen, but saw nothing. I ordered more coffee, lingered over it, thought about the photo book, about Phyllis, about how great it was to be alive, and working, and falling in love.

I had an appointment with Serena Hitchcock that morning at 10:00. So, at 9:30, I went straight there by bus from the restaurant.

"Sit down, Abner," she said, and nodded at the armless, steel-framed chair in front of her desk. "God, you look awfully tired."

"Yes," I said. "I feel tired." I sat, took the signed contracts from my coat pocket and handed them across the desk. Serena took them, gave them a quick once-over. "No problems with these, I assume, Abner?"

I shook my head. "No problems."

"And that July deadline is okay?"

"I'd have preferred a few extra months, but I can do it. I'll just work a little harder, sleep a little less. I'm looking forward to it, Serena."

"Good." She smiled pleasantly and set the contracts aside. "We'll get you your advance check as soon as possible, within a week I hope; it's got to come out of Chicago—"

"That's fine, Serena," I cut in. "I'm not starving." Which was true, thanks to my father's life insurance policy; it hadn't left me independently wealthy, but it had made it possible for me to worry about things other than money.

"Good," she said. "We wouldn't want you to starve, now, would we?" She put her hands palms-down on her desk; it was a signal that I should leave. I stood.

She said, "You really do look tired. You're not coming down with something, I hope."

"No. I don't think so, Serena. I had . . . a long night." I tried in vain to suppress a big, shit-eating grin. I said through it, "I didn't get as much sleep as I needed to, I'm afraid."

She nodded, said, "Uh-huh," and stuck her hand out. I took it. "Well, Abner, it's good to have you on board. I just *know* that you're going to give us one hell of a book."

"Sure I am, Serena." I paused, went on, "Serena?"

"Yes?"

"Is there a man working here, maybe an editor, I don't know—he's in his forties, his middle forties, handsome, I suppose, and he wears a gray, pinstriped suit—"

"A suit, Abner? No one wears a suit."

"No one?"

"Of course not. These are liberated times. We wear what is comfortable; we wear what we can work in. Look at me, for instance."

I did. She was wearing designer jeans and a white,

short-sleeved blouse. She looked casual. "Uh-huh. You look pretty good, Serena."

"Do I?" She sounded pleased.

"Sure. You look . . . informal."

"Informal?" Her tone changed.

"I mean, you look . . ." I was stuck.

"You mean I look 'good' and 'informal,' Abner?"

"No." I smiled an apology. "I mean you look . . . very attractive."

She grinned. I realized that she was toying with me. "No one here wears a suit, Abner. Not any more. Our accountant used to, all the time—the same damned suit every day, a gray pinstripe. It got pretty threadbare, I remember. They buried him in it, which probably pleased him."

"They buried him in it, Serena? You mean he's dead?"

"Yes, Abner." Another grin. "At last report."

"Oh, of course," I murmured. "I'm sorry." I nodded at the contracts on her desk. "About a week, you say then, on the check? It has to come out of Chicago?"

"Maybe two weeks, Abner. It depends on what side of the bed those people get up on, I'm afraid. If there's a problem—"

"No, no problem. Thanks." I shook her hand again, turned, went to the door, looked back. "I should have something to show you in a few weeks, Serena—by the end of the month anyway."

"Good, that's good. I'm looking forward to it."

I opened the door. I heard: "Abner?"

I looked back. "Yes?"

"Get some sleep, okay?"

"I'll try to," I answered. I liked her maternal tone. "I really will try to, Serena. Thanks for your concern," I added, and then I left.

CHAPTER ELEVEN

January 20

These are the things I knew about Phyllis Pellaprat from our first week together at Art's apartment: I knew that she was intelligent, that she was incredibly sensuous, that she liked to play Yahtzee—Christ, she liked to play Yahtzee—and I knew also that she was not a romantic. This disappointed me because I am a romantic; I have always been a romantic—the words *I love you* fly easily from my lips. And when I said to her for the very first time, "Phyllis, I love you," her reaction was not what I had hoped for.

I said it to her after lovemaking, a couple of days into our relationship. I thought that that was probably the best of times to say *I love you*; I figured that most people said it then. So I said it to her. When the screeching and sweating and fun were over and we'd become civilized human beings once again, I whispered, "Phyllis, I love you." I wasn't sure that I meant it; I *was* sure that I *would* mean it, in time, which is all that really mattered.

She was straddling me. She liked to straddle me. I liked it, too.

I felt her stiffen up.

"I really do, Phyllis," I added. It was dark in the room. She likes to make love in the dark. I don't. My hands were on her upper arms, and I could feel her muscles go taut and her knees close hard on the lower part of my ribcage, which began to hurt at once.

She growled.

No, it wasn't a growl. It was a hum. A low, ragged hum. I thought for a moment that she was going to sing again, as she had our first night together, but she didn't sing. Her knees continued to close hard on my ribcage.

"That hurts, you know," I said.

She continued humming.

I slipped out of her then. "You don't want me to say 'I love you,' Phyllis?"

Her knees closed harder.

I was having trouble breathing. The pressure her knees were putting on my ribcage was in turn putting pressure on my diaphragm.

"You can cut that out now, Phyllis," I managed, and pretended to chuckle.

That's when she stopped. And it's when I got angry.

"Christ, Phyllis! Jesus Christ—you act like I insulted you. Christ!" I massaged my ribcage.

She got off me, stood at the side of the bed for a moment, with her back turned. She laughed a low, soft, quick laugh; it sounded just like it was coming from another room.

I remember it gave me a chill.

"Aren't you even going to apologize, Phyllis?"

"I don't give apologies anymore, Abner. I'm through giving apologies to anyone."

"Oh," I said. I didn't want to fight.

She left the room then. I stayed in bed, massaging my ribs, and felt very confused for a long while.

Upon reflection, I don't believe that I loved her that first time I told her I loved her. I believe that I *wanted* her, but not that I loved her. She didn't seem quite vulnerable enough, and that—vulnerability, or at least the pretense of it—is something I've always enjoyed in a woman.

I actually began loving her, I think, two days later, when she brought her parents over to meet me.

They were there, in the apartment, seated with Phyllis at the dining room table when I got home from a day's shooting in Central Park. I saw that they'd been eating something that looked like crumb cake—a small slice of it was left in a pie tin on the table.

Phyllis' father was a tall and awkward-looking man. His skin was a light gray-brown in color, and he was, I guessed, well into his sixties. He had large, round eyes set in a huge, skeletal head that seemed to bob slightly, and at random, as if the connection at the neck were weak.

Phyllis' mother was much like Phyllis herself. She was tall, though not quite as tall as her daughter, and exquisite-looking, with just the whisper of age around her eyes and mouth. She spoke in a low, soft voice that was fully as sensuous as her daughter's and also without a trace of accent.

Phyllis said, as soon as I came in, "Abner, these are my parents. This is my mother; her name is Lorraine." Lorraine said hello and smiled pleasantly. "And this is my father, whose name is Thomas."

I came forward, extended my hand. "Hello, Mr. Pellaprat." He stood, took my hand; his grip was very strong.

"Hello, Abner Doubleday," he began. He spoke at a level that was close to a shout, and I guessed that he was hard-of-hearing. "How are you?" He grinned a huge, toothy grin.

"Cray," I corrected. "My name is Abner W. Cray."

"Yes," he said, grinning wider. "Abner Doubleday. Hello." He let go of my hand and sat down again.

I pardoned myself then, to use the bathroom and to put my camera gear away. When I returned ten minutes later, Phyllis motioned me to sit at the end of the table opposite her. I did it. She said, "I wanted you to meet them, Abner. I wanted them to meet you."

"Yes," I said, nodding at Lorraine Pellaprat and then at her husband. "Of course. I'm really very glad to meet you both." The odor of damp wood was very strong. I supposed that it was a kind of family odor—something all of them shared.

Mr. and Mrs. Pellaprat were dressed nicely, she in a well-cut herringbone-tweed pants suit, and he in a dark blue suit, which was clearly not something off-the-rack, and black, highly polished wingtips. Phyllis had put a fussy white blouse on, and a knee-length, black pleated skirt and beige sandals. I thought they were a good-looking family, if just a tad stiff.

Lorraine Pellaprat told me, "We've been having a little snack," and nodded at the pie-tin, which was now empty.

"But it's all gone," said Thomas Pellaprat. "So I'm afraid we can't share it with you, much as we'd like to."

"You wouldn't enjoy it anyway," Lorraine said. "It's an acquired taste."

I nodded at her plate, which had some remnants in it. "Crumb cake?" I asked.

"Certainly," she answered, and a little, pleased smile creased her mouth. "Crumb cake. Our own recipe." Her smile broadened quickly, then quickly flickered out.

"You are a photographer?" Thomas Pellaprat asked, almost at a shout. "Tell me, please—why do you do that?"

"I'm sorry?" I answered. His question confused me.

"Why do you take photographs, Mr. Doubleday?

Why do you take photographs? Is it to capture the past?"

"It's my job—"

"Because if it is to capture the past, Mr. Doubleday—"

"*Cray*, please. Not Doubleday. I know that the two sound pretty much alike."

"Then you do not need a camera for that," he finished, ignoring my interruption. "And what does a camera give you anyway? It gives you *images*; it gives you *illusions*."

"Of course," I began, "but they are fairly *true* illusions—"

"Like our crumb cake," he cut in, and smiled his huge, toothy smile, which seemed to announce loudly that he was suddenly very proud of himself.

Lorraine looked over at him, her face blank. And Phyllis looked over at him, too.

"Like the crumb cake?" I asked. "I don't understand."

Silence.

"Phyllis?" I coaxed.

She turned to look at me. So did her mother. And then her father. Their mouths opened a little. Their eyes seemed to be in a kind of twilight, half in sleep.

And I felt suddenly as if I were all alone in that room.

"Phyllis?" I coaxed again, and I studied her face. I thought, strangely, that the beauty had gone out of it, that it seemed somehow flat, unresponsive.

That's when I said it the second time, out of desperation, I think. "Phyllis, I love you!"

It got no reaction.

I said it again. "Phyllis, I love you; I do love you."

Her mouth moved. I heard words come from it— these words: "*Do* you love me, Abner?"

I felt a smile flicker across my lips. "I *do* love you, Phyllis." It was as if my words could pull her back from some abyss. "Oh, yes, I *do* love you, Phyllis."

She said it again, as if she were pleading with me. "*Do* you love me, Abner?"

And I said, "Yes, Phyllis, I *do* love you—" And I heard: "Oh, you *must* come and see us, Mr. Doubleday." I shifted my gaze. Lorraine Pellaprat was smiling very broadly and pleasantly at me. "You *must* come and see us, Mr. Doubleday, very soon."

"Yes," I said tentatively. "I'd like that."

"Some evening very soon."

"I'd like that very much."

"*Tomorrow* evening, Mr. Doubleday."

"Tomorrow? I don't know; I'm not sure—"

"Tomorrow evening at 8:30." She stood. Her husband stood, although a little unsteadily because his chair nearly fell backwards to the floor; he caught it. Lorraine went on, "Phyllis will show you the way."

"Of course," I said.

"We're on East 95th Street, Mr. Doubleday. Phyllis will show you the way."

They rounded the table together and started for the

door. Phyllis stood. I stood. Phyllis took my arm and led me to the door with them.

"Tomorrow, then," Lorraine Pellaprat said.

"Yes," I said, "tomorrow."

Thomas Pellaprat extended his hand; I took it. "Good to meet you, Mr Doubleday."

"And you, too, Mr. Pellaprat."

"Until tomorrow, then?"

"Yes, tomorrow. I'm looking forward to it."

"Of course you are."

They left the apartment. Phyllis and I stood in the doorway together and watched as they walked to the elevator. We watched, smiling, as they waited. And, at last, when the elevator came, they waved, and we waved, and the aged man who had been working the elevator a week earlier—and whom I hadn't seen since—stuck his head out. "Hello, sir," he said to me. And I nodded at him and said, "Hello."

I am not going to try and make you believe that what follows is a love story. Because it's so much more than that.

When I hear the words *love story*, I think of Ali McGraw and Ryan O'Neal, Humphrey Bogart and Ingrid Bergman, Woody Allen and Diane Keaton, Taylor and Burton, Streisand and Redford. I do not think of Abner W. Cray and Phyllis Pellaprat.

CHAPTER TWELVE

At the Hammet Mausoleum, Halloween, 1965

I asked Sam again, "Is that some kind of trick-candle or something, Sam?" because it went out a third time, and he relit it.

"Could be," he said. "But it ain't."

"Then what keeps blowing it out, for crimey's sake?" I shifted a little on the cold cement floor because my legs had started to go to sleep.

"Spooks and demons," Sam answered.

"I don't think I believe in demons, Sam. I don't even know what a demon is. And maybe I believe in spooks, and maybe I don't, but I sure don't think they'd hang around here."

"Who's to say?" he asked. "Not me and not you, that's for certain."

We were both seated cross-legged on the floor.

Sam lifted one cheek then, and a long, noisy fart came from him. He looked pleased.

I waved at the air. "Jees, that stinks."

"We can light 'em," he said.

"Shit," I said.

"Light the old demon farts." He chuckled. "Light the demon's breath!" He chuckled again, though lower in his throat, as if to himself. "Demon fire!" he whispered tightly.

"I wanta leave," I said.

"I have demon fire in my shorts."

"You're being real stupid, Sam."

He reached out, stroked the cat's skull very slowly and lovingly. "You're a nice cat, Flora," he said several times as he stroked it. "You're a nice cat, Flora."

"You're giving me the creeps, goddamnit!" I said.

"You're supposed to have the creeps," he said. "We're sitting in here with a bunch of dead people, so you're supposed to have the creeps."

"I wanta leave," I said again.

"Go ahead."

"I mean it," I said.

"No, you don't. You don't mean it."

And he was right. I didn't mean it.

In Manhattan, January 23, 1983

It was a little past 7:00 when Phyllis and I left Art DeGraff's apartment to catch a bus for her parents' home on East 95th Street. She seemed very excited, and I realized that it was the first time we'd been out of the apartment together.

She had dressed warmly—although it was an unseasonably mild evening—in a stylish, white, waist-length mink coat ("Fake," she told me, "but don't let on."), a mid-calf-length green dress, and white, knee-high boots with stacked heels. She looked very sexy.

"You look sexy as hell, Phyllis," I told her. We were walking east on East 79th Street, arm in arm.

"Thank you, Abner." She seemed pleased. "Tonight is very special."

"Yes," I said. "I think so, too."

"They didn't like Art."

"Your parents, you mean?"

She nodded. "They didn't approve of him. Because he was white."

"I'm white, Phyllis."

"And because he had money."

"I have money, too. Not as much as Art does, it's true—"

"And because he liked to hit me."

"He hit you?"

"With his fist. When he got angry."

"Christ, I had no idea, Phyllis."

"He got angry once because his team lost the Super Bowl. He threw me across the room, and then he hit me. Three times. Twice in the face. And then in the stomach. He had to take me to the hospital."

"My God, I never realized Art was like that, Phyllis. I mean, when he was married to Stacy—"

She cut in, "I remember the hospital. It was on the Lower East Side. St. Ignatius. I remember it smelled bad. I remember it was noisy. And I remember I hurt."

I looked at her. She was staring straight ahead.

"I remember I hurt," she repeated. She was speaking in a dead, husky monotone. "I never hurt like that before. Not like that. And I knew that Art had done something bad to me. Something no one was ever going to be able to fix."

I grinned at her, though she wasn't looking at me. I said, "Well, thankfully, Phyllis, they *did*—"

"I heard them say that he'd broken my jaw and that he'd ruptured my spleen, too." I noticed then that she was walking very stiffly, as if she were in pain; I asked her if she was all right, and she ignored me. "They said my spleen had to come out. 'It's got to come out,' they said. So they took it out. And then I heard them say that I had lost a lot of blood, too much blood." We were closing on the bus stop; there were a half-dozen people clustered at it, and one of them, a young black man smoking a cigarette and wearing a gray sports jacket and black scarf, who was hugging himself for warmth—which I thought was odd, because it wasn't a cold evening—looked over, smiled, and nodded.

Someone else at the bus stop said loudly, "There it is," and pointed. I looked and saw our bus a block-and-a-half away. "We'd better hurry up, Phyllis," I said, and walked faster. She kept pace with me. She said, "Too much blood. That's what I heard them say: 'Too much blood.' And I remember looking down at myself and thinking, 'Gee, that really *is* too much blood . . .'' The young man in the gray sports jacket and black scarf tossed his cigarette down, smiled and nodded again. It was then that I realized he was nodding at Phyllis.

"Phyllis?" I said. "Do you know that guy?"

She wasn't listening to me. She was still talking about St. Ignatius, and though she was keeping pace with me, she was still walking very stiffly and was still speaking in that awful, dead, husky monotone. "I saw them put the I-V bags up. I wanted to yell at them, 'Hey, that's not going to do any good.' "

I heard the bus behind us, closing fast; we were a good fifty feet from the bus stop. "We'd better run, Phyllis," I said, and began jogging toward the stop. I soon realized that Phyllis had fallen behind. I looked back.

She was trying to jog. She was trying very hard. But she was keeping her arms straight and stiff at her sides. And her knees were not bending correctly as she ran; they were bowing slightly outward, as if her thigh muscles had become very weak, and the only connection between her thighs, knees, and calves was in the bones themselves. And she had her head held high, too, so her chin was jutting forward, and a pathetic, tight-lipped, wide-eyed look of grim determination was on her face.

I stopped jogging at once.

She caught up with me. I put my arm out so it fell

across her chest and so my hand was clutching her left shoulder. She stopped. "Phyllis . . ." I began.

The bus pulled up to the bus stop. The small crowd of people started getting on.

"You okay, Phyllis?"

And she answered, her voice a long, shallow wheeze, "I don't think I'm used to the exercise, Abner. Forgive me. Please forgive me. It's the cold air—"

"What's to forgive, Phyllis?"

She said nothing; she looked confused.

"C'mon," I said. "That bus isn't going to wait forever."

Thomas and Lorraine Pellaprat lived in what appeared, at first glance, to be a long-abandoned apartment house not unlike several thousand others in Manhattan. It was a ten-story building, the color of dirty cream, with tall, narrow windows, and it was streaked brown here and there from air pollution. Several of the windows visible from the street had been covered by plywood, and a few others appeared to be broken.

"This is where your parents live, Phyllis?" I said. I was confused; the Pellaprats had looked very much like they had money.

She answered, "Apartment 506, Abner."

"We'll probably have to walk up, right?"

"Probably."

"I was going to bring them a bottle of wine, some rosé—"

"No," she cut in. "They don't drink. They used to, but not anymore."

"Not at all?"

"Not a drop."

We were standing at the base of the wide, crumbling cement steps. I held my hand out toward them. "Shall we?" I said.

And Phyllis said, her eyes on the middle of the building, apparently on her parents' apartment, "This is a very special night, Abner. You have no idea how special. This has not been done before." And she started quickly up the steps, her movements now very fluid and graceful.

I followed.

At the Hammet Mausoleum, Halloween, 1965

Sam said to me, "We're just having some fun, Abner. Don't you think this is fun?"

I shrugged. "I'm getting cold, Sam."

"It's the demon's breath on your bones."

"Shit, too!"

"What are you—afraid we're going to get caught?"

I shrugged again. "Maybe."

" 'Cuz who's gonna catch us, you know?" He nodded to his right, then his left. "You think these people here could care less? Shit, they're probably happy for the company."

"Uh-huh." Another shrug. "Maybe we should go, Sam. Maybe this wasn't such a good idea."

"We won't *touch* 'em, for Christ's sake!"

"Who said anything about touching 'em, Sam? *I*

didn't. I'm not *sick*—" I changed my position again on the cement floor; my entire right leg was asleep. "Jees, Sam, if we stay here much longer my whole damn body's gonna be asleep."

"Quiet!" he said, and his finger went to his mouth. "Shh!"

"Gimme a break—"

"Quiet! I *hear* something!"

I put my hand on the floor, prepared to stand.

"Sit *down*, Goddamnit!"

I sat.

"I really do, Abner." A short pause. "I hear someone talking."

CHAPTER THIRTEEN

I have learned this, too, in the past six months; I have learned that even the dead are ignorant.

Phyllis and I had to walk up to Apartment 506. The elevator clearly was not working; its doors were stuck open, and the car itself was stalled several feet below floor level.

"When was the last time you visited your parents, Phyllis?" I asked.

We started for the stairway, to the right, across the lobby. The lobby was dark, but not pitch dark; there were several low-wattage, bare bulbs installed at regular intervals in dull beige, leaf-motif ceiling fixtures.

Phyllis answered, "Not for a long while, Abner."

The building's interior was clean—which I'd

expected, despite its outward appearance, because the Pellaprats had appeared to be very clean people.

"Have your mother and father been here long, Phyllis?" I asked.

We started up the stairs. They too were lit by the same kind of low-wattage bulbs in the same kind of ceiling fixtures. She answered, "Yes, Abner, I believe that they have."

The stairs were made of metal, so her high-heeled boots made a lot of noise.

"You don't keep in touch with them, do you?" It was more a statement than a question.

"We find it difficult to keep in touch, Abner. We always have. We have different . . . approaches to living, I think."

We got to the second-floor landing. I looked up, toward the third floor; there was no light. "Be careful, Phyllis," I said.

She did not answer. She was walking several feet ahead of me, to my right, and as we climbed toward the third floor, I found that the only way I could tell where she was, exactly, was by her white coat and her white boots and the sound her high heels made when they hit the metal stairs—a kind of rhythmic, echoing *clop-clop* noise.

I heard her say: "They liked you, Abner. They didn't like Art. Art was cruel. And Art had money."

She was speaking, again, in the same, low, husky monotone I'd heard her use when we were making our way to the bus stop. "Yes," I said, "you told me about Art." I quickened my pace on the stairs to catch up with her, but she stayed several feet ahead of me, though the timing of her heels on the metal steps didn't change. "I still can't believe it, Phyllis—"

"I remember St. Ignatius, Abner. I remember I hurt, and I remember that I bled."

I took a chance, then, and mounted two stairs in one stride; "It must be awfully painful to remember," I began, and found that she still was several feet ahead of me, her heels clop-clopping on the metal steps. "I've never had surgery myself, Phyllis."

"And I don't blame him anymore, Abner. I did at first—in the first couple of days."

"That's very generous."

"I remember thinking, Abner, how strange it was that there still *were* days."

"I'm sorry, Phyllis. I don't understand that."

"Of course you do; of course you understand it, Abner."

We got to the third-floor landing. I stopped a moment, to rest, because the air here was stale and hard to breathe. "Want to hold on a moment, Phyllis, until I can catch my breath?" She kept walking. "Phyllis?" I called. I saw her white coat and white boots merge with the darkness. I still could hear the clop-clop of her heels on the metal steps, and I called to her again, "Phyllis, hold on, okay?" And I sensed something like desperation in my voice. I grinned, as if to chase it away. "Jesus, it's pitch dark down here, Phyllis." The clop-clop of her heels ended. She called back, "Abner? Are you there?"

"Yes, right here, Phyllis. Hold on." I started up the stairs, toward the fourth floor.

"Abner, where are you? I can't see you!" And now I could hear desperation in her voice.

"It's okay, Phyllis!" I called, and quickened my pace. "It's okay; I'm coming!"

"Abner, I can't *see* you; where *are* you?" It was more than desperation that I heard in her voice now. It was something closer to panic.

"I'm right down here, Phyllis. I'm coming up to you."

"Abner, please, Abner—"

"Don't worry, Phyllis; I'm coming!" I got to the fourth-floor landing. I stopped. "Phyllis?"

"Abner, where are you?" She was pleading with me.

"Here, Phyllis. Just below you." I looked up the stairs, toward the fifth floor. I saw nothing. "Where are you, Phyllis?"

Silence.

"Phyllis?" I started for the fifth floor. "Phyllis, are you up there?" I could see the suggestion of light above me. "Phyllis, please answer me." I heard nothing.

I became aware of a cold draft from above, apparently from the fifth floor. "Phyllis?" I called again. Still nothing. The light was brighter now. I could see that there was another leaf-motif ceiling fixture with a bare low-wattage bulb installed in it. I could see, also, the top edge of the fire door that opened onto the fifth-floor hallway.

I called to Phyllis again. And again I heard nothing. I thought, *This is a kind of game she's playing.* I didn't believe it. I didn't believe she was capable of such games.

"Phyllis?" I called. I had reached the fifth-floor landing. "Phyllis?" I pulled the fire door open all the way and stepped into the hall.

Apartment 506 was directly in front of me. I stepped across the hall and knocked softly on the door.

Phyllis answered my knock at once. She was smiling playfully, and I could see Thomas and Lorraine Pellaprat behind her, in the apartment—he still in his dark blue suit and highly polished wingtips, and seated in a big, high-backed wooden chair near the far wall, and she in her nicely tailored herringbone-tweed pants suit, in a small, rose-colored upholstered rocker beside him. They had their hands folded on their laps, and they were smiling small, pleasant, friendly smiles. They nodded at me, first Thomas and then Lorraine. Then Phyllis said, "Come in, Abner, come in. Where have you been?"

I stepped in. The apartment, what I could see of it—the living room, the dining area, and a small kitchen—was sparsely decorated. The wallpaper was a slightly shabby but very delicate blue-on-white bird print with a blue-striped border, and the only piece of furniture besides the chairs the Pellaprats were sitting in was an ancient, overstuffed red couch that was standing against the left wall, kitty-corner to the Pellaprats. There were no rugs on the hardwood floors, and when Phyllis moved across them, her heels made

sharp, clicking noises, like a tap dancer's—I got
the idea that these people did a lot of dancing because there were numerous scuff marks on the floor.

I had a pleasant evening. They gave me a wine-
glass half-filled with what tasted like coffee liqueur—
which, because it was very bitter, I nursed until we
left at 10:30—and we sat around the edges of the
room and talked about light, inconsequential things.
Mr. and Mrs. Pellaprat stopped calling me Abner
Doubleday, though Phyllis had to remind them who I
was exactly: "He's my *boy*friend; you remember.
And he's not at all like Art." They nodded at this,
and smiled oddly, as if they weren't quite sure who
Art was.

We talked about the book I was doing, about the
various crises around the world, about life in Manhattan, about roaches—"We used to have them, Mr.
Cray," Lorraine told me, "but not anymore. All you
have to do is take away their source of nourishment."
—about baseball, on which Thomas Pellaprat apparently considered himself something of an expert,
though his knowledge clearly was centered on the decades of the forties and fifties. And just before Phyllis and I got up to leave, I was invited back: "Come
any time you'd like, Mr. Cray," Lorraine told me.
"With Phyllis, by yourself. It doesn't matter. We're
very informal people."

"Very informal people, Mr. Cray," echoed Thomas
Pellaprat.

I was pleased. I said "Yes, thank you" several
times. I said that I'd had a very pleasant evening,

which was essentially true. And Phyllis and I went back to Art's apartment and made love until early in the morning.

Then she left the apartment.

Which was the beginning of a routine I am only now beginning to understand.

CHAPTER FOURTEEN

Art called the day after Phyllis and I visited her parents. He was clearly upset.

"Abner, I might come home early; I don't know—this is just not working out for me here, it's just not working out for me."

"Jesus, Art, you sound awful."

"Yes, I know. I'm sorry. I tried to call Stacy, like you said. I tried to call her. But her mother told me she was in New York. What's she doing in New York, Abner? Why is she in New York? Is she looking for me?"

"Art, I don't know what in the hell you're talking about."

"I'm talking about the *accident*, Abner." He paused, chuckled humorlessly. "That's not what the cops call it, of course." Another pause. "And maybe they're right."

"I still have no idea what you're talking about, Art. You're going to have to spell it out."

"I thought you knew, Abner."

"Knew what, for Christ's sake?!"

Without hesitation, he answered, "That I killed someone."

I didn't hesitate either. "You *killed* someone, Art?"

"Yes. Her name was Phyllis."

"You killed someone named Phyllis?" I made no connection to Phyllis Pellaprat. As far as I was concerned, she was quite wonderfully alive.

"Yes," Art answered.

"When?"

"A month-and-a-half ago, just before I left. Actually, Abner, it's *why* I left."

"Christ, Art!"

"But it's not working out here. It's just not working out; I feel so alone—"

"Art, tell me who she was. Was she someone you knew?"

"Of course she was someone I knew. You think I go around killing strange women, Abner?"

"Is that supposed to be a joke?"

"No. I'm sorry." A pause. "I called to let you know that I'll probably be back sometime before May—"

"Wait a minute," I interrupted. "Wait a minute. Are the cops looking for you?"

A brief hesitation. "Maybe. I don't know. Maybe.

I thought it was all straightened out; I had *hoped* it was all straightened out." A quick chuckle of clearly pretended impatience. "But maybe it isn't, Abner. There's this homicide captain—hell, I don't even remember his name. He was there, at the hospital; his name was Whelan, I remember now. His name was Kennedy Whelan. He might show up at the apartment one of these days. You'll probably have to talk to him, I'm afraid. And he was there, Abner, at St. Ignatius, when I took Phyllis there, and he's been calling it manslaughter right from the start—"

"Did you say St. Ignatius, Art?"

"Yes. It's on the Lower East Side."

"Art, I don't understand; this is very strange—this is very, very strange. Listen to me now, because when I got here, to your apartment, I found this woman here and she told me her name was Phyllis; she said she was your girlfriend—"

"Phyllis is *dead*, Abner. She died at St. Ignatius Hospital a month-and-a-half ago. I know that because *I* killed her, so whoever this woman is, she cannot be Phyllis Pellaprat."

"She showed me a picture, Art. She got it off the mantle. It's a picture of you and her together—"

"Yes, Abner. I know the picture."

"Art, listen to me, please. Listen to me. Phyllis and I have been living together. Here. At your apartment."

"No, Abner. It's not Phyllis, it can't *be* Phyllis. You understand that. You must understand that." He was speaking slowly, his enunciation crisp, as if he were talking to a small child. "You are sharing the apartment with *someone else*, Abner. I don't know who. But my very strong suggestion is that you get *rid* of her!"

"I can't do that, Art. I love this woman; I really do love this woman."

"Jesus!" He was clearly at a loss for words. "Jesus, Abner—"

"We'll move out if you'd like, Art."

"I can't ask you to do that." He sounded uncertain.

"Art, I *trust* her."

"Of course you do. I just want to know who she is, Abner; you can understand that."

"She said her name was Phyllis; I don't know— she showed me the picture. Hell, Art, she even introduced me to her parents."

"Phyllis Pellaprat's parents are dead."

"Well, for Christ's sake, I met *someone*, Art."

"I believe you. I do believe you. But now I think, for your sake, and for my sake, Abner, that you have to find out who the woman is. There are lots of con games going on, and obviously someone read about it . . ." There was a short pause; when he continued, his voice had altered slightly, had become higher in pitch. "Someone read about the shooting—"

"The shooting?"

"Yes." Another pause. "That's how Phyllis died, Abner. I shot her."

"Good God!"

"I had a gun. I was cleaning it. Christ, it's the same old story, isn't it? I was cleaning the gun, and I didn't know it had any live rounds in it, and it went off—''

"What in the hell did you have a gun for, Art?"

"For protection. You need a gun in Manhattan, Abner. Ask anyone. It's not like Bangor."

"She told me you hit her. She said that you hit her in the stomach and you ruptured her spleen and she went to St. Ignatius . . ."

"Abner, please, find out who this woman really is, okay?! Because she is *not* Phyllis Pellaprat."

"Yes, I realize that."

"I've got to go now."

"Can I have your number, Art. In case I need to get hold of you?"

"Sure, Abner. I'll see that you get it. Good-bye." And he hung up.

CHAPTER FIFTEEN

I called Stacy's home in Bangor immediately. Her mother answered.

"Hello, Aunt Jocelyn," I said. I sat in a dining room chair near the phone. "It's Abner."

"Hello, Abner." She sounded strained, as if she didn't want to talk. "What can I do for you?"

Jocelyn Horn and I never got along. She guessed right from the beginning how I felt about her daughter, and I knew that she harbored deep-seated feelings of anger and resentment toward me because of it. She also thought I was a tad perverse; Stacy *was* my cousin, after all.

"I'm calling from Manhattan, Aunt Jocelyn. Could I talk to Stacy, please?"

"No, I'm afraid you can't," she said.

"She's out?" I asked.

"No. She's away."

"Oh? Away where?"

"Abner, Paul and I have been discussing you."
Paul is Stacy's father, Jocelyn's husband.

"Uh-huh."

"And it's not that we don't like you, Abner. We do. *I* do, anyway. And I think Paul does, too. He's never actually said that he does, but he's never said that he doesn't, either."

"What are you driving at, Aunt Jocelyn?" She's the kind of person who has lots of very firm and very well-thought-out opinions, but who also finds it extremely difficult to express them. She needs to be prodded. "Just tell me what you're driving at, okay?"

"What I'm *driving* at, Abner, is you and Stacy."

"What about me and Stacy?"

"My God, Abner— My God, what if she were to get pregnant?"

"You're not making any sense, Aunt Jocelyn."

"The world's already full of idiots, Abner. It doesn't need any more of them."

"Oh, for God's sake, Aunt Jocelyn—"

"And it's not that I don't like you. I *do* like you; so does Paul—you're my sister's boy, so you're really a part of me, sort of, in a way—"

"Could you just tell me where Stacy is, Aunt Jocelyn?"

"And I think the real problem is *you*, Abner, and this . . . unseemly attraction you have—"

"Is she in New York? Just say yes or no, Aunt Jocelyn. Yes or no."

"I can't tell you where she is; I *won't* tell you where she is, Abner. Paul and I have been discussing this, and Paul and I have come to the conclusion—"

I hung up, an act which I regretted at once because I liked Jocelyn (despite her opinions of my relationship with Stacy, opinions which were essentially true and good and moral), so I redialed her number, waited for two rings, and hung up again. I've never liked confrontation very much.

Phyllis came in then. She came in very quietly, snuck up behind me, and put her hands over my eyes. "Guess who?" she said, sounding playful.

"Art called," I told her.

"Art?" She kept her hands over my eyes.

"Your former boyfriend. Art DeGraff. The guy who owns this apartment; you remember him."

"Art DeGraff?" She kept her hands over my eyes.

"Uh-huh. He called and we had a good long talk."

"Did you?" She sounded unconcerned; her hands stayed over my eyes. I put my hands around her wrists; her skin was cool, the muscles taut.

"Please," I said, "take your hands away."

She didn't. "I hate him," she said. "I will always hate him." Her hands tightened. "He should be punished for what he did to me."

"Phyllis, please—" I tried to pull her hands away. I couldn't. "Phyllis, what in the hell are you doing?"

"Guess who?" she said, in exactly the same playful tone she'd used a minute earlier.

"I don't know," I answered, trying for a tone of deadly seriousness. "I really do not know."

"Yes," she said. "How could you?" And she laughed. I tried again to pull her hands away, but in vain. "Phyllis, you're hurting me."

"I'm sorry," she said. "I don't want to hurt you." I believed it. I tried to stand, but her incredibly stiff arms and hands kept me seated. "Please don't do that, Phyllis."

"Do you love me, Abner?"

"Please, Phyllis, let me up."

"Do you *love* me, Abner? Do you *love* me?" It sounded strangely like an ultimatum.

I answered, "Yes, I love you."

"And will you take my pain away?"

"I will, Phyllis. Yes. I'll try." I had no idea what she was talking about.

"Because I want so much to love you, too, Abner." Her fingers tightened. "But I reach backward, and I reach inside, and I try to find it; I try to find what love is, and it's not there—it's just not there, and I wonder what it is. I wonder what it *was*."

Silence.

"Phyllis?" I said.

I became aware that her hands were no longer over my eyes.

"Phyllis?"

I heard nothing. I turned my head. The dining room was empty. I called, "Phyllis?" and stood, went into the kitchen, called to her again. I went into the bedroom, the bathroom. I did not find her.

I went out, into the hallway. It was empty, too. I went to the elevator, pressed the button for service, waited. Eventually, it came. Empty.

The Hammet Mausoleum, Halloween, 1965

I asked, "You know what I'm talking about, Sam?"

"No," he answered.

"I mean about the spooks not wanting to hang around here."

He answered again, "No," grinned, added, "Why don't you tell me."

I readjusted my position on the cement floor so my left leg was out straight and pointing to the left. Another of the candles set around Flora's skull went out; Sam ignored it. "What I mean is," I began, "that they didn't *die* here, so why should they want to *hang around* here?" I grinned a big, self-satisfied grin because I had just uttered what I felt quite certain was the crowning profundity of my young life and I wanted to let it linger for awhile.

Sam said, "Asshole!"

"No," I said, my voice low, "I don't think so."

"Sure you are. Shit, what do *you* know? You don't *know* anything, for Christ's sake."

"Neither do you, Sam."

"The shit I don't, the shit I don't. I know this, Abner—I know that all these people here—" he gestured expansively to indicate the six vaults—"could be standing around laughing. *That's* what *I* know. And I know that they could be making love or they could be hunting out something to eat—"

"Why would they need to eat, Sam?" Another profundity, nearly as great as the first, I thought. "Why in the hell would they want to eat?"

He ignored me. He picked up where I had interrupted him. "They could be doing just about anything, Abner. That's what *I* know."

"That's not much to know, Sam. All you're saying is you don't know anything."

"I know *I'm* going to die," he said.

CHAPTER SIXTEEN

The following morning, at a little after 9:00, I called to arrange to have the locks in Art's apartment changed. I was given a tentative date of February 3: "If we can get to you by then, and I'm not sayin' we *can*, I'm sayin' we *might*," the locksmith said. "That's a little longer than I was hoping for," I said, and told him I'd get back to him, which was a lie. The whole idea seemed pretty foolish anyway, because I knew well enough that if Phyllis found she couldn't get in, there'd be no chance I'd keep her out. And that scared me. *She* scared me. She scared me in a way that I'd never been scared before; it was like having a constant, dull ache that probably signifies something serious but you won't have it looked at because you don't want to know the truth. I didn't want to know the truth about Phyllis. I wanted to believe that she was exactly what she appeared to be—a captivating, incredibly passionate, and vaguely eccentric woman with whom I was sharing Art DeGraff's apartment, at least occasionally. I wanted to believe that I was being made the brunt of some stupid joke, that she and Art had cooked the whole thing up between themselves just to rattle me. Lord knew why.

And yet I did call to have the locks changed. It was a kind of sideways affirmation of my fear and my ignorance, I realize now.

I knew that the only rational thing for me to do was to find another place to live. I also knew that I wouldn't do that either, because if I did, I'd probably never see Phyllis again.

I was lovestruck, you understand. I still am. And I was scared, too. And still am. And I think I knew that something very, very profound was happening to me. A transformation. A metamorphosis. As if I were a bottom-dwelling, all-but-blind fish who was very slowly and steadily bringing himself up into the light.

The advance check for the photo book arrived that afternoon. I went to my bank, on East 44th Street, deposited most of the check, pocketed some of it, and had a celebration lunch at a place called Marty's, on East 50th and Third Avenue. This was my first book, and I thought a celebration surely was in order, but the food—several bowls of what was purported to be homemade oyster stew, a creme-de-menthe parfait, and three glasses of scotch—began churning about in my stomach shortly after I left the restaurant, and by the time I got back to the apartment was just about ready to make its second appearance.

I sat in one of the dining room chairs, put my head down, close to my knees, clasped my hands, closed my eyes, and fought back the nausea. I'm very good at that kind of thing. Sometimes I can actually will pain to stop, if it's not awfully severe, and nausea, too, and after a few minutes my stomach calmed. I made my way to the bedroom, lay face down on the bed, and, before sleep came, noted the faint odor of damp wood, Phyllis' odor, on the pillow.

I called St. Ignatius Hospital early that evening. I tried the Admitting Office first, got transferred to the Emergency Department, and ended up talking to a Pakistani doctor named Mubarek, who told me that, "Indeed, yes, a young woman named Pellaprat, a tall black woman, sir, was admitted here, on December 10th. I was not working in the Emergency Department, you see; I only read the report the next day."

"Do you remember who worked on her, Dr. Mubarek?"

"Could I ask, please, your interest in this young woman?"

"I'm with the police," I told him. "I'm working with Kennedy Whelan, in the Homicide Division."

And Dr. Mubarek said, "Then you know that name, of course, sir." He paused very briefly, then went on, "Isn't that so?" And hung up.

*   *   *

At times it is imperative that we grab hold of something that seems real, something that has mass and weight, something that can cut, something mechanical, soulless, gauche, temporary.

We need such things when we feel certain that we are going to be caught up, suddenly—or already are caught up—in something exquisite, and eternal. Like death, or love. Or both.

And we need such things because they can help affirm for us that we are, ourselves, soulless, gauche, and temporary. Sure it's a lie; I know that it's a lie, but it's how most of us make it from one day to the next.

I tried to get hold of Kennedy Whelan. I couldn't. "He's on an assignment," I was told, so I asked whom I could talk to about a recent accidental death.

"What exactly did you want to know?" I was asked. It was a Detective Sergeant I was talking to—a woman named Spears. She was pleasant and efficient, and I got the idea right from the start that she wanted to pump me.

"I'd like some information about the victim, if that's possible," I told her.

"Yes, sir. I'm sure we can accommodate you on that. Could I ask what your interest is in this case, please?"

"Yes. She was a friend. A close friend."

"Of course. And your name is?"

I hung up and left the apartment almost immediately.

I'm not quite sure why. Paranoia, I think. The phone rang as I was leaving. I let it ring. I convinced myself that it was Detective Sergeant Spears calling back—because wonderful, new, and secret methods of tracing telephone calls had been instituted—and that she had a few questions to ask me.

I took my Nikon F. with me. I'm rarely without it—it's a kind of prop; it tells people what I am and what, approximately, they can expect from me. Everyone should be able to carry such identifying props.

I went out to East 79th Street and turned toward Central Park. It was a very cold night, probably down into the teens, and I found myself walking quickly to keep warm.

On Fifth Avenue I headed downtown. It was a route I had taken a week-and-a-half earlier, I remembered.

I saw the man in the ragged T-shirt, jeans, and sandals when I was still a good distance from him, several blocks at least, and I stopped immediately and whispered to myself, "My God, he's *still* there!" I turned to a middle-aged woman walking toward me and nodded at the man. "He's *still* there!" I said, and I smiled. I was trying to share something wonderful with her, something that could happen, I supposed, only in New York, and since she looked like a New Yorker, I thought she'd appreciate it. She ignored me. Her short, fat legs carried her quickly and purposefully past me, and I realized, as she passed, that she was talking to herself in a low, husky whisper.

I looked back at the man in the T-shirt, jeans, and

sandals. He seemed to be in exactly the same position I'd last seen him—leaning against a doorway, head twitching every few seconds. hands in front and folded, I guessed, though I couldn't be sure because I was seeing him from behind. I made my way toward him; the sidewalk was all but empty, except for him, the middle-aged woman, and four teen-aged girls trying to hail a taxi.

I stopped again, about a block from the man in the T-shirt and sandals. The block was not long, so I had a pretty good view of him now, and though I could not yet see his face, I was sure it was the same man I'd seen three weeks earlier. I didn't believe for a moment that he had actually been leaning against the building all that time, head twitching. I believed that that particular spot was probably his *favorite* spot, Lord knew why, and that he came to it every now and again to watch the events of Fifth Avenue unfold.

I remembered, then, what was on the front of his T-shirt. *War is not healthy for children or other living things*. I remembered thinking how quaint that was, remembered that it gave me a little pang of nostalgia—*A middle-aged hippie who never quite got it together*, I decided about the man. And then I realized that he wasn't middle-aged. He was in his early twenties, at most.

I made my way toward him. I passed him. After half a block, I looked back and nodded at him. He didn't acknowledge me. He kept on twitching. And it came to me that when I passed him, I had heard him say, as he had the last time I'd seen him, "Ain't we *all* doin' a book?"

And I saw, also, that the four teen-aged girls—who were behind him a couple of yards, all of them tall and perilously thin—were still trying to hail a taxi. I saw one pass them by, and then another several seconds later. I called, "Do you need a hand?" and realized, as soon as I'd asked it, that they were doubtlessly just as good at hailing taxis as I, and that I probably sounded pretty strange to them.

They were in a tight cluster at the edge of the sidewalk, near the corner of Fifth Avenue and East 61st Street. As one, they turned toward me.

I called—loudly, so they'd hear me above the noise of traffic—"I thought you might need a hand." I was trying for a note of apology. "I guess you don't. Sorry." And I started toward Central Park South. When I glanced back, moments later, they still were staring at me. I could see no sign of anger in their faces. They weren't glaring. A cat sitting on a porch and watching a passerby has much the same look of quiet, studied indifference.

Then a cab pulled up to the curb, and a moment later the cabbie yelled, "Well, c'mon, for Christ's sake, I ain't got till doomsday, and there ain't no one else gonna pick you up." The four teen-age girls turned, very slowly and very stiffly, and got into the cab.

At the Hammet Mausoleum, Halloween, 1965
I said to Sam Fearey, "What do you mean you know you're gonna die? Everybody knows they're gonna die, Sam."

He nodded, grinned; in the candlelight his face looked like a pumpkin. "Yeah, well I *know* I'm gonna die, Abner."

"Why don't we get outa here, Sam. This isn't much fun. I'm cold, and my whole body's about to go to sleep and what if we get caught—"

"What do you think, Abner? You think we oughta take a little peek at Joe Hammet? You think that would be in the nature of an educational experience, Abner?"

My mouth dropped open slightly; I could say nothing.

"It's why we came up here, Abner." Another of the candles went out. I figured, then, that there must have been a draft in the room.

I nodded at the candle. "D'joo do that, Sam?"

He grinned again, and his head bobbed, like an apple in a basin filled with water. "We got the means, Abner—to get a little peek at Joe Hammet. It wouldn't take much; I've done it once or twice before."

"Shit, you have."

His head bobbed more furiously. "I have, Abner. Coupla years ago, me and another guy, a guy named Fred—you remember Fred; he got killed by a drunk, remember? Got thrown offa his bike?"

I nodded. "Yeah, I remember."

"I was there when it happened, Abner. I saw it happen. Jees, he got thrown maybe fifty feet, maybe a hundred feet, and then he went *splat*, right into the pavement. I knew he'd bought the farm when I heard that splat. And anyway, Abner, it was me and him, me and Fred, and we broke into this funeral home across town and we had a peek at some woman who'd gotten shot by her husband—'' He stopped in midsentence, put his hand up. "Quiet!" he said.

"What do you mean, 'Quiet!'? You're the one who's talking—"

"Quiet, I said." We both fell silent for several seconds. "I hear something again, Abner."

"Me, too," I whispered. And it was true. I could hear a very faint whispering sound. "I hear somebody *whispering*, Sam—"

"Yeah, so do I. Shit, Abner—I really do!"

CHAPTER SEVENTEEN

When I got back to the apartment, the phone was ringing. I let it ring quite a few times, gathered up courage from somewhere, and answered it.

It was my cousin, Stacy.

"Stacy?" I said. "Where are you? Are you in New York?"

"Yes, Abner. I'm at the Algonquin. Do you know where that is?"

"Yes, I know where it is. What are you doing in New York, Stacy?"

I heard her sigh.

"Stacy?" I coaxed. "Are you here because of Art? Does it have something to do with Art?"

"Can you come over here, Abner? As soon as possible."

"Sure I can. I'll be there"—I checked the clock on the stove—"at 8:30. Is that okay?"

"Yes. 8:30. I'll see you then." She hung up.

Let me tell you a little bit about Stacy Horn.

She's a knockout—a genuine, old-fashioned, gee-what-a-body, I-wouldn't-kick-*her*-out-of-bed kind of woman, the kind of woman that *women* turn around and stare at. I had known her all her life, of course—she was a year younger than I—and up until her sophomore year in high school, my junior year, we were really no friendlier than cousins ought to be. We saw each other often—at family gatherings, and when her parents came to visit my parents—and we started a casual and harmless flirtation when we were entering adolesence. I think I figured at the time that I was *practicing* how to flirt and that, since Stacy was my cousin, it wasn't going to go anywhere, so no one was going to get hurt, and no one was going to care.

But then, at the middle of her sophomore year, something clicked. I was on my way to American History; she was on her way to Algebra. We passed in the hall. I winked at her; she winked at me—it was a game we'd been playing for a couple of years—and I realized that, at last, we both *meant* it, that the game had suddenly turned serious, that I wanted her and she wanted me, and that, if we could have, we would have jumped on each other right then and there. It scared the shit out of me. I stopped flirting with her; I stopped *seeing* her—when she and her family came to our house or my family and I went to hers, I only nodded at her, avoiding her eyes, and she nodded at me, avoiding mine, I think, and it wasn't until nearly a year after that wonderful wink between classes that she and I tried to get together. She was, in fact, the first girl I was able to lay my hands on, not counting a girl named Jacqueline in sixth grade, whose tiny, soft boobs happened to brush up against the backs of my fingers on a science field trip—a happenstance for which I was soundly scolded. As for the first girl I almost made it with, those honors were to go to a girl named Luanne Stephens, late in my senior year at Pierpont High.

Another thing that stopped Stacy and I from getting together right away was the fact that she was very smart, smarter than I am by a long shot, which, I remember—in the less-than-progressive early sixties—scared the shit out of me, too. How could I *fuck* her if she was smarter than I? It was a question that resolved itself very quickly: I couldn't. When push came to shove, when wink came to nudge, and nudge to snuggle, at last, I went as soft as a ripe banana.

We were at her house, a big Victorian monstrosity that her parents had done up in shades of black and brown and gray and had filled with mouldering antiques. And we were on her bed—which was about the only piece of furniture in the house, I thought, that wouldn't crumble beneath our combined weight—and we were both naked. Her parents had gone out somewhere, to a Grange Meeting, I think. They were Grangers; he was a Rotarian, as my father was, and an Elk and an Odd Fellow, and Jocelyn was a member of The PTA. I've always thought they were nice people, and I've never blamed them a bit for not being the kind of people who could have understood or appreciated what was going on in their buxom young daughter's bedroom that night. Especially in the less-than-progressive early sixties. And I tell myself, even today, that that may have been the overriding reason why I went limp. Because I was convinced that Stacy's parents were going to come home while Stacy and I were in the throes of passion, that they were going to come very quietly up the stairs, and that her father was going to beat the living crap out of me. I know today—being, of course, much older and much wiser than I was then—that I went limp because Stacy intimidated me. She intimidated me with that unbelievable body of hers, and she intimidated me because she was so much smarter than I—in an era when that sort of thing was cause for great concern—so I went limp.

"Gee, I'm sorry, Stacy," I managed.

"That's okay, Abner. You'll make it up to me, I'm sure."

And I did. When we were in college together, and I had learned to accept certain very basic facts of life—not the least of which was that women, after all, like to get it on just as much as men.

I was a sophomore at Brockport State College, in New York, when she got there. She enrolled as a philosophy major, with a minor in Latin and archeology, and a course load that I considered barbaric, but which she seemed to take in her stride. I hadn't seen her since graduating from Walter Pierpont, and although we were cousins and had been pretty close friends—to say nothing of would-be lovers—we had fallen out of touch.

The first thing I noticed about her, that hot early September morning in 1968, was that she seemed to have mellowed a bit. In high school she had been all too aware of herself and her obvious attributes, and that had caused her, I think, to assume a hard outlook on life and on what lay before her—because, Christ, what if she loused up what she had? What if she didn't make the best and most appropriate use of it?

She was at the back of a long registration line that had formed in front of one of the science buildings. She had her hands folded in front of her and was wearing a gray pleated skirt and simple white blouse. These were miniskirt years—nice years—and she looked fetching. I watched her a few moments; I had known, through my mother, that Stacy was going to enroll at Brockport State, but it was a surprise seeing her.

She was not quite five feet, nine inches tall and on the gracefully proportioned side of slender, with very long, very dark brown hair, large brown eyes, and a face that retained some of its baby fat, but with the unmistakable thrust of well-chiseled bone beneath. It was not a beauty-queen kind of face; there was too much character in it, and the hint of pain.

I made my way over to her; she had her back to me and I was hoping to surprise her, but she turned when I was several yards away, smiled, said "Hello, Abner." And that is when I realized she had mellowed. Because it was that kind of smile. The kind that is as much internal as external. The kind that is genuine, and inviting. I took it to mean all that I wanted it to mean. And that evening, in my dorm room, we finally finished what we had begun two years before.

She was sitting on a deacon's bench near the entrance to the bar at the Algonquin when I came in. She saw me, stood, came quickly over, extended her hand—which I thought was a strangely formal gesture—and I took it.

"Hello, Stacy." I bent forward to kiss her on the cheek; she started to back away, stopped, let me kiss her.

"Hello, Abner. It's good to see you."

She was wearing a bulky, long-sleeve, purple and white knit sweater and a knee-length, pastel orange skirt, the kind of stiffly casual outfit she'd been wearing quite a lot in the last few years, since breaking up with Art. "You look nice, Stacy."

"I feel awful, Abner." She nodded toward the bar. "Can we go in there, please? I need a drink."

"Sure." We started to go in; a hotel employee came forward with what looked like a boy's-size brown sports jacket in hand. "Here you go, sir." He smiled a polite, firm smile. I took the jacket, tried to put it on, found that it was much too small, put it over my shoulders, and went with Stacy into the bar.

We found a little table in a corner; I ordered a

scotch, she a daiquiri, and when the waiter was gone, Stacy leaned forward, with her elbows on the table and her hands clasped high above it, put her head down, and said, her voice quaking, "That bastard! Goddamn him, Abner—God*damn* him!"

I reached across the table, put my hands on her hands—it was an awkward and uncomfortable gesture. "You mean Art?"

"Of course I mean Art." She looked up. "Where is he, Abner?"

"He's in Europe." I took my hands away. The waiter came with our drinks. I went on, "He's in Nice. He called me yesterday, in fact—"

Stacy cut in, "There is a man, Abner, who says he's a detective here in New York, and he came all the way up to Bangor looking for Art. He thought Art was with *me*, for God's sake! He said Art *killed* someone; he said Art killed a woman and that there's a warrant out for him." She stopped, took a breath, closed her eyes, shook her head slowly. "This man came to *my* house, Abner; he talked to *my* mother and father, and he upset them terribly. So I have come here to find out what exactly is going on."

"Jesus," I whispered.

"Do you know anything about it, Abner?"

I hesitated, thought, answered, "Yes, I do. It's why he called me, in fact."

"Go on."

"He said it was manslaughter. He said it was an accident; he said he was cleaning this gun he has—"

"Oh, horseshit! Art would never own a gun, you know that, Abner. He hates guns!"

I shrugged. "That's what he told me. He said he was cleaning this gun and it went off. He said that the woman he shot was named Phyllis." A brief pause. "And he said, Stacy, that he . . . loved her."

Stacy chuckled coldly. "Do you believe *everything* Art tells you? He never loved anyone, Abner."

I shook my head. "I'm merely repeating what he said to me. Just repeating it. I believed him, yes—at least when he said the shooting was accidental. I believed him. I don't think he's capable of murder."

"I do," she cut in. "I *know* him, Abner. *I* lived with him, so I know him, and I *know* that he's capable of murder." She took a quick sip of her daiquiri, grimaced.

"No good?" I asked.

She ignored the question. "He used to hit me, Abner; you know that, of course."

"No," I said. "I didn't know." I paused. The news surprised me, but not very much, especially after what Phyllis—or at least the woman who called herself Phyllis—had told me. "I didn't know. I'm sorry."

"It's why we split up—it's why I left him." She took another sip of the daiquiri, licked her lips, went on, "I don't think that he enjoyed it, the way some men do. I think it was a kind of . . . aberration. And he didn't do it often—we were married for five years; he hit me only three times in those five years, and never very hard—a slap across the face. And it hurt, sure, but it didn't do any damage. Then one day he came home complaining about a taxi driver, about how the guy took him way out of his way and got an extra couple of dollars from him, and I said, 'Maybe he thought you were a tourist.' I was just trying to inject some humor into the situation, I guess, because he really was angry, which made me nervous.'' She paused, took another sip, nodded at my scotch. ''You're not drinking, Abner.'' I picked up the glass, said, ''So what did he do then?''

''He—'' she grinned crookedly—''punched me out, I guess you'd say.''

''He punched you out?''

She nodded once, that crooked grin still on her lips. ''He hit me in the stomach, then in the jaw—with his fists—and then in the stomach again. I doubled over—Jesus, I couldn't breathe. Then he hit me in the arm. Then in the jaw again.'' A short pause. ''And that was that. He stalked out of the apartment, and I fell to the floor. I moved out the next day, after spending the night in the Emergency Department at Bellevue. They said I was pretty tough; they said he didn't do any permanent damage.''

''My God. Nobody ever told me a thing—''

''I didn't tell anybody, Abner. Not even my parents. I toyed with the idea of having him arrested—maybe I should have . . .'' She shook her head. ''I still loved him. I love him even now, I think. I know that's stupid—but you don't stop loving someone because they're messed up, do you, Abner?''

"No," I said. "I guess you don't."

"And he *was* messed up. He still is. Except now he's killed someone, and he's in trouble." She downed half of the daiquiri. "Are you going to help me, Abner?"

"Help you?"

She nodded. "Yes, to find him."

"But he's in Nice."

She shook her head, smiled slightly, knowingly. "I doubt that very much, Abner."

"I don't. He called me . . ."

"And have you tried to call him?"

"No. Not yet. But I could."

She took a pack of Merits from her purse, offered me one.

"No, I stopped smoking; I didn't know you'd started."

She nodded. "A little while ago. I don't like it. I don't know why I do it." She lit one of the cigarettes, inhaled of it very deeply.

"This detective who came up to Bangor said that Art's *here,* in New York." She took another drag of the cigarette, wiped a tear from her eye, apparently caused by the smoke. "He said Art's hiding out somewhere. He said Harlem, probably." She saw that I was shaking my head. "You don't believe a word of this, do you, Abner?"

"How can I, Stacy? I told you, I've *talked* with him in Nice."

"Oh, for Christ's sake, Abner." She angrily butted out the cigarette. "How do you know he was in

Nice? How do you know? Did an operator come on the line and say she had a call for you from Nice? Did he reverse the charges? How do you *know?* Shit, don't be so damned dense." She shook her head, downed the rest of the daquiri, attempted an apologetic grin. "No, forgive me, Abner. Please. That was uncalled for."

I picked up my glass of scotch. Some of it sloshed onto my lap. I cursed, dabbed at the stain with the drink napkin. "It's okay, Stacy. I've always been dense. Not stupid. Just dense."

"And klutzy," she offered.

"That, too," I said.

She grinned quickly. "So are you going to help me or not?"

I didn't answer at once, though I knew what my answer would be. I took a moment, dabbed at the stain some more, glanced around the bar, looked back, said, "I can't, Stacy. I'm sorry. I can't. I'm . . . involved." I felt a self-conscious smile start and fought it down. "I'm very involved."

Stacy looked confused. "With your work? You mean you're involved with your work?"

I shook my head. "No. With a woman." This time I could not fight that smile down. "A very . . . special woman."

Stacy said, "I don't understand you, Abner." She was getting upset. "I need your *help* here. I'm asking for your help."

"It's a . . . complicated relationship, Stacy. It's an awfully complicated relationship—"

"I don't give a shit how *complicated* it is! I thought we were friends. Jesus, I thought we were *more* than friends. And I thought Art was your friend, too."

I took a breath, then said, "I've got to go now. I'm sorry."

"Go? Go where?"

"Home. To Art's apartment."

"I don't understand."

"I'm confused, Stacy. I'm very confused. Some things have been happening and I have quite a lot to think about. I'm sorry. I wish I could explain it to you because I do love you. We *are* friends, and if I could help you, I would. But I can't."

"Fuck you, Abner!"

I continued looking at her a moment. Then I said, "Whatever you do, Stacy, don't go into Harlem alone. Promise me that."

She stood abruptly, glared down at me. She said nothing.

"Stacy," I said. "Please—"

She cut in, "I'm going to find him, Abner. I *need* to find him!"

"Yes," I said, "I imagine you do."

At the Hammet Mausoleum, Halloween, 1965

I asked, "You think it's mice, Sam?"

"Mice don't *whisper*," he said, and grimaced as if at some abominable stupidity. "I think it's Joe Hammet. I think he's trying to communicate with us. I think he's trying to *tell* us something."

"Like what?"

"I don't know. How the hell should I know? Maybe he wants to send out for a pizza. If you'd shut up, maybe I could find out."

I shut up. We listened a few moments. I heard, faintly, the rush of traffic on Route 23A; I even heard Sam's breathing. My own, too. I said, at a whisper, "It's stopped, Sam. I don't hear it anymore; I don't hear it anymore."

"Me neither."

"So what do we do now?" I asked, still whispering. "You think maybe we should just . . . go away now?"

"Maybe *we* should try talking to *him*." Sam was whispering, too. He looked to his right, at the plaque marked "Joseph William Hammet." He said to it, aloud, "What you want, Joe?" and giggled softly. "You tell us what you want, Joe." His voice had risen in volume and it echoed hollowly against the cement walls. "C'mon now, don't be a damn wimp, Joe, just 'cuz your dead, okay?"

"God, you're disrespectful, Sam." I grinned. I liked Sam's sense of humor, but I thought I had to say something. "They're gonna getcha for that."

"Whatchoo want, Joe?" he said to Joe Hammet's vault. "You want pepperoni; you want anchovies? If you want *anchovies,* you sure as shit better stay away from *me*." He chuckled quickly. I chuckled. The sound of our chuckling came back to us almost at once from the cement walls.

"Did you really break into that funeral home, Sam?" I asked.

He shrugged. "Sure. Why not?"

I shrugged. "I don't know. It just seems kinda . . . I don't know, purposeless, I guess."

He laughed out loud. "You're a shit, Abner. You're a real shit."

I shrugged again. "Maybe," I said.

"You know what a nebbish is, Abner?"

"Sure I know what a nebbish is, Sam." I was surprised that Sam knew. "Why?"

" 'Cuz you're in real danger of becoming one, that's why." Then he turned his head, faced Joe Hammet's vault again. "C'mon, Joe, don't be a wimp just 'cuz you're dead, okay?"

"Okay," we heard.

CHAPTER EIGHTEEN

I'm not going to try and make you believe that this is a love story. It isn't. Not, at least, in the usual sense of the phrase. When I hear the words *love story*, I think of Ali McGraw and Ryan O'Neal, Humphrey Bogart and Ingrid Bergman, Woody Allen and Diane Keaton, Taylor and Burton, Streisand and Redford. I do not think of Abner W. Cray and Phyllis Pellaprat.

Phyllis didn't come back that night. When I got back from talking to Stacy, I waited for her. I sat on the big, black leather couch, watched some cable TV—Jesus, I watched *Smokey and the Bandit*—and, at a little after midnight, I shrugged out of my clothes and went to bed.

I woke at 8:30, called Serena Hitchcock's office, and begged out of a 10:00 appointment, pleading sickness. "Some kind of flu, Serena; I'm very sorry, but I have quite a few shots for you to take a look at—" which was a lie: I'd done precious little work on the book in the week and a half since I'd last talked to Serena. "Maybe we can get together early next week—Monday or Tuesday, okay?" She said okay, she'd call me. But she was pissed.

I'm not going to tell you, either, that this is a ghost story. Because when I think of a ghost story, I think of the flesh falling off a young woman's bones like so much wet and coagulated macaroni, and I think of nine-year-old boys floating outside second-story bedroom windows with rictus grins on their mouths, and I think of Nosferatu *et.al.*, who try so hard to put something over on Mr. Death.

I do not think of four perilously thin teen-age girls hailing a taxi or of men in gray suits who are caught eternally in the act of asking if an elevator can be held.

Phyllis came back to me that evening. It was past eleven, close to 11:30, and I was lying on top of the blankets, naked—Art's apartment got pretty warm at night, and I like to sleep naked. I heard the front door being unlocked, then the *clop-clop* of stacked heels on the foyer's hardwood floor.

Moments later Phyllis appeared in the doorway.

She was dressed in her white coat and green dress—the same outfit she'd worn to her parents' apartment—and she stood very still in the doorway, one hand on her hip, the other clutching a big, dark leather purse.

Only a soft, diffused light came in through the bedroom and dining room windows, so I saw her mostly in
silhouette.

"Hello," I said.

"Hello, Abner." Her voice had the same slight
raspiness that it had the first time we'd made love.

"Care to tell me where you've been?"

"Does it matter?" she asked.

"No." I paused. "Not really."

She stayed in the doorway. She looked for all the
world like a whore, which didn't bother me. I asked,
matter-of-factly, "Who are you?"

And she asked again, "Does it matter?"

"Yes," I answered.

"I am who I told you I am," she said.

The odor of damp wood was in the room, and it
was much stronger than I remembered, much more
offensive.

She repeated. "I am who I told you I am. I'm
Phyllis Pellaprat."

"Phyllis Pellaprat is dead."

She came into the room, let her coat slide to the
floor. "Well, then," she said, "that's her burden,
isn't it, Abner?" And she quickly and gracefully
slipped her boots and dress off. She was naked beneath the dress. She came over to the side of the bed.
In the semi-darkness I saw her glance at her breasts
and nod. "Touch me, Abner. Please touch me."

The odor of damp wood assaulted me. I turned my
head away. She laughed. It was a quick, humorless
noise, as if she were imitating laughter and doing a

poor job of it. She stopped laughing. "You won't like it out there, Abner."

I looked back. I said nothing. I was confused. And I think that, for the first time since I'd known her, I was scared, too.

She stepped backward, toward the window, so she was facing me and so her body was well-illuminated.

"You won't like it out there, Abner," she repeated. She made her arms very straight, held her hands flat against her thighs, and locked her knees so her legs were stiff. Then she closed her eyes and lifted her chin slightly and drew her lips back so they pointed at the base of her ears. It was not a smile. It was more a kind of hard and joyless grin.

I managed, "Phyllis?"

Her mouth dropped open an inch. A white, pasty substance appeared at the edges of her lips. I said again, "Phyllis?" and swung my feet to the floor, stood, took several steps toward her. I put my hands on her waist. It was a desperate gesture. Her skin felt like tepid water; the odor of damp wood was heavy and cloying about her.

And suddenly I felt alone in that room, and I took my hands from her and stepped back, and tried to say her name once more, but it came out as a scream that caromed shrilly off the walls.

Her eyelids popped open. Her eyes rolled upward in their sockets.

I heard a long, low, rasping noise come from her, like air escaping.

But I loved her, you see. The truth is, I loved her. I loved her as I have loved no one else.

And that's why I came forward again, put my hands around her waist—she was cold now—and held her close.

For what might have been hours.

Until I felt her skin begin to warm again and her muscles loosen. And I heard a low, ragged humming noise come from her, which, over the space of a minute or so, became speech: "You won't like it out there, Abner."

"I love you, Phyllis."

"Of course you do."

She pushed me gently backwards, toward the bed, and said this, her voice low and husky and playful: "I'm sure a fucking horny bitch, aren't I?"

CHAPTER NINETEEN

And when I think of a ghost story, I think about children shivering around a campfire while an aging man with a long, austere face summons up—in resonant, wonderfully spectral tones—the way the misdeeds of the dead will soon be visited upon the living, and I think about old, gray houses that have somehow had Evil implanted in them, and I think about rocking chairs that rock all on their own, and about crying in empty rooms, about cold spots, warm spots, hot spots, hounds out of hell, men who hang themselves in attics, and in cellars, again and again and again.

And it's all true.

I *know* that it's all true.

But there's a shitload more going on over there, over on the Other Side, than any of us can imagine.

And some of it's very interesting, very entertaining, but some of it smells bad—some of it stinks, in fact—and if you tried to put your finger on it, if you tried to pin it down and say, *yes, definitely, this is what it's all about, this is what Death is all about; sit back now, I'll tell you,* my God, they'd swarm all over you like angry bees, the dead would, like angry bees.

Phyllis left before dawn. She got quietly into her green dress and her fake mink coat, her stacked high-heel boots, and as I watched from the bed, she walked to the bedroom doorway and said, with her back to me, "I love you, Abner. Please love me." And then she left. It was a routine that I didn't understand, but I was growing to trust it, to believe in it. So I didn't get out of the bed and go after her. I said, to myself, "I do love you, Phyllis."

I fell asleep quickly.

The phone on a little table beside the bed rang at a quarter past nine. I cursed it, answered it. "Yes?" I said.

"Abner?" It was Jocelyn Horn.

"Hello, Jocelyn."

"Did I wake you, Abner? I'm sorry."

"No. It's okay."

"Stacy is in New York, Abner."

I could have told her that I knew that, but I realized that it had probably taken a great force of will for her to call me, and I didn't want to puncture whatever good feelings that gave her, so I said, "Where in New York?"

"At a hotel called the Algonquin."

"Thank you, Aunt Jocelyn."

"It's okay, Abner. I *do* like you. Just, *please*—be careful!"

"Yes, Aunt Jocelyn, I'm always careful."

"Jesus, no, you aren't!" she whispered, as if to herself. Then she hung up.

"Be careful!" is something that Jocelyn Horn has been saying to me all my life. She said it to me for the first time when I was two months old, lying naked on my back on a changing table, while she was leaning over me, giving me a change of diapers. "Be careful you don't pee in your own face, Abner," she said. So I peed in *her* face. My mother told me that story a couple of years before she died, when I was fourteen or so and she thought I could handle the whole thing. I told her I thought it was a good story, a funny story, but when I repeated it to Jocelyn herself some time later, she grimaced and looked offended. Jocelyn's not an easy woman to figure out.

I got dressed—jeans, a red flannel shirt, sneakers, the wool-lined denim jacket—got my Nikon F. and went out for breakfast to the same Greek restaurant I'd gone to a week earlier. I sat at the same table, ordered the same food—scrambled eggs, whole wheat toast, fresh-squeezed orange juice, coffee—and ate slowly because I was trying to figure out what I was going to do *after* breakfast. I knew what I was supposed to do. I was supposed to work. I was supposed to get started, at last, on the big, coffee-table photo book that I'd been given several thousand dollars to start. It was why I'd come to New York in the first place.

I finished breakfast quicker than I'd hoped, ordered some more coffee, did some more thinking. I started thinking that New York was not only the Twin Towers and the Empire State Building and Grand Central Station, the U.N., the West Village; it was Harlem, too. More specifically, it was the area around East 95th Street. So I checked the Nikon, found that it was loaded with Tri-X pan, that I had three more rolls of it in my jacket pocket, took a last sip of coffee, and watched as a big, brown roach scooted across the top of the table and disappeared around the underside. I leaned over. The roach had stopped a couple of inches beyond the underside edge of the table; its little antennae were going this way and that. I straightened, reflexively lifted my knee into the roach, heard it crack, heard a dull snapping sound as it hit the grimy tile floor. It came to me that I'd done exactly the same thing on my last visit to that restaurant.

I heard, from my right, "Pardon me."

I looked. A man in a stiff, gray suit and a bulky, black overcoat was standing beside the table. He was middle-aged, with a wide, flat face and dull, gray eyes, and he was trying to smile, though he was not very convincing about it.

"Yes?" I said.

"My name is Kennedy Whelan," he said. "I'm looking for your friend, Art DeGraff. Do you think you could help me?" His smile broadened; he had nicotine stains, like liver spots, on his teeth.

"Art's in Nice," I said.

The man's smile became lopsided. He shook his head slightly. "I'm afraid that's incorrect, Mr. Cray."

"How do you know my name?"

He ignored that. "Your friend is *here*, in Manhattan."

"No, I don't think so."

"We believe he's in Harlem, as a matter of fact."

"We?"

He pulled a shield out of his jacket pocket, flashed it, put it back. "I'm with the NYPD, 22nd Precinct, Homicide Division."

"Uh-huh." I stood. The man was not as tall as I, a good five inches shorter, in fact, but at least thirty pounds heavier, and that intimidated me. I said, looking down at him, "If I could help you, Mr. Whelan, I would, but I can't, I really can't; now, if you'll excuse me—"

He put his hand firmly on my arm. "When was the last time you heard from Mr. DeGraff, please?"

I sighed, as if losing my patience. "I heard from him two days ago. He called me. From Nice."

"And what did he tell you, please?"

I considered a moment. I thought it was likely that Art's phone was tapped and that, if I lied, Whelan would know. I decided to tell the truth. "He told me that he had killed someone. A woman. He told me it was an accident, but that the police were looking for him and that he would probably be home early, before May—I'm subletting his apartment . . .''

"Yes, I know," Whelan cut in. His smile reappeared; it was genuine now. "Thank you." He nodded to his right, to indicate the door. "You can run along."

I sighed again; he let go of my arm. I asked, "Is Art's phone tapped?"

"That's restricted information, Mr. Cray." He sat at the table I'd used, shrugged out of his coat, looked up at me. "Thank you, Mr. Cray. We'll talk again, I'm sure."

"Believe me, Mr. Whelan," I said, my voice rising in pitch because I was nervous, "if I could help you, I would. That's the truth."

"Of course it's the truth, Mr. Cray." He picked up a menu, started glancing over it. I watched him a moment, decided he was playing games with me, shrugged, and left the restaurant.

Understand that I *was* concerned for Art, he was a friend—hell, he had been a very close friend at one time—and I did not like the idea that the police were looking for him. I liked the idea even less that he had actually killed someone, that her name had been Phyllis Pellaprat, and that there seemed to be some strong connection between her and the woman I'd fallen in love with. I had no idea what that connection was. The woman in the snapshot over the fireplace was indeed the woman I'd been sharing the apartment with. But I'm a photographer, so I know that photographs are not always truth-telling ("But they are fairly *true* illusions, Mr. Pelleprat." . . . "Yes, like our crumb cake."), and despite her eccentricities and her odd comings and goings, I did not believe for an instant that the woman I knew as Phyllis Pellaprat was the woman that my friend Art DeGraff had beaten to death in December.

No. That's a lie.

It was snowing lightly when I got to the building that Phyllis had taken me to for an evening with her parents. I stood out in front of it, near the street, put a wide-angle lens on the Nikon, focused, took several shots from various angles. I was pretending to work, and I wasn't even fooling myself. I packed the Nikon away, went up the crumbling concrete steps to the front doors of the building, tried to pull them open, found that they were locked. I put my face to the glass in the doors, peered in, saw pretty much what I had seen with Phyllis—a telephone booth *sans* telephone, several overstuffed chairs, a set of elevators, doors wide-open. I straightened, stepped backward a few feet, looked up at what I assumed were the windows of Apartment 506, the Pellaprats' apartment. I saw that one of the windows had been smashed and a sheet of plywood installed on the inside.

"Shit!" I whispered, because I was certain I was at the wrong building.

"You want somethin' in there, my man?!" I heard from behind me.

I glanced around. I saw a black man—in his early twenties, I guessed—dressed in a battered, grayish-brown winter jacket and shiny blue pants and black rubber, buckle boots, unbuckled. He had the unlighted stub of a cigarette stuck between his lips, and when he talked, it bobbed up and down in time with his words. He went on, "I mean you." He didn't move much. He had his hands in his jacket pockets and his elbows hard to his sides, his shoulders up. He looked very cold.

"I was looking for someone," I told him, and smiled. I nodded at the building. "Her parents live here, I think."

"Only people livin' in there is junkies, my man, and half of 'em is dead, so why don'tchoo go back where you come from."

"Yes," I said, and started down the steps toward him, "I will."

He nodded once at the camera. "An' you can give me that before you go, okay?"

I shook my head. "No. I don't think so." I was half-way down the steps, and he was near the street. I turned right, so I was moving away from him. He came forward, stiffly. I glanced back, saw his left hand move in his jacket pocket, as if he were clenching something.

"I don't want any trouble," I said.

"I'm right behind ya," he said.

"I was just looking for someone, that's all."

"Well, you found him," he said. He was keeping his legs straight as he walked, as if his knees were locked. I realized that I could easily outrun him, if I needed. I turned my head, walked faster. The light snow had grown heavier in the last few minutes; a half-inch or so had accumulated on the sidewalk, and my feet were making slight crunching noises on it.

"I don't want to hurt you," I said, thinking that I sounded foolish. I heard nothing. I turned my head, looked back. The man was once again in front of the Pellaprats' building. He was facing it, his feet were moving slightly in the snow, and he was talking to himself, apparently, because I could see the stub of the cigarette bobbing up and down between his lips.

I clutched the Nikon, hurried to Fifth Avenue, and caught a bus back to Art's apartment.

The electricity went out at around 10:00 that night. I looked out the front windows, at East 79th Street, and realized—because the street lights were out, too, and there were no lights on in any of the houses I could see—that we were in the midst of another blackout, like the ones in November of 1965 and July, 1979. It was a wonderful photo opportunity, I thought—New Yorkers coping in a sudden crisis; New Yorkers making the most of an abominable situation; New Yorkers taking what they could before the electricity, and then sweet reason, returned.

I loaded the Nikon with some very fast film, a flash unit, and hurried from the apartment house.

Someone in a big, dark Mercedes pulled up at an

angle on the sidewalk so that his headlights were on the front doors of a house just down the street. A woman, in her seventies, I guessed, and dressed in a white nightgown and a short, brown coat, was being carried from the house. She had her arms thrown around the man carrying her—who looked nearly as old as she, but who was tall and solidly built—and she looked terrified. I saw all this in the glare of the Mercedes' headlights. When the couple moved into the darkness, I saw little, only the Mercedes' door being pushed open by its driver and then, apparently, the woman being put into the back seat.

Just beyond, I saw several people standing on a set of front steps, one of them with a flashlight in hand, and I heard yelling from across the street, as if someone inconvenienced by the blackout was letting everyone within earshot know that he was angry about it.

I turned left, toward Central Park. Fifth Avenue would have more traffic, and hence more light for shooting, plus more action, I guessed, than Lexington Avenue.

I walked quickly. I nodded and smiled at a couple of people who had bravely come out to the sidewalk. One of them, a chunky, middle-aged man shivering in a pair of white pajamas and a black-and-white checkered robe, said, "Ain't this the shits?" I said yes, it was the shits, but that I intended to make the most of it, and patted the Nikon. This seemed to unnerve him. "You some kinda pervert?" he asked.

At Fifth Avenue I turned left. It hadn't been more

than ten minutes since the blackout began, but already a traffic jam had started, and there was a cacophony of horns blaring and curses being shouted. The air was foul and nearly unbreathable from car exhausts; a thick, grayish-white fog was settling in—a temperature-inversion phenomenon, I guessed.

I stopped walking at East 65th Street, swung the Nikon up, took a few quick shots, started walking again. I heard from behind me, "Hey, mister, you want a puppy?"

I did not turn around at once. I let the question swim about in my head a few moments. If I'd been asked to draw up a list of questions I would expect *not* to hear on Fifth Avenue during a blackout, that one would have been high on the list.

I turned. A small boy was staring up at me. He was perhaps seven or eight years old and a little chunky—though that might have been an illusion, because his face seemed to have an excess of baby fat on it. He was dressed in a ragged, brown sweater and a pair of equally ragged, brown pants. At his feet, on the sidewalk, was a cardboard box, and in the box were six black, short-haired, long-eared, apparently mongrel puppies.

The boy said again, "Hey, mister, you want a puppy?" and the most heart-rendingly plaintive smile appeared on his face, flickered a moment, and went out. He had a wisp of a voice, barely audible below the noise of traffic and shouted curses.

I got down on my haunches, reached into the cardboard box, scratched a few ears and lifted one of the puppies out; it tried valiantly to stretch its neck out far enough so that it could lick my nose, and the sour sting of its breath hit me. I looked down at the boy again. "Where do you live? Do you live around here?"

He answered, in the same small voice, "I don't. I don't. You want a puppy. You can have one cheap. Two dollars."

"Do you live over that way?" I pressed on, and nodded to my right, toward East 66th Street. "Would you like me to walk you to where you live? I'll carry the box if you want."

He didn't answer me.

"It's too cold for you to be out doing this, don't you think?" I asked.

His smile flickered on again, then off. "I'm used to it," he said. "You want a puppy. You can have one cheap. Two dollars."

I took a deep breath, thought a moment, brought the puppy a little closer to me so it at last had a chance at my nose. I remember its tongue was warm and wet, and it took a real effort to keep from turning my head away from the sour smell of its breath. I said to the boy, "If I take one from you, will you let me walk you home?"

He answered, "Can't. My mother's there. My mother's always there."

"Uh-huh," I said. "Is she the one that sent you out here?"

He nodded.

"To sell these puppies?" I went on. "She sent you out here to sell these puppies?"

He nodded again.

"And where does your mother live?" I asked.

"She don't," he answered. "You want a puppy? You can have one cheap. Two dollars."

"Sure I do, but as I said, if I take one from you, you're going to have to let me walk you home. Is that a deal?"

He nodded once. "Yeah. Sure. Which one you want? I got six here. I got two boys and four girls altogether. Which one you want?"

I nodded at the puppy I was holding. "This one will do just fine," I said. "Does he have a name?"

"His name's Mahoney," the boy answered.

"Mahoney? That's a nice name. Where'd he get a name like that?"

"From me," the boy answered. "Mahoney's my name, too." He was beginning to sound less and less timid, and slightly more petulant than at first. "My name's Mahoney," he said again. "So my pup's name's Mahoney, too."

I stood, Mahoney the puppy still in hand. "You want to show me where you live now?" I asked.

The boy answered, "My mom says it's 'unfinished business.' She says it's why I gotta come out here. I been out here a long time. You want a puppy? You can have one cheap. Two dollars."

"Yes. This one will do fine, just fine; two dollars is a good price."

"That's Mahoney."

"Yes, you told me that." I was growing impatient.

" 'Unfinished business,' that's what my mom says."
He sounded much more petulant now—a little angry.
"You want a puppy? You can have one cheap. Two
dollars."

I glanced around, hoping to see a passerby who
might lend a hand. No one was on the sidewalk, just
the boy and his box of puppies. On Fifth Avenue, the
traffic was beginning to move very slowly, which
didn't have any effect at all on the blaring car horns
and shouted curses. I looked back at the boy. I did
not remember putting Mahoney the puppy back in the
box, but he was there, with his five brothers and
sisters, and the boy was staring up at me and giving
me his heart-rendingly plaintive smile again. "Hey
mister, you want a puppy?" he asked once more.
"You can have one cheap. Two dollars."

I did not answer.

I had begun to have an understanding of, and
appreciation for, what exactly was happening to me,
and of the world I was being allowed into.

So I backed away from the boy. I nodded, smiled.
I said, "Maybe later," and watched as he picked
another of the puppies out of the box and held it out
to me. "Hey, mister, you want a puppy? You can
have one cheap."

I turned then, and walked quickly away from him,
back to the apartment.

BOOK TWO

CHAPTER ONE

Let's forget the heartbreakingly cute kid with the box of puppies for a moment. Let's forget the four painfully thin teen-age girls hailing a taxi, the man in the threadbare, gray, pinstriped suit, the young guy with the ragged T-shirt, the man in the unbuckled rubber boots. And let's go back a few years.

It pertains. Hell, everything does. Which is something else that I've learned in these past six months. That everything pertains. Everything's germane. What has gone before goes again. And again. And again. And what will be is. And ever shall be.

Let's even forget Phyllis Pellaprat. Let's set her aside anyway. Very gently.

And let's stuff Art DeGraff into a box somewhere. Into a very small box. It's where he belongs, after all. It's where he very well may be at this moment.

And let's go back to a time before I was screwing my cousin Stacy, to a time when my parents both were alive and avoiding each other around the house.

It was a big house. The kind you see quiet a lot in Maine—white clapboard siding, black-shingled roof, wraparound porch. A very functional and livable house, good for sleeping in, and for eating Thanksgiving dinner in, and for waking up in on Christmas morning.

Quite a few people were laid out in that house. Several uncles, an aunt or two, a young cousin who fell through the ice on Miller's Pond early one March morning. She was five. A nice little kid. And, Christ, there was a lot of crying the day that she was laid out.

The house had two living rooms. One was called a parlor, though it was architecturally identical to the other. It had a red brick fireplace in it, and oak floors. A small, dark-blue-and-white braided throw rug had been put at right angles to the big arched entranceway, and another parallel with the front of the fireplace and five feet out from it. The room was well furnished, with carefully chosen pieces from the late Victorian period. We never had a TV at home—my father wouldn't allow it—but he did install a Zenith table radio in a corner bookcase in the parlor. The radio was used occasionally by my mother, who liked to listen to a Bangor top-40 AM station; it dismayed my father, who was of the opinion that the only real music was baroque, though, to his credit, he never said much about it.

The cousin who went through the ice was laid out

in the center of the room in an open coffin. Her name was Rebecca. I remember going over and looking at her and thinking that it was too bad a little kid like that had to die. I was not quite thirteen at the time, and I remember that Rebecca's parents had told her more than once not to go out on Miller's Pond. And I remembered that Rebecca had protested that if she was old enough to do this and old enough to do that, how come she wasn't old enough to go out on Miller's Pond? To which her parents could answer only, "Because we said so." I remember they were there, too, in the parlor, both weeping softly in straight-backed, wooden chairs set up close to the coffin.

Rebecca was buried the next day.

The day after that, I went to Miller's Pond myself, out of sheer morbidness, I think. Twelve-year-olds seem to have a propensity for it, this particular twelve-year-old, especially.

Miller's Pond was near a long-abandoned gravel pit just a mile or so from Lewis Street, where we lived. It was ten feet deep at the center, several hundred feet wide at its widest point, and it was sheltered on all sides by deciduous trees—maples, oaks, and tulip trees especially, which were very tall. These trees were bare then, because it was still only the first week in March, and there were wide, irregular patches of snow everywhere.

The pond itself was iced over, except randomly near the shore, where brackish water was visible, as it was at the center, where Rebecca had fallen in and where her would-be rescuers—a sixteen-year-old boy

named Hymie Simms and his older brother, Timothy—
had also fallen in. They had been able to swim to
safety. Rebecca's body was pulled out an hour later
by a local volunteer fireman. She hadn't drifted far;
Miller's Pond was stagnant, without currents.

No one was there the day after she was buried. It
was a still, cool afternoon, the sunlight pushing through
a high haze and diffusing into a pleasant, soft glow.

I saw a child, dressed in a green snowsuit, appear
at the edge of the pond across from me, hesitate for a
moment, and then step out onto the ice. I called to
her: "Hey, you shouldn't do that!" She looked up at
me, across the pond, a distance of several hundred
feet, appeared to smile, kept walking out onto the
ice.

I cursed. It was the first time that I'd cursed, and it
made me feel very adult. I called to the child again:
"You shouldn't go out there!" But she continued
walking. She moved the way small children do, in
quick, anxious steps. She was clearly enjoying herself,
clearly enjoying the very act of being alive.

I cursed once more. I knew that I'd have to go out
there and get her. "A little girl fell through the ice
just the other day, you know," I called. The girl in
the green snowsuit looked up again and shouted back,
"It's okay. I can do it now."

And that's when I saw that the little girl was
Rebecca.

At least I know now, twenty-one years later, that
she was Rebecca. At the time, I told myself that the

girl was only someone who looked strikingly like her, and I believed it.

So I stepped out onto the ice, to go after her. And fell through. "It's *okay*!" I heard as I scrambled through three feet of ice water back to shore. "It's *okay*!" she shouted with great, childish exasperation and annoyance, the way kids announce, one day, that they do not need help anymore tying their shoes or buttoning their jackets.

"It's *okay*! I can do it now!"

But that was a fluke, a mistake, something that was never intended. For a few moments I became— like lots of other people, I believe—an unwilling trespasser into a world that, until then, had easily kept me out.

CHAPTER TWO

But no more. Now it had me, and I knew that it had me. I knew it when the little ragamuffin with the half-dozen puppies tried so hard to get his "unfinished business" done.

It is not what you might think—this world I trespassed briefly into at twelve, and nearly got trapped in at thirty-three. It is some of what you might think, certainly. But it is so much more.

Go, answer the door, peer through the little security peephole at whoever has come to call. You see a face, a smile perhaps, a pair of eyes. And they tell you—open the door. Or they tell you—do not open the door. But if you have shut yourself up on the wrong side of that peephole for too long, they tell you very little. They tell you only what is within

169

arm's reach, not what is above, or below, or to the sides, or behind that smiling face.

And a lot of them do smile.

Rebecca smiled.

Phyllis Pellaprat smiled. Phyllis Pellaprat slipped her clothes off and offered herself to me. And I took her. And enjoyed her.

At the Hammet Mausoleum, Halloween, 1965

I said to Sam, at a whisper, "I heard Joe Hammet say 'Okay,' Sam. Didn't you hear him say 'Okay'?"

Sam shook his head briskly. "It was an echo. It was just—" he paused, looked around, then went on, his voice sharply higher in volume—"an *echo*!" The word "echo" came back to us from the cement walls almost instantly. He grinned at me. "Just an echo, Abner."

"Uh-huh," I said, disappointed. "An echo."

"Just like all of us are gonna be someday."

"Sure, like all of us."

"You understand that, Abner?"

"I understand it. I'm not stupid."

"You're sure?"

"I think we should get outa here, Sam. That's what I'm sure of."

"Shit, why, Abner? We've only been in here thirty minutes or so. And the witchin' hour ain't till 12:00. We gotta stay here until then anyway."

"I can't stay here till then, Sam. Jees, I gotta get home before 10:30—"

"*They*," he cut in, "gotta stay here forever, and you don't hear them complaining, do you?"

I readjusted myself on the cement floor. "I'm cold, Sam."

"So are they."

"No, they aren't. They're dead."

"Which means they're *cold*, Abner. Don't you understand that?"

"Sometimes I think you're fulla shit. I really do, Sam. Sometimes I think that."

He grinned yet again. It was a slow, wide grin, and the candlelight on his round, freckled face made him look once more like a big pumpkin. He said, "So are they, Abner."

"So are they *what*, Sam?"

"Fulla shit."

"Who?"

"Them." He nodded quickly to his right and left. "Them. These dead people here."

"Oh, c'mon, Sam."

"Think about it. They've been handed a bill of goods—"

"By who?"

"By us. By you and me, and by their wives and husbands, and mothers and fathers, and by everyone, that's who."

"I'm leaving."

"So they're gonna hang around, you know—"

I stood. Sam reached into the plastic bag, withdrew a Mallo Cup, began munching noisily on it. "These are better than Reeses Cups, you know.

They're *gooier*." He stuck his index finger into his mouth and sucked some chocolate off.

"Sam," I said, "you gotta have some respect."

He grinned up at me. "You think they mind, Abner? Hell, it's good for 'em. It tells 'em there's *life* out here—Sit down, goddamnit!"

"No reason to get angry, Sam."

"Sure there is. We're all dead. That's why I'm angry. We're all of us dead. You and me and everyone."

"You sound like a lunatic, Sam."

"I wanta *always* be a lunatic. When I'm shoveled into the ground, I wanta be a lunatic."

I sat down again. I was beginning to worry about my friend, Sam Fearey.

Serena Hitchcock called the morning after the blackout. "Can you come into the office, Abner?" she asked, and I sensed that something was very wrong.

"I can't, Serena; I really can't . . ." I was straining to think of some excuse when she cut in, "Abner, we're not going to be able to do the photo book. I'm sorry."

I said nothing.

"The company's going into reorganization, Abner, and a decision has been made, by the Board, not to do any more big, expensive books. They don't sell as well as they used to—"

"Mine would, Serena," I interrupted, but it was a feeble protest.

"*I* know that, Abner, *You* know that. But the Board doesn't. And they've overruled me. Why don't you come in; we'll sit down, and maybe we can come up with some other ideas. I still like your work, Abner."

"Yes," I said, "I'll do that. I'll call you."

"You don't sound terribly enthusiastic, Abner."

"You're right." A pause. "I'm going to take a small vacation, Serena."

"Vacation from what?"

It was a good question. "I've got something else I want to do—something I *need* to do."

"This all sounds very cryptic, Abner."

I chuckled. "It does, doesn't it? I'm sorry."

"So am I, Abner."

It was just past dawn, late in January, when Phyllis reappeared.

I was sitting on the edge of the bed wondering when I'd get some sleep, because I had lain awake all night watching the digital numbers on Art's alarm clock change. She was dressed in her fake mink coat, her white boots, her green dress, and she stood quietly in the bedroom doorway a long while with a slight, playful grin on her mouth. At last she said, "I lied, Abner."

"Did you?" I asked. "Did you lie?"

"Yes, Abner. About several things." Her slight, playful grin stayed, though her tone had become quiet and apologetic. "I lied about several things. About myself. About Art. About the accident. Several things. And I must apologize.'' She was still grinning, and it was making me nervous. "Will you accept my apology, Abner?"

"I don't know," I answered. It was the truth. "I want explanations first, I think. That's reasonable, isn't it?"

"Do you think I'm capable of that, Abner? Do you think I'm capable of being reasonable?"

"I don't know." I paused. "Could you stop grinning, Phyllis? Please."

"I lied to you about myself, about Art, about the accident. I lied to you about several things. And I apologize. I can't, Abner."

"Can't what?"

"I have to grin. I'm coming apart."

"I don't understand. Coming apart? Tell me what that means."

"I reach inside, and I try to find it, but it's not there; it's just not there, and I wonder what it is—I wonder what it was."

"I don't understand you, Phyllis."

"And I thought it was very surprising, Abner, that there still *were* days."

I got out of bed, stood next to it, watched her.

"But there are days, Abner," she said. "And we mark time in them."

"Phyllis, I love you, I need you." I stopped. I found that I wasn't talking to Phyllis anymore. The room was empty.

*   *   *

I stayed in the apartment for five days. It was a time of transition. I did a lot of pretty intense thinking in those five days. I got no sleep; I ate very little. Sometimes I turned cable TV on, with the sound off, and sat on the big, black leather couch. And I tried to make sense of Phyllis's words: "But there are days, Abner. And we mark time in them." And again and again, there on the big couch, with some crummy movie on the tube, I'd answer her: "But don't we all mark time, Phyllis?" Which just took me around in a circle and got me to biting my own tail.

Imagine this: Imagine being horny, and scared, and quivering with anxiety, and claustrophobic, all at the same time. I felt like a mound of drooling jello on the couch there, waiting for Phyllis to reappear and knowing, somehow, that she wasn't going to— that, after all, I was going to have to go looking for her.

It was an idea that made me queasy, an idea that made me sad and confused and frightened.

Because I did love her. More than I ever loved anyone. But I didn't know if it was enough. Because love isn't always enough. Sometimes it is, but not always. Sometimes it's better to run from it.

I didn't run from it.

CHAPTER THREE

I have learned this, too: Pettiness survives. And jealousy. And pretentiousness, fear, loneliness, depression. I have learned that the living have not yet cornered the market on misery.

On the third of February, I left the apartment for the first time in five days, went out to the street, and hailed a cab. It pulled up across the street; I ran to it, hopped in, and said to the cabbie, "Can we ride around a little bit?"

"Sure we can ride around," he answered, and pulled slowly away from the curb. "Anywhere in particular you want to ride around?"

"I don't know, the city," I answered, and realized that that was a good way to get taken to Queens, so I added, "Midtown, I think."

He turned down Fifth Avenue. He drove the way most New York cabbies drive, as if they're in amusement park bumper cars, and he was talkative. According to his ID card on the visor, his name was Matthew Petersak. He was chunky, round-faced—an everybody's uncle kind of guy.

"I got a sister," he said; we were nearing East 73rd Street and getting caught in one of those traffic jams that seem to erupt out of nowhere in New York, like a bad cough, "and she's a looker, you know what I mean? I mean she's a real looker; nothin' like me, you understand. I mean she ain't fat like me. She's a looker. And she's got all these guys comin' round tryin' to get into her little panties, you know what I mean? Tryin' to get into her little panties, but she won't let 'em, she won't let 'em; she chases 'em away; she says to 'em, 'You get away, you don't get into my little panties.' " He laughed; ahead, several pedestrians were trying hard to make it across the street, on a crosswalk, but since traffic wasn't stopped completely—it was just inching along—they wisely chose to stay on the edge of the sidewalk.

The cabbie babbled on, "You wanta know her name? You wanta know my sister's name, fella? It's Loretta, and she's twenty-nine years old and she's still a virgin. You wanta know how I know she's a virgin? I know she's a virgin 'cuz I ask her every time she comes in. I say to her, 'You still a virgin, Loretta?' I can tell if she's lyin', and she ain't lied yet. And she's still a virgin." One of the pedestrians, a young blonde woman dressed in a black vinyl raincoat, stepped very cautiously off the sidewalk. " 'Cuz she ain't married," the cabbie went on. "That's the way it should be for the women, don'tcha think? Not for the guys, just for the women, 'cuz they're different, you know. They don't want it the same as us, or need it—" the blonde woman took another step out into the street—"the same as us." He was looking at me in the rearview mirror; the cab was moving slowly forward. I nodded at the blonde woman; "Watch out there," I said, and he said, still looking at me, "Don'tchoo agree, don'tchoo agree?" And the blonde woman took another step into the street, hoping, apparently, that the cabbie would stop. He didn't. He hit her with his right front bumper and sent her spinning sideways, with her arms wide, and a look of tremendous surprise and fear on her face. It looked like she was doing some crazy kind of dance, and I found myself fascinated by her. She spun a long way, trying all the while to keep her balance. At last, she hit a police call box, first with her forehead and then with her torso; her arms encircled it, although her hands did not clench, and she collapsed there in a kind of kneeling position, with her knees and calves in the street, her belly and chest up against the call box, the side of her face mashed into it, and her arms thrown around it in a kind of loose hug. Her eyes were open very wide, and her mouth was moving a little: She was clearly in shock.

I said to Matthew Petersak, "Jesus Christ! You hit her!"

"And I'll tell you another thing," he said—traffic

cleared suddenly; he picked up speed—"all this talk
about a A-bomb—"

"Fuck the A-bomb!" I broke in. "You just hit a
woman back there!" I looked back; a crowd had
gathered around the woman, and a couple of men
were beginning to jog after us, on the sidewalk.
"You might have killed her."

"Shit," he said, "it wouldn't be the first time."
The men jogging toward us picked up speed; Matthew
Petersak picked up speed—he turned onto East 73rd
Street, which was relatively clear of traffic. I yelled
at him, "What in the hell are you doing?"

He looked back. He grinned. "Only what I've
always done," he answered. "I'm only doing what
I've always done."

And he came to a quick, jolting stop at Lexington
Avenue. That's when I jumped out of the cab.

He hit his accelerator hard, turned down Lexington
Avenue, and I quickly lost him among the hundred
other yellow cabs on Lexington Avenue, all of them
darting about, jockeying for position, and all of them
precisely the same as the cab driven by Matthew
Petersak.

At the Hammet Mausoleum, Halloween, 1965

"Like if I'm a lunatic now, I wanta always be a
lunatic, you understand that, Abner?"

"No," I answered. "You can't *always* be *anything*,
Sam, except dust. You can always be dust." I smiled
to myself; I had uttered yet another profundity.

"Shit, Abner—I ain't dust now, so how can I always *be* dust? What kinda deal is that, anyway? You got shit for brains, or what? You know what I think?" He farted again.

"Don't do that, Sam."

He ignored me. "I think," he said, and he fingered the wax that had dripped to the floor from one of the candles as he talked, "that we get put here, and we get into habits, and we like them, and then we die, and we keep our habits, and we live happily ever after." He took another Mallo Cup from the plastic bag, popped it into his mouth. "Neat, huh?" he said as he chewed. "Don't you think that's neat, Abner?"

"Sure, that's neat. So what are you going to be doing after you're dead? Are you going to be coming back and scarfing up Mallo Cups?"

"Maybe." He grinned, lifted his fingers—they had wax on them—to a couple of inches in front of his eyes and examined them closely. "But there wouldn't be any taste to 'em, I don't think."

"Why not?"

He shrugged. "I don't know. I'm just talkin', Abner."

"Sure," I said. "And what do you think I'm gonna be doing, Sam? After I'm dead?" I could feel myself being sucked into the mood he was trying to create.

"You won't," he answered.

"I won't what?"

"Come back. I'll bet you won't, anyway."

"Why won't I?"

"I don't know—you're not the type, I guess."

"And who is?"

"I am. People like me."

"People who're addicted to Mallo Cups?"

"Sure. And people like Joe Hammet over there, 'cuz he was a nice old fruit, and people like . . . like my Aunt Marie. 'Cuz she's so fuckin' neat."

"You're fulla shit, Sam."

"Maybe," he said.

CHAPTER FOUR

. . . they'd swarm over you like angry bees, the
dead would, like angry bees.

I had walked a good distance on Lexington Avenue.
To my left, on my side of the street, and stretching
to Park Avenue, stood a row of typical East 80s
townhouses. They were four stories high, with tall,
narrow windows, and they were painted variously
gray, white, and blue. One, near the middle of the
block, was a light shade of orange. Each townhouse
had a set of concrete steps, and all of these were of
the same length. Most of the steps had a black iron
railing attached. In front of the townhouses, between
the nicely kept sidewalk and the street, there were a
number of young trees surrounded by circular fences,
approximately one tree for every two houses. None

of the trees was more than ten feet tall; they looked like the results of a recent block beautification program.

The other side of the street was almost a carbon copy of my side, except that there was no light orange house, and a good tenth of the block, directly opposite me, was taken up by a square, two-story, red brick building. On the side of the building, close to the back, and halfway between the first and second floors, was a large, stylized picture of a smiling mouse, and the words THE MOUSETRAP: AN- TIQUES in stiff, dark-blue block letters just above it.

At the far end of the street, near Fifth Avenue, and on the south side, I could make out two people walking toward me. An old couple. He was wearing a hat and a dark overcoat, and was carrying a cane, or an umbrella. She was stooped over slightly, was wearing a brown coat, and was apparently holding onto his arm.

On my side of the street, in front of the light orange townhouse, two children were playing catch with a softball. They were dressed for early February, in cream-colored snowsuits and mittens. One of the children was facing me; he looked about ten or eleven, and he was short, with a long, thin face. His nearly continous laughter drifted over to me as a slight, tinny noise, like dimes falling.

I heard a stiff, cracking noise across the street, in the antique shop. I looked. Directly beneath the styl- ized mouse, there was a door that I hadn't noticed earlier—probably, I decided, because it had no win- dow in it and had been painted a shade of red that was much the same color as the building itself. The door had been opened inward, and a man was standing in the doorway. He was thin, middle-aged, with long, gray hair, and rimless glasses, and was dressed in blue jeans and a long-sleeved yellow shirt. He was motioning with his hand for me to come over.

I watched him a few moments. He continued motioning to me—a kind of upside-down wave—and a little smile appeared on his mouth. At last I crossed the street to him. His smiled increased as I drew closer, and he motioned again, to indicate the inside of the antique shop.

"In here," he said, his voice a creaky, high tenor.

I stopped walking. "No," I said. "I don't think so."

And he said, "Of course you do."

I considered a moment, then followed him inside.

As I walked behind the thin, gray-haired man, through the shop—through aisles that were narrow and cluttered with odds and ends—I heard a small, tinkling noise to my right, as if he had put bells on the front door and a customer was coming in. But when I looked, there was a big pine cupboard in my way, so I saw nothing.

The shop was even larger than was suggested by its outside. The floor was bare wood and gritty. Here and there, it squeaked as I walked on it, and in several spots it actually gave under my weight.

"This way, please," the gray-haired man said, his

voice now small and friendly, as we made our way through the aisles, past old rocking chairs and battered cupboards and mantel clocks. I had no idea where he was taking me, of course. But I was more than willing to be led. I wanted to be led. It was very fitting, I thought, that I should be there, in an antique shop called The Mousetrap. I had the idea that there were answers here, that this man had answers for me, because I needed answers from someone.

He stopped in front of a huge, rolltop desk that was cluttered with old papers and notebooks, and nodded meaningfully at the end of the desk opposite him. "Could you get that, please?" he said.

"Sorry?" I said.

"That end. Could you get that end?"

"What for?"

"So I can move it, of course," he said.

"So you can move it?"

"Yes. Over there." He nodded to his left at an empty spot near a kerosene heater. "It's warmer."

"You asked me in here just so I could help you move your desk?"

"That's right."

"And that's all?"

He smiled patiently. "Yes, I'm afraid so."

I turned, walked quickly through the store and out, onto East 81st Street. I squinted at the bright sunlight, cringed at the noise of traffic on Lexington Avenue, and cursed repeatedly—at the gray-haired man, at myself, at Phyllis, and Art, and the eight million people around me.

I felt someone tugging at my sleeve. "Mister?" I heard. I looked. It was the thin-faced boy in the cream-colored snowsuit. He was tugging at my sleeve with his left hand, clutching the softball in his right, and had a look of urgency about him. "Mister?" His eyes were green; a swatch of reddish hair stuck out from under the hood of his snowsuit, and there was a scratch, like a cat scratch, just above the right side of his jawline.

"Yes?" I said.

It seemed to please him that I'd finally responded. He smiled a broad, appealing smile, turned, walked quickly down the street, toward Park Avenue. I called after him, "Where's your friend?"

He glanced back at me, said nothing, continued walking. When he reached the light orange townhouse, he turned his head, and his smiled broadened as he went up the steps, opened the door—which was apparently unlocked—and went inside. It seemed very much like an invitation.

The massive oak and glass front door of the townhouse was indeed unlocked. I opened it, stuck my head into the house, saw the boy's legs as he disappeared up a bright green carpeted stairway to the right.

"Hello," I called.

I heard at once, very faintly, from the second floor, "Come in, please, Mr. Cray."

"Sorry?" I called. I got no reply. I stuck my head in further, put one foot in. "Hello," I called again.

"Come in, please," I heard. It was the same voice, a woman's voice, from the second floor. "Go into the parlor, please, Mr. Cray."

I stepped into the house, pulled the door shut, checked to see if it had somehow locked automatically. It hadn't. "Where is it?" I called.

"Just to your right," I heard.

"To my right?"

Nothing.

"To my right, you said?"

"Yes, Mr. Cray." I noted the hint of impatience in the voice now. "To your right."

"How do you know my name?"

"Go *into* the parlor, Mr. Cray. Please."

"Uh-huh," I said, and took a few cautious steps forward toward a set of closed mahogany doors to my right. There was an identical set of doors to my left, closed as well, and at the end of the short hallway, halfway up the wall opposite me, a big, oval mirror, in a smooth, beige frame. I found that I couldn't help watching myself in it, half in amusement, as if I were watching someone else. I nodded at myself, grinned.

"What the *hell* are you doing here?" I whispered.

And from the second floor, I heard: "Please, Mr. Cray!" I went immediately to the set of mahogany doors, pulled them open, and went into the parlor.

It reminded me very much of my childhood home in Maine. It was spacious, not awfully well lighted—

because two sets of heavy, dark drapes on tall, narrow windows that overlooked East 81st Street were closed—and there were mid-Victorian pieces everywhere: a velvet rococo couch, covered in plastic, to my right, between the windows; two Windsor chairs to the left; a tall, dark cherry Queen Anne secretary straight ahead; several Tiffany lamps, in varying degrees of repair; a black upholstered Morris chair—the upholstery, like the rococo couch, also covered in plastic—near it.

I heard shuffling noises from above, as if someone were moving about, and then, faintly, I heard voices. One sounded like the voice of a child, the other that of the woman who had invited me in, her voice now apparently raised in anger. Presently, the voices stopped and a door closed above, on the second floor. I turned and listened as someone moved down the stairway. I went back, through the double mahogany doors. I saw a woman coming down the stairs. She was dressed in a faded pink, floor-length nightgown, a strange thing to wear so late in the morning. She'd gathered the nightgown together, at the top of her breast, with a safety pin.

"Hello, Mr. Cray," she said, her voice now a pleasant, high tenor.

"I didn't mean to wake you," I said.

Her chest heaved, in a sigh. She was in her late forties, I guessed, and had a look of extreme weariness about her. Her hair had clearly been dyed brown—it was raggedly graying at the temples—and it was obvious that she had once been quite attractive.

"You didn't," she said. She was at the bottom of the stairway now. She nodded toward the parlor. "Shall we go in there, please?"

We went into the parlor together, she just ahead of me. She seated herself in the Morris chair, crossed her legs, nodded at one of the Windsor chairs, several feet from her, and said, "Sit down, please."

I sat. She said, her eyes not on me but on the windows across the room, "Who brought you here?"

"I'm sorry," I said. "I don't understand."

"Was it one of the cabbies?"

I thought for a moment. "Yes," I said.

"Petersak?"

"Yes. Is that significant?"

She frowned slightly. Her gaze settled on me; I noticed, then, that her left eye was blue, the other one brown. She asked, "Do you know what's happening to you, Mr. Cray."

"No," I answered. "Do you?"

"Yes," she said. "I do." She looked away again, toward the windows. She continued, "Perhaps you should think first. Perhaps you should know that this new . . . vision you have can be taken from you. It has been taken from others, and they were better off without it." She said this almost as if by rote, almost as if she were reciting it.

I said, "Who are you?"

She ignored the question. She waved toward the windows as if to indicate the outside of the house. "Of course, all of them *see*, but they have no idea *what* they're seeing. They think they're seeing . . . life."

She stopped a moment, looked at me again, smiled coyly. "And in a way, they are." She paused again, briefly, went on, "You probably don't understand a word I'm saying to you, isn't that right?"

I answered, "That's right."

Her smile broadened, then quickly dissipated. It was a nice smile; she had good, straight teeth and full lips. She said, "What do you believe in, Mr. Cray?"

The question took me by surprise. I said, truthfully, "I'm sorry. I don't understand."

She took a quick, agitated breath. "I think you do, Mr. Cray."

"How do you know my name?"

She ignored me again, uncrossed her legs—which, I guessed, had also once been quite attractive; now they were laced with varicose veins—pushed herself to her feet, and went to one of the windows. After a moment she said, her back to me, "Do you believe in *life*, Mr. Cray?"

"I'm afraid I don't understand that—please, you're going to have to tell me what to call you."

"Madeline."

"Madeline," I said. It seemed to fit her.

"Again, do you believe in *life*, Mr. Cray?"

"Do you mean," I began, and she cut in angrily, "I mean *life*, for God's sake! I mean *life*!"

"Yes," I answered, "of course I do."

"And so you believe in death as well?"

I nodded, though her back still was turned. "Yes," I whispered.

"Good, I think we're getting somewhere." I imagined from the tone of her voice that she smiled. "And do you believe that you know the difference— between life and death?"

"Yes," I answered, "I do. They're opposites."

"That is the popular mythology, isn't it?" And again I imagined from her tone that she smiled. "The popular mythology," she repeated, as if she liked the phrase. "Up/down, dark/light, near/far, life/death— all opposites."

"Yes," I said.

"No, Mr. Cray. They aren't. It's a matter of how you look at it, a matter of how you *see*."

"I don't understand. See what?"

"Life, death, dark, light. All just a matter of how you see. Like sunspots, Mr. Cray. You think sunspots are dark—they aren't, of course; they're very bright. They only *appear* dark because the rest of the sun is so much brighter. That's a good analogy, don't you think? I've used it before, and I've been told that it's a good analogy." Again I got the idea that she was smiling, pleased with herself.

I said to her, my voice low and tight, "I want to know what's happening to me. Can you tell me what's happening to me?"

She turned abruptly. She had a broad, pleased smile on her face. "Of course I can, Mr. Cray. I've told you I can. It's why you're here." She went back to her chair, sat, crossed her legs again; leaned forward with her hands clasped. "Would you like some coffee, some tea? Gerald can get it for you."

"Gerald?"

"The little boy in the snowsuit. Gerald. My son."

"No. Thank you." I was growing impatient.

"Of course you don't." Again she smiled. "You want me to tell you what's happening to you."

"Yes."

"And I will. Of course. That's why you're here."

"Yes, you said that."

Her smile vanished at once. I saw, then, that Gerald—the thin-faced boy in the cream-colored snowsuit and shock of red hair, Madeline's son—was standing beside her. He still had a softball in his hand, and the thin scratch I had noticed at his jawline seemed wider, more inflamed than I remembered. He was grinning playfully at me.

Madeline said, "You don't really want tc know what's happening to you. And if you did, I couldn't tell you anyway. I don't even know what's happening to poor Gerald." She reached up, lightly touched the scratch at his jawline. "This is a cat scratch, Mr. Cray. He got it from a big, mangy tom he was trying to befriend. And, of course, as sometimes happens with cat scratches, it's become infected."

"Take him to a doctor," I suggested.

She smiled thinly as if at a tasteless joke. "Of course, Mr. Cray. I'll do that. But not in time."

"What do you mean, but not in time? Call now—take him in now."

"Oh, you really do have a thick head, don't you?" I said nothing.

"I'll tell you what is happening to you, Mr. Cray. You are an all-but-blind and bottom-dwelling fish, and you are coming up, into the light. And you are not going to like it—no, not at all!''

Gerald grinned at me again. I believed that I grinned back. And he said, ''Not in time, mister. Too bad.''

''He's always had a sense of humor,'' Madeline said. ''I think it's important, don't you?''

I said nothing. I felt like I was watching some kind of perverse sideshow.

She stroked her son's cheek affectionately—he was still grinning at me. ''Do you know, Mr. Cray,'' she said, ''that cold is really just the relative absence of warmth? Do you know that there are *degrees* of warmth?'' She paused a beat and smiled as if I had understood what she was saying, and was happy for it. Then she went on, nodding at her son, ''My poor Gerald is not awfully warm, Mr. Cray. But neither is he awfully cold. He's just a little colder than you or I.''

I took a quick, agitated breath. I desperately did not want to be in that house.

Madeline went on, ''You may leave, of course, whenever you wish.'' She hesitated; I stayed where I was. She smiled again, a quick smile. ''But, of course, you're not going to. Not at the moment anyway. You're going to stick around. You're confused, and I can't blame you for it. We are *all* confused, Mr. Cray. Even Gerald here is confused, and that poor man you left twitching on Fifth Avenue and those girls hailing a taxi. They are all confused. How different do you suppose their world is from ours, Mr. Cray, merely because it is the world of the dead?"

"I don't know how to answer that," I said.

"And neither do I," she said. "I wish I did—God, I wish I did. But I know really as little about their world as I do about our own. One springs from the other, so I believe that they are equally complex—and equally terrifying. I can tell you what I know about Gerald. I can tell you that I love him and that he is a comfort to me, and that he has pain, Mr. Cray—oh, intense, unbelievable pain. And I can tell you that someday he will leave here; he will leave this house, this street, and he will go somewhere else. I don't know where. And I can tell you that I used to cry. I used to cry quite a lot. But I don't cry anymore.

"And I can tell you this, too. I used to go to where we put him, where we buried him, and I used to stare at the place he is, and I have no idea now what I saw there. Or what I felt. Because I have him with me again. Almost." She stopped a moment, then went on, a clear note of strain in her voice, "Not to watch him grow up, and not to have hopes for him, and not to worry about him. And he will never give me grandchildren, of course. All that is stopped, I think. All stopped. Those are things, I believe, that death stops once and for all.

"And all the other Geralds are out there, Mr. Cray—they are all out on those streets, and in those houses. They are driving taxis, shoplifting, weeping. They are all there. All the Geralds, and all the men in ragged T-shirts. You don't want to hear this, but you are being made to *see* and so you must hear it. They are all there. Whole and in pieces, buying stocks and doing laundry and watching cable TV. But hear this, too; you are allowed to know them and to see them, but not well, Mr. Cray. Not well at all. Only as well as you know and see the living. Which is why *I* stay in this house and talk to people like you. Because I have only Gerald here. And I love him—cold as he is. I love him.

"You may go now."

And I did. I went out onto East 73rd Street. I stood at the top of the steps, watched a snowfall start, and thought about Phyllis again.

CHAPTER FIVE

And realized that I still loved her, that I missed her, and that I would go looking for her.

As if I were some kind of super sleuth. A Sam Spade. A Sherlock Holmes. And I thought it would be an exciting adventure. Something to savor and to enjoy.

The snowfall grew heavier and I vomited there, at the top of Madeline's steps. What else was I going to do?

At the Hammet Mausoleum, Halloween, 1965

Sam told me, "So that's why I ain't afraid too much to die. 'Cuz I got it figured out."

I said, "You're scary, Sam. Sometimes you're scary."

"Uh-huh. Sure I am." He fingered the wax dripping from one of the candles. "I scare *myself*, sometimes, Abner." He repositioned himself on the cement floor so he was lying on his side, his right hand propping his head up. He went on, "What do you say, Abner—we gonna try to call up old Joe Hammet or are we gonna jabber all night long?"

I got a call from Serena Hitchcock soon after I got back to Art's apartment. She was concerned about me.

"I really do want to talk with you about other books, Abner. That wasn't bullshit."

"I know it wasn't bullshit, Serena. And I appreciate the offer."

"But?"

"But I have other things I want to do."

"Have you gone to another company, Abner?"

"No."

"I wouldn't blame you if you had."

"I haven't gone to another company, Serena. I merely have other things that I want to do."

"In the way of photography, you mean?"

"No."

"Am I meddling?"

"No. I appreciate your concern, believe me, I do—"

"But mind my own business?"

"Not at all."

"Are you going to stay in New York?"

"I think so. It depends."

"Oh? On what?"

"On a couple of things. On what I find here, I suppose."

"And what are you looking for?"

"I've got to go now, Serena."

"I'm sorry."

"It's all right. Really. I'm just a little confused—nothing manic. Just a little confused."

"Abner?"

"Yes?"

"If you ever need someone to talk to, think of me. Okay?"

"Thanks. I will."

"I mean it, Abner."

"Yes. Good-bye." And I hung up.

It came to me that I had to go about my search scientifically. It came to me that I had to make a list of all the things that I knew about Phyllis Pellaprat. A numerical list of things. So I got a pen and sheet of paper from Art's desk—a sturdy-looking, three-drawer, dark cherry library desk that he'd set up on the east wall of the living room, opposite the fireplace—and I sat down at the desk and made my list:

1. Phyllis Pellaprat is a black woman, 28-30 years of age.

2. She's very, very attractive.

3. Tall. Nicely put together.

4. Intelligent.

5. A games player.

6. Her parents live on East 95th Street.

7. Their names are Thomas and Lorraine Pellaprat.

8. Lorraine Pellaprat looks much like her daughter.

9. Phyllis was once Art DeGraff's girlfriend. He beat her up early in December.

I got stuck there. I think that I sat grinning stupidly at the list for quite a few minutes, and then I crumpled the paper up in my fist.

Supersleuths didn't make lists. Supersleuths had *brains*, for Christ's sake.

I was drawn very quickly onto the street again. I remembered what Phyllis had said to me and what Madeline had said to me: "You're not going to like it out there, Abner." I wanted to prove them wrong. I wanted to make my way down Fifth Avenue, past all the little specialty shops on Madison, through the little knots of people waiting for buses or going to work, and I wanted to prove them wrong. I wanted to prove Phyllis wrong, and Madeline wrong, and Barbara W. Barber wrong. I wanted to jostle people and get angry when they jostled back. I wanted to enjoy the crazies, ogle the women in tight jeans, be annoyed by the noise of traffic; I wanted to convince myself that Manhattan was a place where the living played out their lives, went about their business, saw sons and daughters born, made careers, got in the way, did stupid things and marvelous things and then died, and were buried. I didn't want to believe I was a part of anything more than that.

But I was, of course.

*   *   *

It was 12:15 P.M., on the sixth of February, and I was out in front Art's house, with my back to it and my eyes on the house across the street. There was nothing special about it. It was very much like Art's house. But someone was watching me from a second-story window: a child, I supposed—a young girl with long hair who was holding the curtain aside with her right hand and apparently did not care much if I saw her looking at me.

We watched each other for quite some time. Eventually I got the idea that her hair was dark—it was difficult to be sure because the sun was creating a glaze of light on the surface of the window—that her skin was very pale, and that she was dressed in a pair of pants and a short-sleeved shirt.

Eventually, someone came up behind her—an adult, I imagined, who looked out the window at me, too, for half a minute. Then, together, they backed away from the window and the sun put a heavier glaze of light on it.

I remembered then: "And they are all out there, Mr. Cray. All out on those streets, and in those houses. They are driving taxis, jaywalking, shoplifting, watching soap operas, weeping. They are all there."

Phyllis, too. And I remembered: "I used to go to where we put him, where we buried him, and I used to stare at the place he is, and I have no idea what I saw there. Or what I felt."

Phyllis, too, I thought. *I can go to where they put her*. It was an idea that made me queasy, and I found myself sitting down slowly on the snow-covered front

steps of Art's house and then grabbing hold of the
iron railing to steady myself.

I was looking at the sidewalk in front of my feet
when I saw another person's feet appear there, in
front of mine—a man's feet; he was wearing highly
polished red oxfords and gray suit pants. I looked up
and saw that he was chunky, red-cheeked, and his
eyes and mouth were smiling. He had a small notepad
and a pencil in hand. He said to me, in a voice that
was high-pitched, but efficient, "I can help you now."

I glanced down at his feet and saw that he had left
footprints in the snow. I thought, *This isn't one of
them. This is a crazy. He leaves footprints in the
snow.* I looked up again, at his face. I said, "No, I
don't think so." He jotted something down on the
notepad, his smile softening as he did it. Then his
smile strengthened again, and he said, "If you tell me
who you're looking for, I can help you."

"No," I repeated, "I don't think so. Please leave
me alone."

He nodded to his right. I looked. I saw a green and
white 1961 Chevy Biscayne—the kind with the flat
fins—parked down the street. The man said, "I have
a car. Not many of us do, but I do. Could you come
with me, please?!" It sounded like a command, which
made me angry.

I said, "No, I won't come with you."

He jotted something down again on his notepad,
then looked at me, still smiling. "You *have* to come
with me," he said, sounding petulant.

I stood then. My strategy was simple. He was

maybe five feet nine or ten, a little overweight, not really very healthy looking, despite his ruddy cheeks, and I stand six-foot-two and weighed, then, almost two hundred and ten pounds. I was trying to intimidate him. I smiled a kind of tight, warning smile.

He smiled back, a smile of gratitude. "Good," he said, and started for his car. He got a few steps, stopped, looked back. "Well, c'mon," he said, and continued walking. I followed him, watched him go around to the driver's door, open it—it creaked pitilessly—get in. And I found myself standing beside the passenger door. I bent over and told him through the closed window, "I'll call a cop."

He reached across the seat, opened the door. "I know who you're looking for," he said. "And I can help you."

I got in, but left the passenger door open. The inside of the car smelled of beer. Directly in front of me was a cheap compass on a small suction cup stuck on the inside of the windshield. In the dashboard itself, there was a hole where a radio had once been. I said, my eyes straight ahead, "What do you mean you know who I'm looking for?"

The man started the car. It was noisy; the muffler was going. "Close the door, please," he said. I hesitated, uncertain, then closed the door softly. We pulled away from the curb and started toward Fifth Avenue. I repeated, "What do you mean, you know who I'm looking for?"

"How do you like my car?" he said. "Pretty cherry, huh?"

"I asked you a question," I said, trying hard for a tone of firmness.

"Madeline told me," he said. He came to a stop at Fifth Avenue, waited for the light. It changed to green almost at once. He stayed put. A car came up behind us; its driver leaned on the horn. "Uh-huh," he said, "Madeline told me all about it, about how you got this little girlfriend, this little black girlfriend and how you wanta—" the driver behind us was still leaning on the horn—"how you wanta get hold of her again. Can't blame you for that, those black girls—"he shook his right hand in the air—"min*ga*." He glanced back, leaned out the window, threw the bird to the driver behind us. "Blow it out yer ass!" he hollered, then stomped on the accelerator and took a squealing left-hand turn. He hit the brake hard; I straight-armed the dashboard. There was a truck just ahead. He stared at it. "Goddamned, for crimey's sake!" he muttered. He stuck his head out the window again. "Hey shit-for-brains—get that freakin' piece a tin outa the way!"

I put my hand on the door handle; he glanced over, smiled. "You ain't goin' nowhere," he said. I tried the door. It wouldn't open. I felt the sharp whisper of panic inside me.

"You scared?" he asked.

I closed my eyes.

"Sure you're scared," I heard him say. Then I heard him yell, "I said get that fuckin' piece a crap offa the fuckin' street!" There was a short pause, then he whispered, "Oh Jesus!" I opened my eyes.

The driver of the truck, a beefy, dark-haired guy, was walking very slowly toward the car with a big, shit-eating grin on his face. When he got to the car he leaned over, looked in the driver's window—which had been hastily rolled up—and said tightly, the shit-eating grin still on his face, "Your ass is grass, my friend, and I'm the mower." The man I was with put his hand inside his suit jacket; I saw something gleam darkly in there. He said to the truck driver, "I don't want any trouble here."

"You already got it!" bellowed the truck driver.

" 'Cuz I'm on an errand of mercy," said the man I was with, and nodded at me.

The truck driver bent over and looked at me; his grin broadened. The man I was with grabbed hold of the thing inside his jacket.

And I frantically tried the door again. It opened. I looked dumbly at it a moment and scrambled from the car.

I saw a woman coming my way. She was wearing a long, red wool coat and carrying a large, black purse, and she was staring disapprovingly at me. I stared back a moment, then looked at the Chevy again. I saw that it was down on the right front end, as if one of its springs was broken, and that its right rear tire was going flat. When I leaned over, I saw that the car was empty, and I realized that it could easily have been just one of the thousands of junked cars that litter New York City's streets.

"I'd find a *decent* home if I were you," said the woman in the red wool coat.

I turned to her. "Yes," I said. "I have one," and she turned her head and quickened her pace to get away from me.

I saw no truck, either, and no murderous driver with a shit-eating grin on his face.

I saw Madison Avenue.

I saw, across the street, a furniture store called Rick's Rattan and Wicker, and next door to it a little bar called Raoul's, and next to it a place that sold cigars and men's magazines.

And I saw people moving purposefully about, eyes straight ahead usually, heads down a little. It is the way New Yorkers walk, as if they're going someplace and are already late getting there.

Go, answer the door, peer through the little security peephole at whoever has come to call. You see a face, a smile perhaps, a pair of eyes. And they tell you—open the door. Or they tell you—do not open the door. But if you have shut yourself up on the wrong side of that peephole for too long, they tell you very little. Only what is within arm's reach, not what is above, or below, or to the sides, or behind that smiling face.

At the Hammet Mausoleum, Halloween, 1965

"Hey, Joe Hammet, Joe Hammet, come to us, Joe Hammet." Sam was trying to speak the way he'd heard mediums speak on TV, in a kind of high sing-song voice but he couldn't help grinning at the same time, which got me to grinning, too. "Hey, Joe

Hammet," he went on, and glanced slowly about the room as he spoke, "you old fruit, come on, *tauuulk* to us, *tauuulk* to us." He stopped, listened a moment, went on, "Give us a sign, Joe Hammet, anything, give us a sign." He looked at me. "What you grinning at, Abner? This is fucking serious business, here."

"Sorry," I said, and forced myself to stop grinning.

"Good," Sam said, and went on, "A sign, Joe, a sign. Tell us it's a nice day."

"A nice day, Sam?"

"Sure, he said it all the time. Coulda been raining buckets and he woulda said, 'Boy, it's a nice day.' "

"Oh."

"So if we hear 'It's a nice day,' we'll know it's him. *Habits,* Abner, like I said."

"Uh-huh, then how do you know you won't get a nun?"

"A what?"

"A nun—you know, a sister."

"Whose sister?"

"A *nun*, Sam. A Catholic nun."

"Why would I get a Catholic nun?"

"Forget it."

"Anybody ever tell you you got a sense of humor like a stone, Abner?"

"Yeah. *You* have."

"Well, you do. You say these incredibly dumb things, and you think they're so fucking funny, and they're not. I'm only tellin' you this 'cuz I'm your friend, Abner—"

"Okay, okay, can we get on with the seance?"

"This ain't a seance."

"Whatever it is—can we get on with it; I gotta get home."

"Sure, Abner. In a moment." He lifted a cheek, grunted; nothing happened. He smiled. "Must be all dried up, Abner."

"Could be," I said. "That's disrespectful, you know."

"Joe *Hammmmm*et, Joe *Hammmmm*et!"

"Christ," I whispered.

"Come out, come out, wherever you are. Is it a nice day, Joe? Is it a nice day over there?"

CHAPTER SIX

I saw Phyllis, too. I saw a black woman anyway, across Madison Avenue, near the corner of East 80th Street. A patch of sunlight was on her, and she was wearing what Phyllis always wore—a white, waist-length fake mink coat, white, stacked heel boots, and a green silk, mid-calf-length dress.

Her face was obscured by sunlight, I guessed, but I got the idea that she was staring at me, and I stared back. After several minutes, I said her name to myself. "Phyllis."

She turned away.

"Phyllis!" I called.

She vanished down East 80th Street.

"Phyllis!" I called again, and made my way around the front of the Chevy, moved cautiously into the street with my arm extended, palm out. A big Lincoln came to a quick, reluctant halt inches from me, it's driver cursing.

"Please," I murmured. "Please."

Traffic was slow and I made it easily across the street to the other side, then to the corner of East 80th. I saw the woman I hoped was Phyllis half a block away, and I smiled and ran hard to catch her.

"Phyllis!" I called repeatedly as I ran.

She did not turn her head.

I gained on her very quickly. She was starting up the steps of a brick apartment house when I caught up with her; I stopped at the bottom of the steps.

"Phyllis!" I said.

She turned. She said to me, smiling a big, willing smile, "Whatchoo want with Phyllis, honey, when you can have some time wif me?"

"I'm sorry," I said.

Her face was lined and aged, the nostrils flared, the mouth hard, the eyes flat and tired.

"I'm sorry," I repeated, and added, "I thought you were someone else."

She smiled again, playfully. "I ain't no one else, honey—I ain't never been no one else."

Her voice was Phyllis', almost. It was brassier, less appealing and, like the eyes, a little tired. She went on, "But I can be whoever you want me to be."

"No," I said, not unkindly. "No. I'm sorry. Forgive me."

She shrugged, turned, walked up the steps and into the apartment house. I stood in front of it for quite some time waiting for her to come out: *That is Phyllis!* I told myself. *That is my Phyllis! Coming apart.*

I waited quite a while for her. Fifteen minutes, at least.

But she did not come out.

So I went in.

My odyssey began there, I think. In that house.

The front door—solid oak painted a dull violet, which put it in sharp contrast with the red brick of the building itself—was unlocked. It opened onto a long and dimly lit hallway that appeared to run the entire length of the building. There were six doors on either side of this hallway, each painted the same dull violet as the front door. Beside each of these doors stood a spindle-legged, dark wood wash-stand with a white porcelain wash basin and matching pitcher. Several women dressed in bra and panties were washing themselves—around the pubic area especially, and when they did this, they pulled the waistband of their panties down—when I came in. A short, blonde woman with a large nose and an excess of makeup looked up, smiled in the same way that the woman I'd hoped was Phyllis had smiled, and said, "You want me? I ain't taken."

"I'm looking for someone," I told her. She was wearing a pair of black lace panties, a black garter belt, bra. The effect would have been appealing, had it not been for a large, blue-black bruise on the inside of her right thigh and the fact that her skin was very pale, almost white. "I thought I saw her come in here," I went on.

The woman dried herself off with a cream-colored towel from the washstand, come over to me, put her hands flat on my chest. She was even shorter than I had first guessed, no more than five feet tall, and she smelled strongly of soap.

"You won't find better than me," she cooed, and made a show of licking her lips; I noted that her tongue was nearly as pale as her skin and that it apparently was dry, too, because it left no sheen of moisture on her lips. "I'm tight; I'm good—you come with me and find out. I want you come with me and find out."

"No," I said, my voice low. "Thank you. No."

She licked her lips again and her knee came up slowly and cautiously into my groin.

I told her, "Please, don't do that."

She kept doing it.

I grabbed hold of her wrists, hard, and tried to push her away. I couldn't. She said again, "I'm tight; I'm good—you come with me and find out; I want you to come with me and find out."

"Thank you," I said, and I heard a little tremor in my voice. "Thank you. No. Some other time. Some other time, soon."

"I'm clean, too," she said. "I'm tight; I'm good; I'm clean—you come with me and find out."

I looked past her, down the hallway. Several other women were staring at us. One of them—an older woman with stiff black hair and thin legs—was smiling at us, as if amused, and another woman, in the act of cleaning herself, looked at me very much as the girls hailing a taxi had, with quiet and studied indifference.

The short woman still had her knee in my groin and her hands on my chest. I gripped her wrists harder, hoping to push her away, but it was impossible. I felt, strangely, as if I had just come into a room filled with flies and they were beginning to alight on me.

I said to the short woman, trying hard for a soothing tone and missing it, I think, "Tell me your name. I want to know your name."

The question made her smile gratefully. "You wanta know my name? You really wanta know my name?"

"Yes," I said.

"My name's Sheila."

"That's a nice name. I've always like that name."

Her smile broadened. She looked very pleased; her knee lowered from my groin. "Yeah," she said, "ain't it?"

And from behind her I heard, "Sheila!"

I looked. I saw only that the older woman with the thin legs and the other woman were both furiously involved in cleaning themselves now. I felt Sheila's muscles loosen and I let go of her wrists. She slid away from me, her mouth open a little, her eyes wide, as if she had been surprised, and she backed away slowly, without much grace, as though she was having trouble making her legs work properly.

I heard again, "Sheila!" It was a young man's voice, I guessed, someone in his late teens, and it had a distinct tone of forced authority to it.

He appeared then, from within a room several doors down the hallway. He was eighteen, perhaps nineteen, and was several inches shorter than I, with a head of unruly, brown hair, small, dark eyes, and a grin on his round, pink face that was like the grin I'd seen on the face of the murderous truck driver—a kind of slick shit-eating grin which seemed to announce loudly that he was very happy with himself.

He said to me, "Ain't this great? Ain't this fantastic?" and came forward a few steps, looked back, toward the women still cleaning themselves; he held his right hand up, snapped his fingers. The women disappeared quickly into their rooms. "Ain't it great?" he said again. Then the grin left his face abruptly. "You got to keep 'em in line, that's all. It ain't hard. Shit, it wouldn't be, would it? Which one you want? You want Sheila?"

"I'm looking for someone," I said.

He ignored me. "I got one named Ruth, and one named Cathy, and one named Wilhelmina; she's my favorite."

I felt myself backing away, toward the door.

"Course, they're all just marking time, you know," the boy said. "You ask 'em; they'll tell ya—hey, where you goin'?"

I reached behind, found a doorknob, I assumed it was the one to the front door.

"You gotta pay first," the boy called frantically.

I turned the knob. "Thank you, no," I murmured, and pushed the door open, my eyes still on the boy. I felt a pair of hands at my waist, from behind. I glanced around, saw a flat, gray face, a mound of dark brown hair, a set of gray teeth.

The boy called "And besides, she's all done, so you ain't gonna have no fun with her." I looked at him again; he came forward. "Let me," he said, and straight-armed the woman. She stumbled back, into her room. "Jesus," the boy whispered; he smelled abominably of beer and sweat. "Christ almighty!" And he shut the door, though clearly with effort, as if the woman were pulling on the other side of it. He got a key from his pocket, locked the door, grinned at me again. "She's *leavin'* tomorrow, early; so *you* can't *have* her," he said. His grin altered. " 'Less of course, you like 'em that way."

I told him again that I was looking for someone. And again he ignored me. He said, "Some guys do. I try to keep 'em out, but it's hard, it's hard—you can't keep the sickies out; there's no way you can keep 'em out, not all of 'em. Some get through; the live ones get through—"

"Please," I cut in, "I need your help."

"Can't," he said. "I want to; really, I want to. But I go out that door—" he nodded glumly at the front door—"and you got a real loony on your hands. I mean a real class A loony. In here—hey, it's okay. I like it. Kind of a feast for the eyes. Most of the time. Till they start comin' apart, you know. Then it ain't so good. They you gotta start cleanin' up after 'em, you know, and they start gettin' real desperate, real horny, 'cuz they're desperate, you know, and then you gotta kinda keep the door locked when you're takin' your naps. But the rest of the time—'' His grin reappeared suddenly. "It's great. It's fantastic, better than watchin' my sister and her goddamned girlfriend, that's for sure. I mean, you gotta be a real wacko—'' He stopped. His grin faded; he lowered his eyes, took a deep breath, scratched idly at the inside of his elbow. "Damned place's got lice," he murmured. "Every day, every *fuckin' day*, I gotta take a fuckin' shower with fuckin' lye soap to get rid of the fuckin' lice. Damn it all to hell—''

"Have you seen her?" I cut in. "Have you seen Phyllis?''

He turned away suddenly, violently, still scratching at his elbow. He moved with great agitation toward the room he'd just come out of. "Goddamn it all to hell, shit fuck! Next I'll get roaches in here— next I'll get roaches; I'll get silverfish. All the time cleanin' up after 'em, all the time cleanin' up their little messes—'' He was at his door now; he went into his room, babbled on furiously, "All the time gettin' in my hair, fuck you, fuck you, fuck you!" And he slammed his door shut.

I saw other doors open then. Immediately. Down the hallway. I saw a few faces stick out, some smiles. I heard the door behind me open—the door that the boy had closed and locked—and far down the hall, half in darkness, I saw what looked very much like the woman I had followed into the house. She was standing with her back against the wall; she had her arms wide, her legs wide, and she was naked.

From behind me I heard a low, ragged humming sound, as if someone were trying to whisper with her mouth closed. And I saw also that several more faces had appeared from within the rooms lined up down the hallway.

And the woman at the end of the hallway, the woman standing half in darkness, was opening her mouth and closing it, very slowly, and a noise was coming from it—a long, low noise. This noise:

"Ahhhb—"

Followed by this noise:

"baaaahhnnerrr—"

CHAPTER SEVEN

Abner, of course. The woman standing half in darkness was calling my name. Or trying to. And so I called to her: "Phyllis!"

And she repeated, "Ahhhhbaaahnnnerrr—"

The low, ragged humming noise behind me drew closer. I felt something touch my arm and I glanced around, not for long, then back again, very quickly, at the woman at the end of the hallway. I saw that she had turned sideways to me and that she was moving off, to what had been her right. The touch at my back grew stronger. I glanced around once more and saw the mound of dark hair, the flat gray face, the pitiful approximation of a smile. The smile changed. The mouth formed this word: "Please." And these words: "Keep me here!"

And I ran from it, past the faces sticking into the

hallway, past the smiles. I ran very clumsily; I knocked over several of the washstands and heard them clatter to the floor behind me, then I heard the wash basins and pitchers shattering.

I got to the end of that hallway and found only the odor of the woman who had been there—the odor of damp wood, Phyllis's odor. I inhaled very deeply of it.

I saw the boy appear from his room, saw his mouth drop open when he caught sight of the shattered porcelain and the washstands lying about. He shook his head slowly, looked down the hallway at me, and said, his tone one of tortured disbelief, "You can't *do* this!" And he started toward me, head still shaking. "How are they going to clean themselves now? I'll get silverfish in here; I'll get roaches in here . . ."

"I'm sorry," I said.

He said, "You'll have to leave. This is not orderly. It has to be orderly. We have to have some order. Who will want them if there's no order?" He was very close to me now, within arm's reach. I said again, "I'm sorry."

Phyllis's odor mixed with his odor—the odor of nervous perspiration and stale beer, a combination that was sickly sweet and made my stomach churn. "Please . . ." I said.

And then his small, moist hands were around my neck, squeezing hard, though not as hard as Phyllis could have or Sheila could have, not hard enough in fact that I couldn't plead with him to stop at the same time, because I could see myself doing something that I didn't want to do, having always been something of a pacifist.

I said to him, "Please don't *do* that!"

But he continued to babble on about roaches, lice, silverfish, about having to clean up, about needing *order*, and something in my brain screamed that he really wasn't worth much, that he was only a guy who took care of a whorehouse in the middle of Manhattan.

And I was glad my brain said that to me.

I lifted my knee hard into his groin. It broke his grip on me at once, and a look of intense surprise and pain spread all over his face, which made me happy. I smiled. He doubled over. And again I brought my knee up, into his mouth this time. His top front teeth went through my pants and settled deep into my skin; then he thudded backwards to the floor, where he lay with his hands to his groin, his arms stiff, his knees bent, his mouth oozing blood, and a constant, low, moaning sound filtering up out of his throat.

And I was still smiling. I thought he looked like a beetle that had gotten turned on its back in the sun.

I noticed the women then. They were walking very slowly and very stiffly to the door that opened onto East 80th Street. Sheila got to the door first. Then the older woman with the thin legs, then a tall brunette. They bumped into each other, like cartoon characters. They got to the door, bumped into it, bounced back a little, took another step forward, bounced back.

I remember thinking that it was kind of comical, like watching *The Three Stooges* or *I Love Lucy*.

And then I heard someone weeping. Sheila, I supposed, because the weeping stopped as quickly as it had begun and a voice—Sheila's voice—said, "We are not zombies!" I heard a tremendous, quivering anger in the words.

And then weeping again. A chorus of it—low and soft. And all the while, through it—through the weeping—they kept walking into that door and bouncing back a little. It seemed to jar them; their bodies shook, like wood hitting stone.

To my right, where Phyllis might have gone, I thought, a door was standing open. I stepped through it, into a small, dark room that had only a small cot, like an army cot, in it—no sheets or pillows—which smelled as I might have imagined it should—of come and sweat.

The room had one window. It faced a brick wall, part of the building next door. I went to the window, started to open it, heard the weeping continue behind me, heard the small, stiff noises of bodies hitting the door at a slow, walking pace.

I said, beneath my breath, "Jesus God in heaven," which surprised me because it was a curse I had never used before, one that had vaguely religious overtones.

Then, because the window wouldn't open, I kicked through it, kicked out the shards remaining at the sides and went out into the narrow, paved service passage between the buildings.

It was dark there. And cold. And quiet. I went way back into the service passage, far from the window I'd come out of. At the front of the service passage, I could occasionally see people walking past, traffic.

It was good to be alone. It was good to be out of that house.

I heard a cat purring loudly nearby. I looked. It was a big, orange and white cat—*marmalade* is the correct term—nursing at least half a dozen newborn kittens. I smiled at the cat. I said hello to it and congratulated it. It continued purring, and I continued talking softly to it for quite some time. After a while, I sat down near it and fell asleep.

At the Hammett Mausoleum, Halloween, 1965

"Joe says it's a nice day, Abner."

"Shit, too."

"You callin' me a liar? I'm not a liar. Joe says it's a nice day—he says it's *always* a nice day over there."

"What time is it, Sam?"

"How'm I supposed to know what time it is? What do you think?—You think I'm fuckin' Big Ben or something? I don't know; it's 10:45, 11:00. Who gives two shits?"

"I do. I gotta get home. You're getting awfully hostile, Sam."

"I'm gettin' hostile? We're all *dead*, Abner—'course I'm hostile."

"I thought you brought a watch along."

"I did. It stopped. The spooks got to it and made it stop. John Cameron Swayback gave it to 'em and said, 'The spooks got it now, and we'll see in a couple million years if the Timex is still running.''

"Who's John Cameron Swayback?"

"So I don't know what time it is, Abner. Sorry." He put his hands over Flora's skull, his arms straight; he was seated Indian-style again. "I mean it this time, Joe Hammet. Give us a sign, goddamnit, or we're gonna do something sleazy, I promise."

"I'm not doing *any*thing sleazy, Sam."

"Wimp. I'll tell you something, Abner. I may not live very long, but I sure as hell am gonna have some fun, and that's more than you're gonna do. You'll probably end up being a damned encyclopedia salesman, or a muffler installer or a social studies teacher."

"I'm gonna be a photographer, Sam."

"Yeah? Well, you gotta be able to *see* to be a photographer, Abner. You gotta be able to *see*, you know. And you don't see nothing'. I'll bet you don't even see old Joe Hammet standing right there—'' he nodded—"beside ya, grinnin' away. How do, Joe?"

"Eat shit and die, Sam."

"I'm already dead, Abner. Why ain'tcha lookin'? He's there; he really is."

I looked, quickly. Sam laughed. "Gullible bastard!" he said.

"Trusting," I said.

"You'll probably sell lamps or something; you'll probably be a TV repairman."

"I told you what I'm gonna be, Sam. I'm gonna be a photographer. I'm gonna take photographs."

"He really is there, Abner. I'm not kiddin' this time. He's there, and he's reaching out to touch ya; he wants to touch ya—he's very . . . *sens*ual."

I felt something touch my left shoulder lightly, like a moth settling down.

CHAPTER EIGHT

When I got back to Art's apartment, Kennedy Whelan was there. He'd made himself some perked coffee and was putting sugar in it when I came in.

"For Christ's sake!" I muttered, shrugged out of my coat, hung it in the closet. "This is private property, Mr. Whelan."

"No," he said, and seated himself at the dining room table, withdrew an ugly cigar from an inner pocket of his suit jacket, stuck it in his mouth and began chewing on it. "This is a crime scene, Mr. Cray." He stopped, give me a once-over. "You look like shit, Mr. Cray. You look like you've been sleeping in an alley." He grinned. I went over to the cupboard, got a coffee cup, poured some coffee for myself, went to the table with it and sat down across from Whelan. He sniffed conspicuously. "You stink, too," he said.

I sipped the coffee. "What do you want, Mr. Whelan? I'm very tired."

He rolled the ugly cigar from one corner of his mouth to the other; he was clearly trying to strike a pose, trying to intimidate me. It was working. "I want to ask you about Art DeGraff."

"Uh-huh."

"I want to ask you where he is."

"I don't know where he is, Mr. Whelan. You know as much as I do about that, probably more."

"I don't believe you, Mr. Cray." He leaned forward, took the cigar from his mouth, jabbed the air with it as he spoke. "I think you're hiding something from me. I think you know where your perverse little friend is, and I think you're protecting him."

"You're wrong," I said simply, and sat back in the chair.

He sat back, put the cigar in his mouth again, grinned. "And what about this black chick you've been seeing?"

This came as a surprise to me. I shook my head. "That's none of your concern, Mr. Whelan."

He said nothing for a moment. He let a grin slowly come and go; then he said, "You're right; it isn't." He stood abruptly, reached down, took another sip of coffee, went to the sink, poured the remainder of the coffee down the drain, looked back at me. "You know, of course, that I could have you thrown out of here if I wanted. Your friend's case is still open.''

"Is it?'' I said, trying for a tone of impatience and weariness.

"But I'll let you stay. You're good bait. He'll come back here, eventually, because you're here. Then I've got him.'' He went to the front door, looked back, grinned again—the cigar, well-chewed now, still in his mouth—and left the apartment.

Jocelyn Horn called minutes later.

"Abner, this is Jocelyn. Abner, I'm coming to New York. I'm coming to find Stacy. I'll be arriving on the 10th.''

"That's good, Aunt Jocelyn. Enjoy your stay.''

"I want you to meet me at Grand Central, Abner. I think it's the least you can do.''

"The least I can do?''

"Of course, for . . . for doing what you've been doing all these years.''

"That's all over with, Aunt Jocelyn.''

"Well, of course it is; I should hope that it is anyway. But you owe something to Stacy, too, don't you think, and if she's in trouble, as I'm certain she is—''

"She can probably take care of herself, Aunt Jocelyn.''

"*No one* can take care of themselves these days, Abner. I'm sure *you* can't. So, as I said, I'll be arriving on the 10th, at 6:15 P.M., and I'd like you to pick me up at Grand Central.''

"I can't.''

"You can, Abner. And you will. The 10th, 6:15 P.M. Remember!" And she hung up.

The heat started acting up then. The radiators got awfully hot, so the air got hot and dry. I tried to shut the radiators off, succeeded with one, but burned my hand doing it, so I whispered, "The hell with it," and took off my jeans and my shirt—which did indeed stink, as Whelan had said—and got into bed, on top of the sheets, with the lights out and the curtains open. I saw that a snowstorm had begun, and I thought it was a nifty counterpoint to the hissing radiators and the dry heat. I watched it for a long time, for several hours anyway.

And I told myself as I watched it, *This is Manhattan in winter. The snow falls; the radiators overheat; people spend time alone in their apartments; they wait for lovers and friends; they go out. And they stay in. And they die. On a night like this, people die. They curl up under bridges, or on steam pipes, or in flea-bag hotels, and they die.*

I got out of bed at 2:00, put warm clothes on—several T-shirts, a flannel shirt, a sweater, blue jeans over a pair of Art's thermal underwear bottoms, and my denim jacket, which was all I had to serve as a coat—and I left the apartment.

Once, out of love—or what masqueraded quite well for it—I walked fifteen miles in a blizzard. It wasn't a big granddaddy of a blizzard, but it was big enough that I nearly lost three toes to frostbite and almost got run over by a snowplow because of it.

I was sixteen, I think, and had been smitten by a girl named Astelle. She was a year younger than I, had blossomed early and could have passed for eighteen. In my clumsy, adolescent way, I flirted with her for a month or so, and at last she invited me to her house. "It's in Granger. You know where that is?" she asked.

I said yes.

"Good. You come up there sometime. Meet my people."

"Your mom and dad?" I asked.

"Uh-huh. And everyone else. Come up any time, Abner."

So, when that blizzard struck, I thought it was as good a time as any, because she'd doubtless be stuck there, in Granger, with her people.

I tried to call her, found that her family didn't have a phone, put on all the warm clothes I could—and still be able to walk—and set out on Route 45, north out of the Bangor to Granger. I was going to meet Astelle, and "her people." I thought that was awfully romantic. And I thought that nearly freezing to death doing it would be romantic, too, and would impress Astelle.

It did. It impressed the hell out of her. And if I could have gotten her alone, away from "her people," I'm quite certain she would have let me know just *how* impressed she really was. But I was suffering from frostbite when I got there, and I was exhausted besides, and "her people"—all twenty of them, various aunts and uncles and cousins and a grandfather or two, all living in three big, gray farmhouses on two acres of land (because, as someone said then, "There's security in numbers, Abner.")—-were friendly and concerned and happy, and some of the strangest people I have ever met. They were also quite aware of just why I'd come to Granger. "She's a little too young yet, Abner," one of the women whispered to me—one of Astelle's aunts, I think.

"Too young for what?" I said.

"For screwing," she answered simply.

"Oh," I said, "yes. I know she is."

But, even to this day, I think of that weekend and that visit and that blizzard as the very soul of romanticism, and I think that I would do it all over again.

Which is what I was doing, of course, that night twenty years later, when the snowstorm struck New York. I was going to meet Phyllis' people.

I didn't believe that I'd have any trouble finding them.

CHAPTER NINE

From the second floor window of the house across the street, the child I had first seen there a week earlier was watching me. The woman was watching, too. They nodded cordially, in unison, as I came out of Art's house, and I nodded back, from the top of the front porch steps.

It was dark, of course, and a sharp, stiff wind was pushing the snowfall frantically about. But I felt warmth from that window. From the light there—a kind of dull orange-yellow light—and from the child, herself. And from the woman. And I remembered: *They are all there, in those houses, on those streets* . . ., and so I said to myself that if I was in search of Phyllis' people, that was as likely a place to start as any. In that house.

So I crossed to it, went up the steps—I tripped on

them; they were slippery from ice and snow—went through the front doors to the foyer, tried the second set of doors, found them locked.

I checked the directory. There were four names listed for the second floor. There was a Braniff, which didn't seem to fit that woman and child, a Kindheit, which surely didn't fit, a Thomas Ross, an M.S. Arnoni, which I decided was a possibility, and someone named Anja Schone—Finnish, I guessed, and promising. I pressed the button next to "M.S. Arnoni" and the speaker squawked back almost at once.

"Yes?" It was a woman's voice.

I grinned, bent over, said hello into the speaker.

"Hello," she said. "What do you want?"

"I'm the man from across the street."

"Is that of some importance to me?" she said.

"I don't know. I think it could be. I saw—" I stopped. What was I going to say?—*I saw you in your window*. What if this was not that woman?

"You saw what?" she said.

"I saw your name here. On the directory." I was beginning to feel uncomfortable, cold, stupid. It was, after all, past 2:00 A.M. and the chances were excellent that I'd gotten this woman out of bed.

"And?" she coaxed.

I said, "Are you M.S. Arnoni?"

"No. M.S. Arnoni is *dead*." She emphasized the word. "I'm his sister."

"Oh. I'm sorry."

"Did you know him?"

"Yes. A little. Not very well."

"Then why did you ask if I was him?"

"Sorry?"

"If you knew him, you'd know well enough that *I* was not *him*, wouldn't you?"

"I guess that's true."

"So you're lying?"

I hesitated, then answered sheepishly, "Yes, I am. I'm sorry. I was looking for someone else. I'm sorry."

"You apologize too much. Would you like to come up?"

"I don't think so. Thank you. I'm tired—"

"You can come up. We'll talk. We'll get to know each other. One doesn't often get strangers calling at two in the morning. You have a nice voice."

"Thank you. So do you."

"I've cultivated it. I used to be an actress."

"Did you?"

"Some time ago, of course. Hold on."

A moment later, the door buzzed. I stared at it a second, reached for it; the buzzing stopped. I pressed the button for M.S. Arnoni again.

"Yes?" she said.

I leaned over and said very apologetically into the speaker, "I'm sorry; I didn't get to the door in time."

"You're the man from across the street?"

"Yes."

"Hold on."

The door buzzed again, very briefly. I grabbed for it. Too late. I pressed M.S. Arnoni's button.

"Yes?"

I leaned over, said into the speaker, "This is the man from across the street. I'm afraid I didn't get the door then, either. You didn't let it buzz long enough."

"Oh. Do you want to try again?"

"Yes. If you don't mind."

"Hold on."

It buzzed once more. I grabbed for it, got it, pulled. The buzzing stopped a fraction of a second before the door unlocked. "Jesus," I whispered, and rang for M.S. Arnoni again.

"Yes?" she said.

"I'm awfully sorry, but I missed it again."

"Who's this—The man from across the street?"

"Yes, it is."

"You're not very quick, are you?"

"No, I'm afraid not."

"I don't like slow men."

"I don't think it's a matter of being slow—"

"I like *quickness*—" the speaker broke up on the word, she'd said it so loud—"I like speed and strength. You'll have to go away now."

"Sorry?"

"Go away now!" I heard a click.

"Are you there?" I said into the speaker. Nothing. "Miss Arnoni, are you there?" Still nothing. "Is anybody there? Anybody at *all*?" Nothing.

I straightened, considered, pressed the button next to "Anja Schone," waited. Nothing. I pressed it again, waited. Still nothing. I turned to leave.

"Who is it?" I heard from the speaker. It was a

man's voice. I hesitated, my hand on the door's push-plate. I looked back. "Who *is* this?!" the man insisted.

I pushed the door open and went outside.

When I was at the sidewalk, I looked back. The woman and the child still were at their window. They nodded again. I nodded back. Then I hurried down the street, toward Fifth Avenue, my hands thrust into my pants pockets for warmth, and my legs moving me along in short, fast, careful steps so I wouldn't slip again.

When I got to Fifth Avenue, I realized, after a few moments, that the storm was much worse than it had appeared from Art's bedroom window, that it would probably go into the record books. I could hear an occasional car on the avenue, now and then I could see the diffused yellow glow of headlights. But my ears were beginning to ache from the blast of wind and snow on them, and my forehead was getting numb, and because I was wearing only sneakers, my feet were starting to feel like blocks of wood. I decided, reluctantly, that I had done something abominably stupid. Romantic, perhaps, but stupid, so I turned to go back to the apartment. And heard, "Mister?" very faintly, from a couple of feet to my right. I looked. I saw the dark outline of a child there, his features obscured by the blowing snow.

"Hello," I shouted, to be heard above the storm.

"Mister?" he said again, no louder.

I extended my hand, felt his hand—in a knit

mitten—take mine. "Who are you?" I shouted, and
through a quick break in the wind and blowing snow
I could see that he was dressed for the storm, in a
long, dark ski-jacket—I guessed that it was dark
blue—dark pants, and what appeared to be white
snowmobiler's boots. "Who are you?" I shouted
again.

"Ronnie," he shouted back. "I want you to take
me home."

"Whose home?"

"My home."

The storm began to wind down then.

"And where is that, Ronnie?"

The wind began to sputter, as if it were a car
running out of gas, and the snow got heavier and
wetter.

"Over there," Ronnie said, and nodded to his
right, south, down Fifth Avenue. "On 76th Street,
near Lexington, next to the Catholic Church, I want
you to take me home."

"Yes," I said at once. "Yes, I will."

"Thank you," he said. I could see him clearly
now, because the storm had all but died. He smiled
up at me; he was a round-faced boy with very large
eyes, a small nose, lots of tight, dark curls, and his
smile was big, engaging, and contagious. I smiled
back.

"Are you one of them, Ronnie?" I said.

"Sure," he said, and let go of my hand. "Sure
I'm one of them." And he ran off, south, down Fifth

Avenue, across 75th Street, and 74th Street, and that's where I lost sight of him.

I didn't call after him. I decided that it would doubtless do no good anyway. I stuck my hands into my pockets and I started walking south, down Fifth Avenue, toward 76th Street. I thought it was turning out to be a promising night. The snowfall was now fat and luxurious, even warming somehow, and the wind had calmed to a whisper. What few cars there were on the avenue had lots of room to maneuver, and so were quiet. The sidewalks were empty, too, the new snow untouched, white, and fresh-looking where the square bright fluorescence of an occasional storefront touched it. And there was a crisp, almost clean smell in the air that was tinged only slightly by the sharp smells of traffic. I decided that the quick storm had washed the air.

My feet still felt like blocks of wood, though, and it was not a feeling I liked, of course, but it made me less aware of how cold they were, and I thought that I could walk half a dozen street blocks like that.

Which was just about as far as they took me—to 76th Street and Lexington Avenue, to St. Jean Baptiste Church. The building next door to it was a gray-brick, flat-top, row house, art-deco in style, three stories tall. And there were footprints in the snow, leading up the steps, to the front door.

It was about 4:00 A.M., I guessed, and traffic was beginning to pick up slightly. Now and again a yellow cab cruised down Lexington Avenue toward midtown Manhattan, and I could hear the grumbling of a garbage truck a block away, the clattering of garbage cans, someone shouting a block or so in the opposite direction—the sounds of Manhattan very early in the morning.

In the art-deco row house, one light was on, in the third floor, in the center of the left-hand side of the building. I could see a lamp in that window, and the top of an upholstered chair. Nothing else.

I went up the steps of the row house, to the front doors, then inside. The doors beyond the foyer were standing open, and beyond them was darkness punctuated only by the dirty cream-colored shapes of couches and chairs set up in what obviously was the lobby. The building, I thought, was not unlike the building on East 95th Street, where I'd met the Pellaprats, or, for that matter, the whorehouse on East 80th. It was a place where I could find some of Phyllis's people and where, in a way, I could get closer to her.

And that made me happy.

One of the chairs in the lobby was facing away from me. It was big and overstuffed, and as I moved closer to it, I realized that someone was sitting in it. I could see a dark, bare forearm, a hand lying flat, fingers outstretched, and I could faintly hear a soft, rhythmic, wheezing noise.

It was that wheezing noise that scared me. In the early morning darkness, in the lobby of that art-deco row house, with Manhattan asleep around me, it was a very melodramatic noise, and it would have been comical, had it not been something I could *hear*.

Something, goddamnit, that was in the same *room* with me.

It changed.

It slowed.

It stopped.

I whispered to myself, "What am I doing here?" And heard, as if in response, from that overstuffed chair, "Tha's a good question, my man."

I ran. Back out to 76th Street, over to Park Avenue, west to Madison Avenue, to Fifth Avenue, through the early morning darkness—Manhattan at last waking around me—north to 79th Street, to Art's apartment house, up the stairs, so my lungs felt like they were filled with cement and my legs as if nails had been driven into every muscle.

And, at last, into Art's apartment. Which was still hot and dry.

And I slammed the door shut, locked it, put my back against it, and realized that, at last, I had nearly been scared to death.

At the Hammet Mausoleum, Halloween, 1965

"It's the not knowing, Abner, that I don't like. It makes me itchy uncomfortable. Joe Hammmmettt, Joe Hammmmettt. Speak to us, Joe. Give us a sign. Know what I'm talking about, Abner?"

"Sure I do. I'm not stupid."

"Just ignorant. We're all of us ignorant though. Even old Joe Hammet, I bet. You know, you get hold of a spook—I mean if we ever did—and once you finish peein' your pants and catchin' your breath,

what's the first thing you'd wanta know?—You'd
wanta know *How is it over there?* Or you'd wanta
know *What's it all mean?*''

''What's what all mean, Sam?''

''Everything. You know. Everything. And you figure since the spook's been through it all, he'd know,
right? But who's to say?—That's my question.
Nobody; that's who. I bet the spooks are just as
stupid and ignorant as the rest of us. Course it depends on where they've got off, right?''

''Right, Sam.''

''Shit, you don t know what I'm talking about.''

''I do, Sam.''

''Okay, tell me. What am I talking about?''

''You're talking about spirits, and where they go,
and . . . like that.''

He grimaced.

''I don't know. Sometimes you're fulla shit, Sam.
Sometimes you scare me, you're so fulla shit.''

He closed his eyes, put his hands on his knees,
thumbs up, fists closed.

''What're you doing, Sam?''

''Shhh. I'm meditating.''

''You think I'm stupid, don't you, Sam?''

''Shhh.''

''I think Joe Hammet touched my shoulder, ya
know. A little while ago.''

''Shhh, I'm sensing the vibrations.''

''You look awful, Sam. You look blue.''

''I'm holding my breath.''

''Why?''

"Because the dead don't breathe."

"Oh."

He opened his eyes suddenly. He grinned, tilted his head to one side, shrugged. "Maybe they do," he said, "and maybe they don't. If they can walk around, they can breathe, too. Habits, Abner—like I said."

"Yeah, like a—" I stopped.

"Like a what?"

"Nothing, Sam. I'm getting cold. Why don't we get outa here, okay?"

"You can go. I'm staying for a while. I like it here."

I sighed. "You know something, Sam? I bet that if old Joe Hammet came in that door—" I nodded sagely at the mausoleum's door—"you'd faint dead away."

He shrugged again. "Maybe. Like I said, it's the not-knowing that gets you scared. So maybe I would, and maybe I wouldn't. It depends on how friendly he was, I guess."

"Oh, yeah? You mean if he said, 'Boy, it's a nice day,' and gave you one of his big smiles, you'd get up and shake his hand?"

"I don't know. Maybe that'd scare me more than if he was carryin' his head between his legs and pukin' at the same time. I don't know. It depends, Abner. Everything depends."

*   *   *

I stood with my back to Art's door for a very long time. I didn't think for a moment that it would keep anyone out, but I thought the gesture was important.

I watched morning light slowly fill the apartment. I listened to Manhattan come fully awake. I thought that love was often enough, but that sometimes it isn't—sometimes it isn't enough by a long shot.

And I thought, too, that what I most wanted was to be able to work on the big photo book that I'd come to New York to do. I wanted to take ten thousand pictures; I wanted to feel the Nikon in my hands, wanted to push chemicals around in a darkroom, I wanted to make decisions about lighting and about angles, and moments out of time.

CHAPTER TEN

I called Serena Hitchcock at 9:15.

"Serena, it's Abner Cray. Can we get together soon? I'd like to talk about the book."

"Abner, there is no book, you know that; it's been cancelled."

"I want to do it anyway, Serena. On spec. Can I do it on spec? I *need* to do it."

"I'd prefer to talk about other projects, Abner. I have several in mind—"

"I'd really like to do the big book, Serena. The one I *came* here to do." I waited. She said nothing. "Serena, I thought you'd be pleased. Are you there, Serena?"

"I'm here."

"And?"

"And I wish I could help you, Abner—"

"I said 'on spec,' Serena. I'll do the book, and I'll show it to you, and if you don't like it, you can give it back."

"I know that *I'll* like it, Abner. But that's not the point—"

"I'll come down to your office. We'll talk. I *need* to do this."

"You sound . . . manic, Abner. No, don't come here. Please. You can come to my apartment, it's in the West Village—you're familiar with the West Village?"

"Sure I am."

"Okay. Come over after 7:00, closer to 7:30 really. I'm at 230 West 11th. You'll see my name on the directory."

"Thank you, Serena."

"Sure," she said, and hung up.

I went to breakfast at the small Greek restaurant near the apartment. I sat at the same table; I ordered scrambled eggs, fresh-squeezed orange juice, whole wheat toast, coffee.

The owner of the restaurant—a dark-haired, smooth-faced man in his early forties, wearing a soiled, white apron over a short-sleeved white shirt and black pants—said from behind the counter, "I thought you were not coming back," and glanced quickly about, apparently to see if there was anyone else within earshot. There wasn't. A very thin young man with receding blonde hair and a thick mustache was seated at a corner table reading *The Christian Science Monitor*;

a couple of nicely dressed women in their early thirties were talking animatedly in a booth on the other side of the restaurant.

The owner went on, at a high whisper, "I thought our little friends scared you away."

"Little friends?" I said.

"The cock-a-roaches," he said, his accent now plainly in evidence. "The bastard *cock*-a-roaches. I saw you squash one of them and I thought it scared you away. I'm glad for my restaurant that it didn't."

"Your food's good," I said. "And I don't care about cockroaches." I smiled. "It's hard to get away from them anyway, in New York."

He swiped at the counter with a dishcloth. "It's hard to get away from many things in New York," he said.

"Like the pollution," I said.

He swiped at the counter again, his smile stuck on his face. On the other side of the restaurant, the two nicely dressed women still were talking animatedly. In a far booth, the young man with receding blonde hair and thick mustache still was reading his *Christian Science Monitor*. "I'm glad you like my food," the owner said. "All the time I make good food."

"Yes," I said, "you do."

He swiped at the counter again. "Not like some of the others," he said. "Some of the others don't care no more. I care. I always care."

I speared some egg with my fork, pushed it around the plate. "Yes," I said again. The fork scraped shrilly against the plate, sending a shiver down my back. I put the egg into my mouth; the egg was cold.

"Fifty years I been makin' good food for my customers. Gets to be a habit, you know. You want more coffee?"

"No." I stood. "Thank you. No." I fished in my pocket for some change, put two quarters on the table, watched as a fat cockroach scooted up from the underside of the table, across the top, over the quarters, and disappeared around the other side. "No," I said again, and found that I was grinning oddly. "I think I'd better get—" the cockroach scooted across the table top again—"to work," I finished, and started for the door.

"Sure, go ahead," the owner said, that smile still stuck on his face. He swiped at the counter again. "Sure, go ahead," he repeated. In a corner booth, the two nicely dressed women still were talking animatedly. At a table, the young man with the blonde mustache still was reading his *Christian Science Monitor*. "Sure, go ahead," the owner said again.

I looked at the door. It was open; some people were walking hurriedly past, and a light snowfall had started that was already beginning to collect on the single cement step.

"Sure, go ahead," the owner said again. He swiped at the counter. "Go ahead. It's good for my restaurant that my little friends didn't scare you away." He glanced at the women in the corner booth. "More coffee, girls?"

Both of the women looked over. One was a redhead, her skin very pale, her lips thick with bright red lipstick. "No," she said. "No, thank you. We're going to leave soon." And she turned to the other woman, an incredibly well-endowed brunette in a tight, pink dress, who was holding a small, black purse on her lap. "We should leave soon," she said to the woman, and the woman said to her, holding her hand horizontally at her throat. "I'm full up to *here* with coffee. I'll *never* sleep."

"Sure," the owner said to them, "go ahead. Sure, go ahead." He looked at the young man reading the *Christian Science Monitor*. "Some for you, young man."

"None for me," the young man said.

"I'll *never* sleep!" said the incredibly well-endowed brunette in the tight dress. "I'm full up to *here*."

The young man pushed himself away from the table, dropped his newspaper, bent over, picked it up, went to the door, hesitated, went out, turned right, was gone.

The owner whispered, "He didn't pay me," then shouted, "Hey, you come back here!" and ran around from behind the counter, dishcloth still in hand. He stopped, grinned, looked at me, said, "He'll be back. He's one of my regulars."

"Yes," I said. I was making my way slowly to the door. "One of your regulars," I said.

"And you?" he said.

"No," I said.

"It's good for my restaurant that my little friends

didn't frighten you away." He went back around the counter, swiped at it with the dishcloth.

"No," I said. I was at the door now. I went through it, turned right on Lexington Avenue. "No," I said to myself, when I was half a block from the restaurant. I shook my head violently. "Not me," I said.

And a middle-aged man in a rumpled, brown suit who'd been walking parallel to me said, "Got a lot on your mind, huh, bub?" and chuckled, hurried on, said loudly, when he was a yard or so in front of me, "New York's just chuck full of 'em," and chuckled again.

"Not me," I said again. "Not me, mister!" I shouted.

At times it is imperative that we grab hold of something that seems real, something that has mass and weight, something that can cut, something mechanical, soulless, gauche, temporary.

We need such things when we feel certain that we are going to be caught up, suddenly—or already are caught up—in something exquisite, and eternal. Like death, or love. Or both.

And we need such things because they can help affirm for us that we are, ourselves, soulless, gauche, and temporary. Sure it's a lie, I know that it's a lie, but it's how most of us make it from one day to the next.

*   *   *

I went to a small shop called Gifts for Giving, on Madison Avenue, near East 79th. I had been in the shop once before, very briefly, several years earlier, in search of a birthday present for Stacy and I'd found that it dealt in goods that could only be called exquisitely tacky. There were lava lamps—in pastel green and gold—and picture clocks, "Starving Artists" oil paintings, toilet-paper holders with built-in AM radios, battery powered mittens, and even a miniature wooden outhouse whose door opened to reveal a tiny, pantless ceramic man in the midst of urinating.

I went to this shop after breakfast and I happily prowled the all-but-empty aisles unbothered for several hours, until a fat, balding, thirtyish man wearing rimless glasses, a pink shirt, and shiny gray pants come over, said he was in charge, and asked if I could "please loiter elsewhere."

"I'm still deciding," I told him.

"On what?" he said, clearly incredulous.

"On what I'd like to buy, of course. I'm trying to find a birthday gift. For a friend."

"You've been in here for quite a while, mister, and if you haven't found anything yet, I'd say you probably never will."

I shook my head. "No, you're wrong. There's so much . . . *stuff*." I grinned. Nearby, some aprons were on display. I picked one up, looked it over. It was a full length white apron, and imprinted on it, in big, black letters, were these words:

**GOT MORE TIME FOR MISBEHAVIN'
SINCE I STARTED MICROWAVIN'!**

"This is nice," I said. "I think she'd like it."

"Your wife?" he said, sounding suddenly less incredulous. "Is this something for your wife, sir?"

"No. A friend. As I said." I laid the apron down on a display table behind me. "I'll let you know," I said.

He glanced about, picked up a needlepoint picture on another display table, held it up to me. "Perhaps she'd like this, sir. It's a fine sentiment, I'd say."

The picture had these words on it:

**TIME ENDEARS
BUT CANNOT FADE
THE MEMORIES
THAT LOVE HAS MADE.**

I took it from him, studied it a moment, said, "Yes, it is a fine sentiment," and set it next to the apron.

"Can I show you something else, sir?" asked the balding man.

"No, thank you," I answered, "I'd like to browse some more, if you don't mind."

"Take your time, sir."

"Yes. I will."

"It's the only thing any of us have, isn't it, sir?"

"Sorry?"

"Time. All we've got is time." He smiled a wide, flat smile. "All we've *got* is time, sir." His eyebrows shot up, as if he were doing a Groucho Marx imitation. He said it again, "All we've *got* is time, sir." His smile was stuck. His eyebrows stayed up. His head looked like a cueball with a happy face painted on it.

"I'd better go," I said.

"Where to, sir?"

"I don't know. Somewhere else."

"There is nowhere else, sir."

"Sure there is." I started for the door, felt his hand on my arm, looked back. He was still smiling. His eyebrows still were up. He said, "The apron, sir? Do you want the apron?"

"No," I told him.

"Or the picture? It's a fine sentiment."

"No. I'd just like to leave."

"Certainly, sir." He let go of my arm, gestured with his hand, quickly, toward the door. "Go ahead. Leave. Please. We want you to leave."

"I'm sorry," I said.

"So are we," he said.

And I left.

I went, my head down and my hands thrust into my pockets, to a porno movie house off Broadway, on 49th Street. Something called *Vixens In Cellophane* was playing, and I seated myself in the last row, which was empty, in the corner, and I wept.

At the Hammet Mausoleum, Halloween, 1965

"Sam, I'm hungry," I said.

"Ain't nothin' to eat here," he said, and grinned, "unless, of course—" He inclined his head slightly toward Joe Hammet's vault.

"Jesus H. Christ, Sam, that's disgusting!"

He laughed quickly.

I stood. "That's disgusting," I said again. "And I'm sicka sittin' here watchin' you turn blue from not breathing and gettin' cold and havin' my rear end go to sleep."

"I can't help what your rear end does, Abner." He nodded at the spot where I'd been sitting. "But if you're my friend—"

"Course I'm your friend."

"Then you'll sit down." He sounded distinctly and suddenly sullen. "I like it here, Abner."

I thought a moment. I sat down again. I said, quietly, "For real, Sam?"

"For real, Abner. I like it here. I don't know why, but I do."

And I felt, at once, more affection for him than I ever had before.

BOOK THREE

Heaven can wait
And all I got is time until the end of time.
                    —Meatloaf

CHAPTER ONE

It was close to 6:30 when I left the theatre. I did not go back to Art's apartment, though I needed a shower and shave and a change of clothes. I went straight to Serena Hitchcock's apartment. I thought of her and the book and the cancelled contracts as gritty, almost venal links with reality. And I thought of Art's apartment as a link to something else altogether.

Her building was one of a series of three-story, red brick row houses on West 11th Street. It was streaked brown from air pollution and steep, snow-covered concrete steps led to a set of heavy, black-painted wooden doors which opened onto a brightly lighted foyer. I found her name on the building's directory— she was on the third floor—rang her once, then again, and again. She answered on the fourth ring.

"Hi, Serena," I said. "It's me. Abner. You decent?"

"You're early," she said. "You'll have to wait a few minutes, okay?"

"Okay."

She clicked off. I waited with my hand on the doorknob. After several minutes, I rang her again.

"Yes?" she said, clearly annoyed.

"Hi, Serena—"

"I'm not dressed, Abner."

"Oh. Sorry."

She clicked off. I put my hand on the doorknob again. I saw a man and woman, dressed well, as if for an evening at the theatre, come out of a first floor apartment and walk quickly toward the door, the man with his arm around the woman's waist. They saw me, and he grimaced slightly; I smiled at him, let go of the knob. From behind the closed door he said, "You're not coming in."

I pointed toward the ceiling. "I'm waiting for someone," I said.

"Then you'll have to continue waiting," he said. "Back away from the door, please."

I backed away from the door; he opened it, and they walked through. He closed it firmly, and they moved quickly past me, eyes averted, through the first set of doors.

I rang Serena again.

"How's it going, Serena?"

"You can come up now, Abner," she answered, and the door buzzed. I grabbed it, pulled it open, went inside, and climbed the three sets of noisy, wooden stairs—which tilted noticeably to the left, so climbing them was something of an adventure—to her apartment, at the rear of the building. I knocked, she answered at once, and showed me in.

Her apartment was small: a living room, kitchenette, and bedroom, I guessed, the walls a soft cream color, the floors well-polished oak, and the living room furnishings, two chairs, a couch, a loveseat, all of the same type—heavy beige fabric on chrome frames. There were two large chrome-framed prints hanging, one of lilacs with the name Galen in blue beneath, over the loveseat. The loveseat was near a south-facing window that looked out on a spacious, well-lighted garden behind the row house. The other print, near the chrome and glass dining room table, was a colorful, stylized painting of various vegetables—corn, cucumbers, several tomatoes—and the words EXHIBTION, 1964 beneath it in black.

"Very nice," I said, and nodded to indicate the apartment.

"Sure," Serena said. We were standing just inside her front door. She was dressed in black designer jeans, a white, long-sleeved blouse, and she made no attempt to hide the fact that I was imposing on her. She nodded at the dining room table. "Do you mind if I finish eating, Abner?"

"Of course not."

"Fine."

We went to the table; she sat, and immediately started in on what looked like linguini with red clam sauce and a glass of wine. She nodded at the other end of the table, said, "Sit down, Abner," put some of the linguini into her mouth, and chewed it very slowly and delicately. It was clear that she was enjoying it.

I sat at the other end of the table.

"Now, what is it you want to talk about, Abner?" she said, and dabbed at the edges of her lips with a pale violet napkin. "The book?" she went on, and put the napkin on her lap.

"Yes," I said. "The book." I nodded at the linguini. "That looks good, Serena. Your own recipe?"

"Sure," she said. She gave me a quick once-over and pursed her lips, as if in annoyance. "You look terrible, Abner."

I looked down at myself, grinned. "Yes," I said, "I do, don't I? I haven't been home. I spent the day in a theater."

"Oh?" She sipped the wine, and a look of great pleasure spread over her face. She held the glass up. "You want some of this, Abner?"

I shook my head. "No. Thanks." I patted my belly. "Not on an empty stomach."

"Sure," she said, put some more linguini in her mouth, and went on as she chewed, "You want to do the book on spec, Abner, go ahead. I can't promise you anything though." Some of the red clam sauce dribbled down the right side of her chin. She dabbed it away with the violet napkin.

"Yes," I said, "I know that. But this book is

something that I really *need* to do. It's why I came to New York in the first place."

"Uh-huh."

"You don't sound terribly enthusiastic, Serena."

"I'm not." She sipped the wine, set the glass down, pushed her plate away. "I wish I were, but I'm not." She stood, said nothing for a moment, looked confusedly at her plate, then up at me. "I'm sorry, Abner; did you want some of this stuff? It's not very good, but if you're hungry, I'll get you a plate."

I said something about not wanting to put her to any trouble.

"It's no trouble, Abner," she said, and went quickly into her kitchenette, got a plate from the cupboard, went to the stove with it, ladled some linguini onto the plate. She said, over her shoulder, "You have to forgive me, Abner. I've been . . . somebody else, I guess. Since my brother's murder." She turned from the stove, came to the table with the plate of linguini and red clam sauce, set it in front of me. I stared at the plate a moment, looked apologetically up at her. "If you could tell me where the silverware is, Serena . . ."

"Oh, sorry." She turned quickly, went back to the kitchenette, got some silverware, came back to the table. "I really loved him, Abner. I didn't know just how much." She put the silverware down next to the plate. "I guess that's an old story, isn't it?" she went on. "You don't really know how much someone means to you until he's gone." She smiled sadly, hesitated, then went back to her seat at the table.

"You know what I'm talking about, don't you, Abner? You've lost people, haven't you?"

"Yes," I said.

"Who?"

"My parents," I answered. I scooped up some of the linguini; it was quite good.

"They died together?" Serena asked, and I noticed that her tone had changed, had become lighter.

"No," I answered.

"Separately, then?" she said.

"Yes." I nodded at the linguini. "This is very good, Serena."

"They died . . . close to one another?" she asked. "In time, Abner? Within a couple of weeks of each other? That's nice. It happens that way quite a lot, you know."

"No," I answered. "My mother killed herself. My father died several years later." A short pause. "Can we talk about the book, Serena?"

"I'm bothering you, aren't I?" She shook her head slowly. "I'm sorry. Just trying to . . . make some sense of it all, I think."

"Yes," I said, and then, because I could see her pain clearly in her eyes and around her mouth and because I thought she was reaching out to me with it, I hurried on, "I've met some people, Serena."

"People?" She held the bottle of wine up again. "Are you sure you don't want any of this, Abner?"

"No. Thank you."

She set the bottle down. "What kind of people, Abner?" A stiff, flat grin appeared on her mouth.

"I've met a woman," I explained. I ate some more linguini, complimented her again on it, continued, "And she's . . . taught me quite a lot, Serena."

"Does this woman have a name?"

"Yes. Her name's Phyllis."

"Phyllis? I don't think I've ever known anyone named Phyllis." She picked up her fork, popped some linguini into her mouth, set the fork down, dabbed at her lips with the violet napkin. She looked very civilized; I liked that. She continued, "You must love this Phyllis very much." She sipped her wine, set the glass down, picked up her fork again. She nodded to indicate my clothes. "Assuming, I mean, that she's somehow the reason you've been letting yourself go like this."

"In a way, I guess she is," I said.

"What's she like?"

"You mean Phyllis?"

She put another forkful of linguini into her mouth, chewed it slowly, swallowed. "Yes, I mean Phyllis. Tell me about her."

"Phyllis is dead."

The phone rang. Serena stood, dabbed at her mouth again, said, "Excuse me, please," and went to answer it. She said good-bye to whoever had called a minute later, went to the kitchenette, and brought back a small salad and some bread in a wicker basket. She sat, held the basket up, "It's sourdough, Abner. Would you like some?"

"No. Thanks," I said. The linguini was filling me up quickly. "You go ahead."

"Thank you, I will," she said, and spread some butter on a piece of the sourdough. The butter was soft, the bread warm, apparently, because the butter formed little yellow pools on it. Serena took a small bite; some of the butter clung to her lip. "And that's why you look the way you do?" she asked. "Because Phyllis died?" She looked properly concerned.

"No," I said.

She dabbed at the butter on her lip with the violet napkin. "I don't understand, Abner." She ate some more linguini, gathered some salad up on her fork. "Phyllis' death didn't upset you? I would say that that's very unusual, wouldn't you? Assuming, of course, that you were in love with her. Didn't you tell me you were in love with her?"

"I was in love with her, yes. I still am in love with her, Serena."

She put the forkful of salad into her mouth. A small piece of lettuce fell to her lap; she picked it up, set it next to her plate. "Then that's the problem, I'd say. You're in love with . . . you *profess* to be in love with a dead woman. *That's* the problem. When did she die?"

"In December."

She brought the glass of wine to her lips, hesitated. A look of confusion passed swiftly across her face. She sipped the wine, set the glass down. "In December? Was this a woman you knew in Maine?"

"No."

"Where then?" She dabbed at her lips with the napkin, again.

"Here," I answered. "In Manhattan."

"Oh?" She picked up her dinner fork, set it down, picked it up again. "Oh," she repeated. "Someone you had known for some time, then?" This seemed to please her. She scooped up another forkful of linguini, put it into her mouth, and chewed slowly, as if savoring it. "Someone you met before?"

"No, Serena."

She stopped chewing for a moment, started again, swallowed. "I'm sorry, Abner. You're confusing me."

I looked away, out the window that overlooked the large garden behind the row house. The garden was brightly lit and I could see that there were people walking in it, despite the snow—a woman pushing a baby carriage and a man, several yards behind her, dressed in a red turtle-neck sweater and blue jeans, who was walking with his hands in his pockets and his head down. I said to Serena, "I want to tell you something. About Phyllis." I looked away from the window, into Serena's eyes. She looked back expectantly.

"Yes," she said, "go ahead."

A big, quivering grin broke out on my face. I was nervous. I grin when I'm nervous.

Serena repeated, "Go ahead, Abner. I'm listening." She had a forkful of linguini poised halfway to her mouth.

I looked out the window again, at the brightly lit garden. I saw that the woman pushing the baby carriage had stopped and was leaning over it, as if tending to her baby, and that the man in the turtleneck was closing on her. I said, "She's a part of something, Serena, that's . . . much bigger . . ." And I grinned again.

"You mean Phyllis?"

"Yes." I looked away once more, toward the garden. The man in the turtleneck was very close to the woman leaning over the baby carriage. He still had his hands in his pockets, his head lowered, and the woman looked up at him as I watched. I believe that she smiled. I looked at Serena. "Yes," I repeated, grinned once more, forced it down. "We lived together for three weeks."

Serena thought a moment, then said, "You're confusing me, Abner. Please, don't confuse me. You said Phyllis died in December. Isn't that correct?"

"Yes."

"And you said that you met her here. In Manhattan. Isn't *that* correct?"

"Yes."

She picked up her fork, set it down. "You're making me nervous, Abner. You're making me very nervous."

"I can see that," I said. "I'm sorry. I don't want to make you nervous, I want to give you . . . hope." I smiled.

She reached for a slice of sourdough, stopped—her hand halfway there—brought it back, picked the fork up again. "I sweat when I'm nervous, Abner. I don't like to sweat."

I said again, "I'm sorry."

"You're telling me that you lived with a dead

woman for three weeks." And now a small, quivering grin appeared on her lips.

I looked out, at the garden, again. The man in the red turtleneck had passed the woman pushing the baby carriage, who was still leaning over it. I looked back at Serena. I said to her again, "I want to give you *hope*, Serena."

"Dead is *dead!*" she cut in, and speared a piece of sourdough with her fork. She repeated, though without emphasis this time, and with a little whimsical smile playing on her lips, "Dead, Abner, is dead." She began munching on the sourdough. She nodded at the breadbasket. "Eat. You need to eat, Abner. I want you to eat."

"Serena, I'm sorry if I've upset you." I glanced at the garden again. The woman there still was leaning over the baby carriage. I looked back. "But I'm scared, Serena—" I looked at the woman in the garden. She had lifted one foot. I looked back. Serena had speared another slice of sourdough. She was buttering it. Her hand was quivering. *"You're* scared?" she said, and grinned. *"You're* scared?"

"I'm scared," I acknowledged. I looked at the woman in the garden. She was bent over violently at the waist, her right leg at right angles to her left, which was straight. I looked back. Serena was still buttering her slice of sourdough; it was beginning to shred.

"Abner," she said, her eyes on the sourdough, "I'm not going to try and humor you. I'm not going to play any silly games with you. I am going to tell

you again that you are making me very nervous, and
I don't like to be nervous. I sweat when I'm nervous.
I'm sweating now. And you're making me nervous—"
her butter knife went through the bread, spreading
some of the butter onto her fingers; she didn't seem to
notice—"because I honestly feel that you need help
of some kind. Maybe because of the setback with the
book, I don't know. If so, then I'm partially re-
sponsible, and so that makes you—to some small
degree—*my* responsibility. So I'll tell you what I'm
going to do. I'm going to eat this bread, and then I'm
going to phone someone I know who will talk with
you—"

"You think I'm nuts, Serena?"

She looked up suddenly, surprised. "Of course I
think you're nuts." Another grin, short-lived.

"Will you at least listen to me?" I said.

"No. I'm sorry." She took a little bite of the
sourdough and chewed it delicately.

In the garden behind the house, the woman leaning
over the baby carriage had stuck her head further into
it, so her right leg was high in the air. I said to
Serena, "I wish I was."

"Was what?"

"Nuts."

"You *are* nuts, Abner." She took another small
bite of the sourdough, and again chewed it delicately.
"And I wish, I really wish that I could afford to sit
and talk with you about it, but I can't. Please
understand—the luxury of being nuts comes with
certain—" she thought a moment—"certain *miseries*.

And one of those miseries is having to accept the fact that . . . acquaintances—and that's all I am; I am *not* your friend—are not going to listen to you."

I stood. I looked at the garden again. I saw the baby carriage. I did not see the woman.

Serena said, "So if you are not going to have any more food with me, I'd like you to leave." Another grin. "And quickly, please."

I looked at her. *"Hope*, Serena," I said. "There *is* hope, believe me."

She shook her head. "No. There isn't. Now, please, will you leave? For a while you were very entertaining. But no more."

"Yes," I said. "I'm sorry." I pushed my chair back, stood, nodded at the linguini. "Thank you, Serena. It was good."

"No problem," she said.

"And I didn't mean to disturb you."

She said nothing.

I went to the door, looked back. She was not looking around at me. She was sitting with her face buried in her hands. I believe that she was weeping softly. .

I left the apartment and went down to the street, then back, into the garden.

CHAPTER TWO

To the baby carriage there, which was big and black, with lots of chrome.

And empty, too. Except for the face of that woman—a nice face, with large hazel eyes and full red lips:

Which moved and pleaded with me, "My baby, where is my baby?"

It was a long way back to Art's apartment. More than sixty blocks. I ran it. I jogged it. And when I got there, I sank into Art's black leather couch and I watched a cable channel that was showing something filthy. I immersed myself in it. Completely. As I never before had. I got a hard-on; I found myself smiling. It was a retreat, a haven—it was *life*, for God's sake. Tacky as it was, it was *life*.

And I did not know how long Phyllis had been sitting on the couch with me. When I noticed her, at last, I screeched out of fear and surprise, and she turned her face toward me. She was grinning.

She said, her voice lower than I remembered, and harsher, "I told you that you wouldn't like it out there, Abner."

Her face was flatter somehow, her skin tighter; and her smell had changed, too. It had softened, become more subtle, and distant.

She was wearing what she always wore; her fake, white mink coat, her green dress, her white, stacked-heel boots. I said, "I miss you, Phyllis."

She continued grinning. It was hard and humorless. "You have me now," she said.

"Yes," I said, and I took her hand. She stiffened, as if in pain. She said, "No, Abner." And she still was grinning. "No, Abner." And I heard the same kind of quivering anger and grief in her voice that I had heard in the whorehouse East 80th Street. "I am coming apart, Abner."

"I miss you, Phyllis," I told her again.

"I am coming apart," she said. "We come apart. We all come apart." Her grin changed slightly. "The way dolls do."

I shook my head.

"It happens, Abner. It has to happen."

I shook my head more violently. I said nothing.

"We leave, Abner. We go away."

I lowered my head; it frightened me to look at her.

"We leave," she said again. "We go away."

I looked at her. I saw that she was the woman I had stopped outside the house on East 80th Street.

And she said now, as she had said then, "I ain't no one else, honey. I ain't never been no one else."

And I grabbed her, pulled her to me, wept, babbled into her shoulder. I was desperate to keep her; I would have held her for days on end to keep her.

God, I loved her.

I love her even now.

Her body felt like a sack of loose sand. And I held it, weeping, until she slid away from me.

She scared me. Good Christ, she scared me!

But not enough. She slid away from me; her fingers traced lightly down my shirt, my thigh, my calf. I grabbed for her; I grabbed hard.

And got her hand clean off at the wrist.

And watched her slide away, through the floor, like water soaking in.

At the Hammet Mausoleum, Halloween, 1965

"Why do you like it here, Sam?" I asked.

"It's quiet," he answered.

"Yeah, well, *libraries* are quiet, and I know you don't like libraries."

"And it's . . . a place to be."

"A place to be, Sam?"

"Yeah. Forever. You gotta end up being someplace, right?"

"Maybe."

He reached out and fingered Flora's skull. "Like

Flora here. She'll be buried with me, I guarantee it, Abner.''

"That's nice, Sam."

"It ain't nice, Abner. It's the way that things have gotta be. You try and spend forever with something you love. God, Abner, you make bein' dead sound like a Tupperware party or something. Nice, shit! Nothin' is *nice*.''

"You're damn spooky, Sam."

"Sure I am." He pushed himself to his feet suddenly, swiped at the back of his pants, smiled down at me. "You wanta pick those things up, Abner—" he nodded at the candles, which had burned to half of what they were when we got there, and at Flora's skull—"I think we'd better get outa here, okay?"

"Sure enough, Sam." I was happy. "Whatever you—"

"But first," he cut in, "I gotta have just one little look at Joe Hammet. I gotta *touch* him, Abner. I gotta see how real he is. I gotta see how *real* he is anymore.''

CHAPTER THREE

It was an afternoon early in February, the day after I'd gone to Serena's apartment and also the day after Phyllis had come to Art's apartment, that Stacy showed up there. I'd been sleeping fitfully when I heard her knock. I think I knew it was her at once, and when I answered the door, after throwing on one of Art's robes, which was much too short, I realized that I did not want to see her, that I thought of her as an intruder.

She looked awful.

"Jesus, Stacy—"

"Can I come in, Abner?"

I stepped out of the way, held my hand out toward the living room. "Sure. Of course," I said. "Come in."

She came in. She was wearing what must have, at

one time, been a very stylish, blue raincoat, a pair of white jeans, and a ruffled, white cotton blouse that— also at one time—must have fit her quite fetchingly, but hung limply on her now, because she was very wet, as if she'd been standing a long time in a rainstorm. And there were streaks of brownish grit on the coat and the jeans, even down the side of her face.

"Give me your coat, Stacy."

She gave it to me. "I'd like to use the shower, if that's all right."

"Of course it's all right." I nodded to my left. "The bathroom's over there, just past the bedroom."

"Thanks, Abner." She sounded hoarse. "I know where it is."

"Oh," I said. "Yes." And she went quickly down the short hallway to the bathroom.

I made some coffee for both of us, dressed, and waited for her. She took a full half-hour in the bathroom and needed every minute of it. But when she reappeared, she didn't look at all refreshed, only cleaner. She had one Art's shirts on over her underwear.

She sat, legs crossed loosely, her cup of coffee in hand, in a black leather chair opposite the couch. "Could you do me a favor," she began, "and get my clothes cleaned somewhere? The coat has to be dry-cleaned; the other stuff you can take to a laundromat. You don't mind, do you?"

I shook my head. "No, I don't mind." It was a lie. "What have you been doing, Stacy?"

"Searching for Art." She looked pained. She sipped her coffee, set the cup on the floor, and announced, "I found him."

"You *found* him?" I said. "He told me he was in Nice, Stacy. Where'd you find him, for Christ's sake?"

She relaxed; her head was resting on the back of the chair, and she sighed, then explained, her gaze on the ceiling, "On East 100th Street. He's got an apartment there—he calls it an apartment." She brought her head forward; she looked suddenly angry. "It's a goddamned pigsty. He's cleaned it up, of course. He wanted to paint, but they wouldn't let him—Jesus Christ, Abner, he's a goddamned *mess!* You know what he's doing? You want to know what he's doing? He's *hiding out*. Jesus, hiding out! I asked him what good he was doing himself, living there like that, and you want to know what he told me? He told me that he's *free*. Free, for Christ's sake. Free! I asked him—free to do *what?* He said 'free to scratch.' That's what he said exactly. 'I'm free to scratch, if I want.' " She picked her coffee up, sipped it, grinned. "Which is when I told him he was full of shit!" Another sip of coffee. Her grin reappeared, but there was pain in it now. "Which is when he hit me." She touched the left side of her chest, just below her breast. "Here." She touched the back of her head. "And here. With his fists. He likes to hit people with his fists. Not just women. People in general. When we were married, he hit this supermarket check-out boy who was looking at me, just looking at me. People look at other people, right? Where's the harm? He broke the boy's cheekbone. That's awfully hard to do, I'm told.''

"I stood, went over to her, put my hand on her shoulder. "Do you want to see a doctor, Stacy?''

She shook her head. "No. Not here anyway. I'll see my doctor in Bangor. I'm okay.''

"You're going back to Bangor?''

"Yes, tomorrow, I think. Maybe tonight. It depends on what kind of arrangements I can make.''

"You're sure you're okay?''

She nodded, sipped her coffee again. "Yes. I run fast. He can't run.''

"I know.''

"So I ran from him. This is a *dirty* city, Abner. This is an awfully *dirty* city.''

"Here and there,'' I said.

"They'll catch up with him though.''

"Who?'' I asked. "Who'll catch up with him?''

She shrugged. "Whoever.'' She smiled. "Someone.'' She pushed herself to her feet. "Can I stay here tonight if I have to, Abner?''

"Sure you can. But won't you be a little . . . uncomfortable?''

She started for the bedroom, looked back. "He won't come here. This is where he killed her, Abner. He's afraid to come here.''

*   *   *

I slept on the couch, she in the bed. And she left the following morning, early.

I kissed her good-bye. I said to her, "I love you, Stacy," and conjured up a tear or two. She said she was glad she'd come, after all, that she was finally able to admit to herself that Art was "a crud" and unworthy of her, so she could put a big, unhappy part of her past behind her, at last. And then a taxi took her to Grand Central.

I was posturing all the while. I felt like a man on display. Do this; do that; be what she *expects* and *needs* you to be, Abner. I felt the way a visitor from another planet probably feels—stiff and uncomfortable. As if she were in one world and I had one foot in another. I was not at all sad to see her go. Because I do not believe that I felt anything for her. Only for Art. My best friend. Who, deep inside me, was fueling a smouldering anger.

At the Hammet Mausoleum, Halloween, 1965

I shook my head violently. "I'm *not* going to help you break into Joe Hammet's casket. No way, nohow, nowhere—"

"Oh, your grannie's knuckles," Sam said. "I'll do it myself, okay? Just give me the fuckin' screwdriver and I'll do it myself. You don't even have to watch. You can go over there—" he nodded at a far corner of the mausoleum—"and you can hang onto your little cock so's you don't pee your pants. Christ,

Abner, all I wanta do before we go is touch him. What's *he* gonna care?''

I stood, stuck my hands into my coat pockets—my right hand found the screwdriver, clutched it tightly—and said, ''I'll tell you what he's gonna do, Sam. He's gonna sit up and tear your throat out and feed it to the rats, that's what.''

''Ain't no rats here.''

''And then all the rest of 'em—'' my hand swept wide to take in the whole room and the six vaults in it—''will get up and munch on you awhile.''

''Jus' gimme the freakin' screwdriver, Abner, so I can do this and we can get outa here.''

I shook my head.

''I mean it, Abner.''

''No,'' I said.

''I'll beat the livin' shit outa ya, Abner.''

''No, you won't,'' I said. ''You're my friend.''

''Yeah, well, this ain't got nothin' to do with friendship, Abner. This has got to do with stayin' alive.''

''With stayin alive?''

''Yeah.''

''What's that mean?''

He took a step toward me, held his hand out. ''Just give me the screwdriver, Abner, 'cuz if you don't, I'll take it away from you.''

I considered it a moment, then gave him the screwdriver.

"Thanks," he said. He nodded at the plastic bag. "Get me another Mallo Cup, wouldja?"

"Get your own Mallo Cup, Sam."

He grinned. "Sure," he said, and got his own Mallo Cup.

CHAPTER FOUR

I have been to places in the last couple of months that I don't want to go back to, but I know that I will go back because I have learned this, too—that Madeline was right. It really is just a matter of *seeing*, not *what*, but *how*.

I knew that I'd find Phyllis sooner or later, if I looked in the right places. I asked myself, *Who makes a world, and love, and time, if there's no way of keeping it. All* of it? It was a good question.

What a miraculous thing the mind is. It's what computers are patterned after. And the mind can figure out most things (how to get someone to the moon, how to bring someone back from schizophrenia, how to take an old, tired heart out of someone's chest and put a new one in), but it has trouble with other things. Like the things that Phyllis and Madeline and

283

the boy in the house on East 80th Street introduced me to. The mind turns inward. The mind stiffens up and says that it would rather leave such things alone.

Go to bed, it says. *Get some new shoes*, it says. *Turn on the tube and watch* Love Boat, it says.

But the mind cannot fool itself for long. At last it has to admit that it has learned some very frightening things, some very confusing things, but that it is still ignorant, too, and needs to learn a lot more.

Early the morning after Stacy left, the morning of the tenth, I watched daylight come. It is a nice view from Art's living room window—not the view of the skyline, which is barely visible through the bathroom window, but a view of the flat-gray and flat-green painted townhouses across the street, a view from halfway up to the top of the townhouses, and then twenty degrees of sky above that. The sun does not rise behind these townhouses; they are to the north, and when the sun comes up on a still and cloudless morning, as this was, it casts beautifully delineated, very dark shadows across the house fronts, shadows from bits of the houses themselves—roof overhangs, window frames. There is even a pair of pollution-streaked gargoyles on a house just down the street, the far right house visible from Art's couch, that cast marvelously grotesque, elongated shadows.

I found myself smiling at them as daylight came because I knew that I could no longer be spooked very much by things that were intended to spook. Like gargoyles. I'd gone beyond that. I'd graduated, paid my dues; I had taken a quantum leap of the spirit.

I was frightened, yes. But for the right reasons. I was frightened because I was in search of the woman I loved in a world that, only two weeks earlier, I hadn't even realized existed.

But, in those two weeks, I had gone walking in it, sightseeing in it, I had been a part of it. And I knew generally, what it was all about.

That wasn't true, of course. I merely told myself it was true because it was the only way I knew of holding on and of coping.

The great fiction (it's a small world): "Oh," one American says to another, both vacationing somewhere in Europe, "you're from Cincinnati. Maybe you know my cousin George."

I had peered through the little security peephole and I had seen faces that smiled and frowned and laughed and cried. And I had told myself that they had no secrets from me.

How could they?

The dead can't have secrets from the living.

As Serena Hitchcock had very succinctly put it, "Dead, Abner, is dead!"

And, of course, I knew very well what *dead* was.

Everyone knew what dead was.

And that was the big lie that was going through my head there on Art's black leather couch.

With daylight coming.

Dead, Abner, is dead!

With daylight slanting gaily off the townhouses

across the street, off the windows, off the ledges, off the gargoyles.

Because the dead *sing*, and *laugh*, and sit up, and look around, and cry, and want.

And they are confused. They are lonely. They hurt.

And, at last, they come apart. And go off to someplace else.

As Phyllis did. Just as Phyllis did.

At Grand Central Station, the Evening of the 9th

It is a miracle, I think—a testimony to someone's unsung genius with audio technology—that announcements of departures and arrivals are heard by anyone at all at Grand Central. Outside New York, in bus depots and train stations that are barely large enough to sleep in, such announcements sound like recordings of hay bailers or cement mixers. But at Grand Central, it is usually clear that names of towns and cities and track numbers and times are being said.

This is, of course, because departures and arrivals on a very grand scale are what Grand Central is all about. When several thousand people have someplace to go, they must be told how to get to where they're going only once or twice. This way, they can make their exits and their entrances with a modicum of style.

Jocelyn Horn always had style. She was the reason I went to Grand Central that night—to tell her that Stacy had already left for Bangor, so her—Jocelyn's—trip had been unnecessary; sorry, good-bye.

I had tried to phone her in Bangor earlier in the

day, but was told, by her husband Paul, that she was already on the train and "probably halfway to New York by now, Abner."

"Oh," I said.

"I would have come with her," he said, "but there were prior commitments. I'm sure Stacy's all right, don't you think?"

"Sure," I said. "She's all right." Then I said good-bye and hung up. I never liked Stacy's father very much. I always liked Jocelyn—regardless of her clearly ambivalent feelings toward me.

I got a big, freshly baked pretzel at a stand called *Hot Sam's* near the 42nd Street exit. I began wandering about and munching on it because I was several minutes early to meet Jocelyn, who was due to arrive at 6:15.

I felt someone tugging softly at my jacket. "Hey," I heard. It was a man's voice. I turned my head and saw a young man, twenty or twenty-one, no older, wearing jeans and a brown leather jacket. He was smiling at me and nodding at the pretzel. "Hey," he said again, "where'd you get that?"

I pointed to my left. "Over there," I told him. "Near the 42nd Street exit."

"Thanks," he said, turned and walked quickly away, in the direction of *Hot Sam's*.

I checked the big clock on the south wall of Grand Central, between a pair of timetables for the local trains. It read 6:05. I heard a woman shouting: "He grabbed at my purse; he grabbed at my purse!"

She was close by. I looked to my right, saw her near the Amtrak ticket booths, near the entrance to the waiting rooms, and Park Avenue. She was tall, in her thirties, gaunt, and was wearing a loose-fitting red dress. She was standing still and pointing stiffly at a stocky, well-dressed man who was walking quickly away from her with a look of great humiliation about him.

"He grabbed for my purse!" the woman screamed.

The man continued to walk away.

A cop—also stocky, dark-haired, in his early forties—came down the ramp from the waiting rooms. He saw the woman, went over to her—with no particular air of urgency about him—said, "What's the problem, miss?"

She said again, still pointing at the well-dressed man, who was close to me now and shaking his head slowly, hugely embarrassed, "He grabbed for my purse; he grabbed for my purse."

The cop called to the man, "Hold on there, buddy."

The man stopped walking. The cop went over to him, took him firmly by the arm—which was clearly even more embarrassing to the man than the woman's accusations—and said, "D'joo grab for the lady's purse?"

I felt someone tugging at my sleeve. I turned. It was the guy in the brown leather jacket. He said, "Ain't no pretzels over there. Why'djoo lie?"

I nodded again at the 42nd Street exit. "It's called Hot Sam's," I said.

"Nope," the boy said.

"I'm not lying to you," I said.

He nodded at what was left of my pretzel. "Can I have the rest of that?"

From behind me, I heard: "He grabbed for her purse," and "This guy grabbed for that lady's purse."

I thrust the pretzel at the young man in the brown leather jacket. He took it happily, started chewing on it, walked away.

I checked the clock again. It read 6:08.

At the Amtrak ticket counters, several long lines had formed, apparently, I guessed, to try and get last-minute tickets on the 6:45 which stopped at points in upstate New York and terminated in Chicago.

The woman in the loosely fitting red dress was at the middle of the line nearest to me. She took one step out from it every now and then to check its progress, then stepped back and stood quietly, hands clutching her purse. The line was moving very slowly.

I watched as a younger woman, carrying a backpack and looking at a timetable went over to her, stood next to her a moment, hoping, apparently, to be noticed. A man just in front of the woman in the red dress turned his head slightly, noticed the younger woman, gave her a quick and critical once-over, looked back. When, after a full minute, the woman in red didn't acknowledge the younger woman, she cleared her throat and said, "Excuse me, please?"

The woman in red turned her head, looked blankly at the younger woman. "Yes?" she said.

The younger woman smiled. "I didn't mean to

disturb you,"—she held her timetable up—"I was just wondering if you could tell me . . ."

"Get lost!" said the woman in red.

The younger woman looked stunned.

The man in front of her, who'd turned his head to give her a quick and critical once-over, looked at her again. "Yeah," he growled, "get lost!"

"I'm sorry," she said.

The cop came over, put his hand on the younger woman's shoulder. "You givin' these people here a hard time, honey?"

The woman in the red dress said, "Yeah, she is."

"No, I'm not," said the younger woman.

The man in front of the woman in the red dress turned his head again and said to the cop, "She's asking questions, officer."

"Yeah?" said the cop. "What kind of questions?"

The younger woman looked very confused now, and was clearly at a loss for words.

"Why don'tcha just leave 'em alone, okay?" the cop said.

And that's when I went to meet Jocelyn.

Her first words to me were, "You look scared, Abner."

"Too much coffee," I said, and extended my hand to take one of her two, big blue suitcases. She let me take it and I nodded toward the 42nd Street exit. "We can go out this way, Aunt Joceyln."

"I've been here before, Abner."

"Yes, of course you have." We started for the

42nd Street exit, which was all the way across Grand Central. Jocelyn was dressed well, in a blue pants suit and black shoes. She's a nice-looking woman (she'll be described as handsome one day, when her basic feminine attractiveness has begun to fade), and men—certain kinds of men, businessmen in their forties and fifties—turned around occasionally to look at her, which she appeared to enjoy. She said, as we walked, "Where's Stacy, Abner?"

"Stacy's back in Bangor by now," I answered.

She stopped walking. "You mean she's not in New York anymore?"

I nodded. "She left this morning."

A quivering little grin broke out on her lips. She held her free hand out to me and indicated the suitcase I was carrying. "Then I don't know what the hell I'm doing here, do you, Abner? Give me that please."

I gave her the suitcase. "Don't you want to get something to eat anyway, Aunt Jocelyn?"

"No. I'll eat here. Good-bye, Abner."

"Just like that?"

"Just like that. Good-bye." And she turned and walked away from me.

CHAPTER FIVE

Phyllis was buried in a gritty, little cemetery in Brooklyn, between McDonald Avenue and Van Sicien Street. On one side of the cemetery, there was a small tailor's shop which smelled of fresh ironing, and on the other side, a wholesale toy distributor. Dozens of cheap, pastel-colored stuffed animals, most of them faded by the sun, had been set up precariously in the toy distributor's window, and they gave the whole area, including the cemetery, a tacky and impermanent look.

It was a Friday afternoon, two days after I had last seen Phyllis, that I went to where she was buried. I think there were fifty headstones, no more. Most of them were quite old, several dating from the late 1700s, and most of them were in bad repair.

Phyllis was pretty easy to find. She was toward the

back of the cemetery, near a high, brick wall topped with spikes of black wrought iron.

She hadn't been given a headstone. She'd been given a small, rectangular piece of greenish metal—like a miniature of the ones used for roadside plaques to commemorate battles or landmarks—which had been set flat into the ground not too long ago, because the earth around it looked as if it had been very recently turned.

The piece of metal said merely this:

PHYLLIS PELLAPRAT
1958-1983

I wept when I saw it. I wept quietly, with my hands at my sides and my head down a little. I enjoyed myself. I don't believe that I've ever enjoyed myself quite as much. I enjoyed myself because it was confirmation. It was release. It—that piece of greenish metal—was an invitation.

Find me, it said. *I am here, or here, or here. I am!*

A maple tree, small and bare of leaves, stood at the back of the cemetery, near the wall. While I wept I became aware that a man was at the other side of the tree, with his back turned. I could see his shoulders—one on each side of the tree—a right leg in brown corduroy, from the knee down, and a right elbow pointing at the toy distributor's east wall, as if the arm were bent, the hand at the mouth. I saw a small, ragged cloud of smoke appear, and then another.

"You Art?" I heard. It was a young man's voice, and it had an intimidating bite to it.

I answered, "No, I'm not."

"You sure?" Another cloud of smoke appeared, and dissipated instantly on a sudden breeze.

"My name is Abner," I said. I had stopped weeping, but I could hear that my voice was quivering from its after-effects.

"Abner?" said the young man with his back to the tree. "What kinda name is that? Ain't no one named Abner. You fulla shit, my man!"

"No," I said, "I'm not."

"How you know Phyllis?"

I said nothing.

"I asked you how you know Phyllis?"

And still I said nothing. I was not in the mood to be intimidated.

He chuckled. "You pretty hot stuff, you think? You pretty hot stuff?"

"No," I said.

"I think you think so." Another cloud of smoke appeared, hung near the tree a few seconds, then wafted off in several directions on the still air. His elbow went down, then his hand; he let his cigarette fall close to his foot, where it smouldered in the wet, matted grass, letting off a continuous stream of smoke. "You think you hot stuff because you fuck her. Ain't that so?"

I said, "Are you trying to make an issue of a dead woman's sex life?"

He chuckled. "Sure, Art. Everyone else does. You fulla shit, you know that?"

"I'm not Art."

"You are."

"No. My name is Abner."

"You *here*, you *Art!* I don't need no convincin'; my mother didn't raise no dummies."

I took a deep breath. I was losing my patience, and I did not want to lose my patience. I was enjoying myself too much. I said again, "My name is *Abner*," and added, "Abner Cray. And I love Phyllis Pellaprat very much."

He chuckled again. To my right, someone came out of the toy distributor's front door and looked over at me. He was a big, balding, overweight man in his late fifties or early sixties, and he was dressed in a white, short-sleeved shirt and black slacks. He said, his voice high-pitched, a little nervous. "You got some kinda trouble here?"

"No," I said.

The man behind the maple tree said nothing.

The fat man said, "You got some business being here, then?"

"Yes," I said.

"You want to tell me about it?"

"No." I paused a moment. "No. It's my business."

The fat man seemed to think about that. Then he shrugged. "Sure enough," he said, and waddled back into his office.

The man behind the maple tree chuckled again. "You know what he's gonna do?"

"No," I said.

"He's gonna go and call the *po*lice. He been

robbed, you see. So he's gonna go and call the police—he's a *very* nervous man.''

"Uh-huh," I said.

"And that don't bother you?" He seemed vaguely amused.

"No, it doesn't bother me."

"Fuck, you is *really* hot stuff, ain't that right, my man?"

I said, "You're beginning to annoy me." It made me feel very masculine, so I said it once more. "You're beginning to annoy me," and added, "quite a lot."

He chuckled again. "You know I'm gonna take *care* of you?!"

It was a statement clearly designed to scare me. It succeeded. "Jesus!" I breathed.

"We're all of us, *all* of us, gonna take *care* of you, Art. Not right here and now. That'd be stupid. But we *are* gonna take care of you!"

"Jesus!" I said again. "I am *not* Art DeGraff. Christ, you wanta see some ID or something?!"

He chuckled.

I hurried on, "My name is Abner Cray. I'm a photographer. I came to New York to do a book. I met Phyllis Pellaprat and I fell in love with her." He chuckled again. I went on, "I *know* Art DeGraff. He used to be my best friend. And I know that he killed Phyllis; he *told* me he killed her, and he told me that it was an accident." I paused; I could hear the strain in my voice and I wanted to suppress it. I continued,

"You have no reason at all to want to kill me." I stopped. I thought I sounded pretty convincing.

The man behind the maple tree said, "Didn't say nothin' about *killing* you, Art. You dead—big deal! Lots and lots of people are dead, Art, and lots and lots of people ain't, too. It's the ones that ain't that get the most scared, you know what I mean, Art? You ever been scared? Yeah, you been scared. And you know what scares you the very most, Art? I'll tell you. It's not knowin' that scares you the very most. Not knowin' when, or how, or if they's gonna be pain, or how much they's gonna be, or if it's ever gonna end, or if you is ever gonna go back home again and get some rest. Put your feet up. Watch the fuckin' TV. Relax. have a fuckin' beer or two, and *drift*. Know what that is? Know what *drifting* is, Art? Sure you do. It's feeling nothin' and being happy and thinkin' you got everything all taken care of. You wanta piss, you go an' piss. You wanta grab a bite to eat, you wanta play with yourself, you wanta read the sports page, hey, you do it. You know? You do it! But what if you can't *do* none of those things, Art? What if you can't do none of 'em? Like you're in jail, you know? You ever been in jail, Art? I been in jail. Like you wanta go a couple feet *that* way, you can't. You wanta go a couple feet *this* way, you can't. You're stuck. You can't do much of anything. 'Cept piss in the toilet they put in the cell with ya. And eat the bologna sandwiches they give ya. Like bein' in jail, Art. Only the walls are a lot closer; they get right up next to ya and they squeeze hard. And they don't look nothin' like walls neither. They got faces, you know, and they got hair and fingernails, and they don't smell too good nor listen too good neither, 'cuz they is way past listenin'. And they *got* ya, Art! Like you're their little dog, you know. They got ya and where *they* go, you go. You got no choice. *That's* what's scary. It sure would scare the holy shit outa me, Art. It surely would. You think about it. You just think about it a little bit. Think about it a lot, Art."

I clenched and unclenched my teeth. I cursed beneath my breath.

The man from the toy distributor's came out his front door again. He was smiling an odd, crooked smile. "You'd better haul ass!" he said to me.

"Sorry?" I said.

His smile broadened. "I said you'd better haul ass. You're gonna have some people here asking you some questions pretty quick!"

I looked at the maple tree. The man behind it was gone. I looked at the fat man, mumbled something to him about just minding my own business, that I was harming no one. And he smiled his crooked smile while I spoke, and when I was finished, he came forward a step or two, into the little cemetery, said, "Why don'tcha just leave 'em alone, okay?" hesitated, said again, "Why don'tcha haul ass?"

And I did.

CHAPTER SIX

Back to Art's apartment, where I sat at Art's desk, in the living room, and made another list:

1. The man is black.
2. I'd guess that he used to be a friend of Phyllis.
3. He smokes. Should go back and check the brand—might be something exotic.
4. He wears brown corduroy pants, and he
5. Does not speak well.
6.

I put nothing down for number 6 because that's when Art came into the room. I guessed that he'd been in the bedroom, sleeping—he was wearing his blue robe and made a show of stretching as he came in.

"Hi, Abner," he said.

My mouth hung open for several seconds before I could speak. And when I did speak, it was a curse:

"Goddamn you, Art—you son of a bitch!"

He smiled thinly, came over to the desk looked at what I was writing. "What's this?"

"It's a list," I said.

"Yes, I can see that." He picked it up and appeared to read it over. "Someone you know, Abner?"

"No. What are you doing here, Art?"

"I live here, remember." He smiled again. It grated on me because it was the kind of smile which said loudly that he thought he'd put something over on me. "You're being awfully hostile, Abner."

"Of course I'm being hostile." Hot, unreasoning anger was welling up inside me, and I pushed it back, with effort. "You're a real shit, Art."

"We're friends, Abner. Aren't we friends?"

"Fuck you!" I nodded at the list in his hands. "That man wants to kill me. Would you like to know why he wants to kill me?"

Art put the list down in front of me on the desk. His smile vanished. He said nothing.

"He thinks I'm *you*, for Christ's sake," I said. "He was Phyllis' friend, and he wants to kill me because he thinks I'm *you!*"

Art still said nothing. He went to a kitchen cupboard, withdrew a can of ground coffee and looked back at me briefly, no particular expression on his face. He opened the coffee with an electric opener on the counter, set the can aside, and stood for a moment with his hands flat on the counter and his head lowered. Then he said, his voice low and apologetic, "You've been having a pretty miserable time, haven't you, Abner?"

I didn't answer him.

He took a percolator out of a lower cupboard, removed the basket, set it on the counter. He went on, "Phyllis had quite a few friends. I didn't know all of them, only a few of them." He ran water into the percolator, put the basket inside it. "None of them liked me, I guess." He plugged the percolator in. "That guy—" he nodded to indicate the list on the desk—"is just trying to scare you."

"I don't think so, Art."

He smiled thinly again, but this time it was a smile of impatience. The smile vanished; a look of intense earnestness came over him.

He asked, "Did you find out who the woman was, Abner?"

I answered, "Yes. She was Phyllis."

He shook his head slowly, sadly. "No, Abner. No, no. She was *not* Phyllis. You *know* she wasn't Phyllis because Phyllis is dead. *I* killed her, for Christ's sake!"

"I'm aware of that," I said.

He nodded at the coffeepot, which had begun to perk. "You want some of this."

"No," I answered.

He sighed. "I really did think we were friends, Abner. I thought we were pretty damned *close* friends, in fact."

"We were."

"Uh-huh." He shoved his hands into the pockets of his robe, glanced at the percolator, then back at me. He had that look of earnestness about him again. "Have you seen anyone, Abner?"

"Seen anyone?"

"Yes," he explained. "About this fantasy you're having."

I picked up the pen and filled in #6 on the list:

Art says he was not acquainted with most of Phyllis friends.

I said to Art, "I wish it was a fantasy."

The coffee stopped perking; Art poured a cupful.

"It is a fantasy, Abner. And if you believe it, you're nuts."

I sighed, stood, went to the fireplace, got the photograph that Phyllis had shown me a month earlier, brought it back to Art, shoved it under his nose. "Is *this* Phyllis, for Christ's sake? Is *this* Phyllis Pellaprat?"

He looked at the photograph for only a moment, then turned away, his cup of coffee in hand. "Yes," he whispered, "it is."

"Yes?"

"Yes."

"Then Phyllis Pellaprat is the woman I shared this apartment with, Art. And she is the woman I fell in love with."

"No, Abner." He shook his head slowly. "No," he repeated. "Phyllis is the woman I killed, god-damnit." I heard no malice or anger in his voice, only regret, sadness, and resignation. "She's the woman I killed." A very short pause, then: "Did I tell you that it was manslaughter, Abner?"

"Yes," I answered, "You did."

He shook his head again. "It wasn't. It was murder." A quick, nervous smile.

I sat heavily at the kitchen table, leaned back in the chair.

Art said, "Did you hear what I told you, Abner?"

"I heard." I stood, went to the desk, got the pen and my list, brought it to the table, sat down, and wrote:

"7. Art says it was murder, so *of course* the little bastard is after me."

Art looked at the list again, appeared to read #7, said, "You don't care, Abner?"

I shook my head briskly. "No, Art. I don't care. Tell me why I *should* care, and I will."

"You don't even want to hear how it happened?"

I turned my head away from him. I said nothing.

"I have to tell you how it happened, Abner." A short pause. I felt him touch my arm very lightly. "I *want* to tell you how it happened."

Still I said nothing.

"I beat her up," He said. There was a small tremor in his voice, as if he were on the verge of chuckling. Anger began to mount inside me again. He repeated, "I beat her up, Abner. I don't know why; I'm not sure why. Some men are like that. They beat up women. I used to beat Stacy up." I clenched my teeth. "Not a lot. I beat her up twice. I mean, I hit her twice. Several times. I got her black and blue. I broke one of her teeth; she had it capped—'' I grabbed for him, but I was too slow. He backed away, grinned. ''I don't like myself any more than you like me, Abner,'' he said.

''Why'd you come back here, Art?''

Another grin. ''To give myself up.''

''How wonderfully magnanimous,'' I said, paused, went on, ''But why?''

He shrugged. ''Guilt,'' I think,'' he said. ''Guilt can work wonders, you know.'' He paused, then added, ''And fear, too.''

''Fear? Fear of what?''

Someone knocked at the front door. Art glanced sharply at it. His hands began to shake first—some of the coffee sloshed out of the cup and onto the floor— then his arms and his mouth began to shake. ''Jesus!'' he whispered. ''Jesus!''

I smiled. ''I'll get it, Art.'' It occurred to me then that I had grown to hate Art, that as much as I loved Phyllis, I hated him. I wanted desperately to see him hauled away. ''I'll get it,'' I said again, and stood. He stuck his hand out so his palm was flat on my chest. ''No, Abner. Please. Let me.'' He was pleading with me. I sat. ''Sure, Art.''

He went haltingly to the door, his cup of coffee still in hand. He grasped the knob. There was another knock, louder and sharper than the first, and it spooked him, he stepped back. Then, apparently, he screwed some courage up from somewhere, because he reached out suddenly and yanked the door wide open.

It was Kennedy Whelan. He had a cigar in his

mouth, and his hands thrust into his suit pants pockets. He said, "Hello, Mr. DeGraff?"

Art nodded. Some more of his coffee sloshed out onto the floor.

Whelan took the cigar from his mouth, held it near the middle of his chest as he talked. "I've got a warrant for your arrest on a charge of second-degree murder . . ."

Art fainted.

I was glad to see it happen. I laughed, in fact.

Whelan looked over at me and barked, "Clam up, Mr. Cray." I quieted. Whelan leaned over Art—who'd collapsed so he was on his back, with his left arm close to his body, and his right arm out, toward the inside of the apartment, his legs bowed, feet together. He looked pretty ridiculous, too, because his robe had come open. "Help me with him, would you?" Whelan said, and put his arms under Art's arms. I went over, took Art's feet, and together, Whelan and I carried him to the couch.

Whelan said, "It happens."

"What happens?"

"People pass out."

"Oh," I said.

"Why are you still here, Mr. Cray? Don't you find me intimidating enough?" He put the cigar back into his mouth, began rolling it theatrically from one side to the other.

"I live here," I said.

Art started coming around then. His eyelids fluttered; he groaned a couple of times.

"Uh-huh," Whelan said. "Well, it's not important now, is it?" He nodded at Art. "I've got him."

Art mumbled something incoherent, something about Phyllis, I think, something affectionate.

Whelan grinned, as if at a private joke and leaned over him. "Mr. DeGraff?"

Art's eyes opened. He looked frightened.

"Mr. DeGraff?" Whelan said again.

"Yes?" Art managed.

"Mr. DeGraff, you have the right to remain silent. You have the right to have an attorney present during questioning. If you give up these rights—"

Art sat up suddenly, pushing Whelan aside. Whelan started reciting his rights again, and Art waved agitatedly at the air, as if waving at flies. "That's not necessary."

"Certainly, Mr. DeGraff," Whelan said. "Could you get dressed?"

"Sure," Art said.

"We have to go downtown, sir. We have to book you."

Art stood, grinned. He looked suddenly very pleased. "Yes," he said, "I'd like that." His voice was quivering. "I can't tell you how much I'd like that, Detective . . ." He stopped, looked confused. "What's your name, again?"

"Whelan. Call me 'Mr. Whelan.' I prefer being called Mister."

Art nodded, put his hand on the back of his head.

"I think I hurt myself." He rubbed the back of his head.

"Yes, sir," Whelan said. "We'll see that it's attended to." He looked at me. "Mr. Cray, will you be willing to testify that Mr. DeGraff received this head injury as the result of fainting."

I said yes.

"Thank you." He turned to Art. "Now, if you could get dressed, Mr. DeGraff."

Art started for the bedroom. "Yes," he said, "I will. I won't be long."

Whelan followed. Art said, "Please, let me do this alone." After a moment, Whelan nodded. "Okay," he said, and let Art go alone into his bedroom to get dressed. He shouldn't have done it, of course. He was stupid to do it; I suppose he considered himself a good judge of character (grizzled cop, twenty or twenty-five years on the force, gets to know people awfully well, right?). I suppose he felt pretty certain that Art wasn't going to do anything, so he decided to give him a final moment of dignity and let him get dressed alone.

It was a mistake.

When Art had been in the bedroom a minute or two, Whelan said, "Can I get a statement from you, Mr. Cray?"

"About Art's head injury?" I said.

Whelan puffed on the cigar; he seemed to delight in it. "Yes. For the record."

A kind of high-pitched grunting noise, barely

audible, came from the bedroom. We both looked. Whelan, thinking, apparently, that it was nothing to be concerned about, said, "You'd be surprised, Mr. Cray, at the number of suspects who claim police brutality—" He was interrupted by another grunting sound, louder now.

"Excuse me, please," he said, and I watched as he strode quickly—and more gracefully, I thought at the time, than I supposed a man his size could— down the hallway to Art's closed bedroom door, and tapped on it. "Mr. DeGraff?"

Another grunting sound, now as much a screech as a grunt.

Whelan hit the door with the side of his fist. "Mr. DeGraff? Open the door, please." He tried the knob; the door was locked. He cursed, stepped back, kicked the door very hard just below the knob. The door swung open sharply, Whelan pulled his gun out, took up a position to the left of the door, and bellowed this time, "Mr. DeGraff, please come out of there!"

I had been coming slowly down the hallway all this time, and now I was close enough to Art's bedroom to see past Whelan, into it. I saw movement inside, though I heard nothing.

Whelan bellowed again, "Mr. DeGraff, come out of there! Now!"

It was a quick and frantic kind of movement that I saw in that room, as if something furious and silent had been let loose inside it.

"Goddamnit!" Whelan hissed.

"Are you going to go in there?" I whispered.

He ignored me. "Goddamnit!" he hissed again. He was obviously very upset, and more than a little nervous. "Mr. DeGraff, I am going to ask you only one more time to come out of there. *Please* come out of there!"

"I'll go in and get him if you like," I offered. I meant it.

He looked at me as if I were a madman, waved at me with his gun and ordered, "Get *out* of the way; get *out* of the way!"

I stepped back a little.

And Art screamed.

Whelan twitched, cursed again, and launched himself, head-first—so he could tuck and roll—into the room. It was very theatrical, and I enjoyed it immensely. He let loose with the gun moments later. I didn't like that; it was loud, obtrusive—"Christ!" I screamed. "Stop that, you asshole, stop that!" And I ran into the room.

I found Whelan sitting up against the wall to the right of the door, his feet under the middle of the bed. He was still pointing his gun, and his mouth was moving fitfully—small, spittle-laden curses were coming out.

Art was not in the room. His robe was there, lying very neatly on the bed. The window was open; cold air was pushing into the room. But Art was gone.

I grinned. "Great," I said.

CHAPTER SEVEN

I leaned over Whelan. He was flushed; his breathing was shallow, and I guessed that he was in shock, that he had seen something very strange. I patted him several times, softly, on the cheek. It did no good.

I straightened, stared at him a moment. The small, spittle-laden curses stopped; his breathing remained shallow. "Mr. Whelan?" I said. Nothing. I turned and went to the window, stuck my head out, looked down the fire escape, then right and left.

Art was on the sidewalk on East 79th Street. He was dressed only in a pair of dark slacks and a white T-shirt. He was barefooted. Three people—a young, casually dressed woman, a child, a young black man smoking a cigarette—were hurrying him along, left, toward Fifth Avenue. "Art!" I called, and he glanced back. I saw a paralytic kind of fear on his face—stiff, and pale, and wildly incredulous.

Then Kennedy Whelan shouldered his way in next to me at the window, stuck his head out, saw Art, too, and yelled, "Stop right there, Mr. DeGraff! Stop right there!" and stuck his arm out, gun in hand, and pointed it in Art's general direction.

"Jesus," I said, "what's *that* for?"

He shoved me aside, leaned farther out the window, and leveled the gun directly at Art. "Stop there, goddamnit!"

I pushed in beside him, looked frantically toward East 79th Street and the tight little group of people that was all but carrying Art away.

"Damnit!" Whelan breathed. He drew back from the window and headed for the phone on a nightstand near the bed. "Please don't go anywhere, Mr. Cray," he said. I nodded, and then moved more quickly than I supposed I could have. Out the window, onto the fire escape, and, before starting down, I looked back, saw Whelan running through the bedroom, reaching into his jacket for his gun. "Shit!" I whispered, and clattered down the fire escape to the ground. I heard from above:

"Shit, fuck, goddamnit!"

I looked up. Whelan had started down after me, but had gotten the front bottom edge of his suit jacket caught in the fire escape.

I ran to East 79th Street. Behind me, from the fire escape, Whelan called, "You asshole, you fucking asshole!"

I reached the sidewalk. In front of me, a yellow cab came to a sharp halt. The cabbie leaned over, rolled the passenger window down and said, "Cab, sir?"

It was Matthew Petersak.

CHAPTER EIGHT

Keystone Cops

Behind me, Whelan had freed his jacket from the fire escape and had reached the ground.

" Cabbie," he yelled, "I am a New York City police officer and I am ordering you to halt!"

I opened the front passenger door of the cab, hopped in, glanced at Whelan. He was running toward us with his gun pointing skyward and was yelling again, "I am a New York City Police Officer, goddamnit, and I am ordering you to bring your cab to a halt!"

"Jesus!" I breathed.

A quick, hollow chuckle came from Matthew Petersak.

"Jesus!" I said again. Whelan was within fifty

feet of the cab now. "Can we *go?!*" I said to the cabbie. "Please, can we *go?!*"

Matthew Petersak chuckled once again. He opened his door, put one foot out onto the pavement, stood, and yelled to Whelan, over the top of the cab, "Yeah? Well *I'm* a New York City dead man, and I don't give a fuck!" And he laughed.

Whelan stopped. His gun still was pointing skyward, but now his mouth was open.

Ahead of the cab, traffic had come to a standstill—another of New York's traffic jams—though, in the opposite lane, traffic was sparse.

Whelan leveled his gun at me. I leaned far forward, noticed, before my head went below the level of the window, that the barrel was tracking me.

"Stop right there, cabbie!" Whelan yelled.

And Petersak hit the accelerator. "Madeline wants to see you," he said.

Whelan fired.

I heard a noise to my right, like a hand slicing into water. I looked. I saw a very small, yellowish hole in the side of Petersak's head, just below and behind his temple.

"Jesus!" I breathed again. "Jesus, Jesus—"

"Hurts," Petersak said, winced, and swung the cab hard around so we were in the opposite lane. I straightened, saw a car brake furiously, heard someone yell a curse.

"Hurts," Petersak said again. He brought the cab to a halt, put it in reverse, backed up, stopped, put it

in first. I heard another shot. Several square inches of
dashboard shredded in front of me.

"Hurts," Petersak said.

Outside the cab, people were cursing all around
us.

"Hurts," Petersak said.

"Please," I said, and slid down as far as I could,
so my rear end was nearly on the floor. "Please, let's
go," I said.

Petersak hit the accelerator.

Madeline was very angry.

"You are stupid, stupid man, Mr. Cray. You cannot,
I repeat, you *cannot* interfere with these people. Do
you understand that? You cannot!"

We were in her living room; she was in the same
chair she'd been in the last time I saw her, and she
was wearing the same blue nightgown. Gerald was
standing beside her, grinning. The cat scratch at his
jawline was terribly inflamed. Madeline went on,
"Do you think you can actually *find* Phyllis Pellaprat?
Is that the delusion under which you are laboring,
Mr. Cray?"

"Is it a delusion?" I asked. I was seated on the
rococo settee near the two tall, narrow windows halfway across the big room from her.

She stared at me a moment, in much the way that
Whelan had and Serena Hitchcock had. "Yes, it is."
She said it very slowly, her enunciation crisp.

"That's not what you told me the last time I was
here," I said.

"I don't give a hoot or a holler or a tinker's damn—" She stopped and composed herself. At last, she nodded toward Gerald, who was looking blankly at me. "This, Mr. Cray," she said, "is all that you can expect. No more than this."

I leaned forward in the settee. "No," I said. "I don't believe that. I've seen evidence—"

She cut in, "The house on East 80th Street, Mr. Cray? Is that what you're talking about?"

"Sorry?"

"The whorehouse on East 80th Street, damnit! Do you know what you did there? Do you have any idea at all what you did to those poor creatures?"

"No, I don't," I said, "I hadn't really thought about it . . ." I faltered.

"You probably imagine that you *helped* them in some bumbling way." She stopped, thought, went on, "Suffice it to say, however, that you didn't. Just as you did not help the man in the ragged T-shirt or, for heaven's sake, that poor boy selling puppies. Don't you realize, Mr. Cray, that they are in *transition* and that you cannot *do* anything for them. You cannot do anything for *any of them,* including Phyllis Pellaprat. She is in transition. Just like Gerald. You may love them and you may even *need* them, but you cannot *help* them. Do I make myself clear?"

I said, "I'm sorry, no."

She looked surprised. I think she was a lot like Kennedy Whelan—unaccustomed to resistance. She smiled stiffly. "And what precisely is it that I have not made clear to you, Mr. Cray?"

"All of it's clear, Madeline; all of it's very clear. I just don't believe it."

That upset her. "And who, Mr. Cray, just *who* in the name of heaven are you to tell me that? I *know* these people, I've lived around them for a long, long time. For twenty years." She stopped, took a tissue from a box of pink Scotties on a small, round table near her chair, dabbed at her mouth with it, put the used tissue on the table. "And," she continued, "I have never seen them suffer the way you have made them suffer. You confuse them. Do you know that?"

"I don't mean to," I said lamely.

"The ignorant don't *mean* any of the harm that they do." She stopped and put her arm around Gerald, who was standing next to her. It was an affectionate and touching gesture, and he smiled slightly, as if in appreciation of it. "Tell me what you expected to find at the place Phyllis Pellaprat is buried, Mr. Cray."

I thought a moment. I answered, "Nothing. Nothing at all."

She smiled a flat, impatient smile. Gerald's smile strengthened. "You cannot ask me to believe that you went there expecting to find nothing. You went there because that's where her body is, isn't that correct? And *because* that's where her *body* is, then, naturally, she'd have to be there, too. It's a reasonable assumption. Ignorant, but reasonable."

"Please don't patronize me," I said.

"Oh, why ever not, Mr. Cray?" She was annoyed. "Why ever not? Do you think that you're somehow above it. You're not above it. You're a meddler; you're an intruder. And you are confusing them. All of them. Phyllis Pellaprat, too. They're in transition. Do you know what that means? It means they're *going* somewhere. Even Gerald here.'' She squeezed him. ''And Matthew Petersak, all of them are, in their own time, *going* somewhere. I don't know where. I wish to God that I did. But I don't.''

I stood abruptly.

''What are you doing, Mr. Cray? We're not done here—we're a long way from being done.''

''You're wrong.'' I started for the door, then stopped. ''I think you're as ignorant as I am, Madeline. I think that you fool yourself because you've been around them so long. But I think you're just as ignorant as I am. And just as scared. I'm going to find Phyllis Pellaprat. I'm going to go and find her because I love her.''

Madeline sighed. ''Yes, you probably do. And you'll probably find her, too. But I doubt very much that you'll like what you find. And I also doubt very much that you'll be able to hold onto her.''

I went to the living room entranceway. She called after me, ''Mr. Cray?''

''Yes?'' I looked around at her.

She said, ''The man at the cemetery—''

I cut in, ''I think he found what he was looking for.''

She smiled. ''Perhaps. I don't know what they're going to do with your friend; I have no idea. But it would be—" another smile, slightly perverse—"very entertaining to find out."

And that's when I left.

I went back to the little cemetery in Brooklyn the next morning; I stood above that ugly green plaque, and I tried hard to peer past it to what lay beneath.

And when at last I did, I saw flesh coming apart and falling away, a brain shriveling up, a yellow-white skull grinning up through the earth at me.

And I thought, *This is Phyllis. This is my Phyllis. Why do I need more than this?*

Because there is more, I answered myself. *Because I can have more, and because I want more.*

Inside that skull, which was like the inside of the earth itself, the brain was shriveling up, and the memories were drifting away from it like dreams: they come and they go; they come and they go.

They come apart, and they go together again.

I felt people around me. Millions and millions of people. And I felt sunlight on me. I heard voices raised in anger, and I sensed love and excitement and happiness.

And I remembered one voice especially.

The voice of the man behind the maple tree.

"We gonna take good *care* of you, Art," it said. "We gonna take good care of you."

At the Hammet Mausoleum, Halloween, 1965

I said to Sam Fearey, as he worked hard at trying to pry open Joe Hammet's vault door, "It's gonna knock you right over, Sam."

"Yeah," he said. "What's gonna knock me over?"

"The smell."

He shoved the big screwdriver I'd brought along, and which he forced me to give him, under the bottom edge of the door and hit it with the palm of his hand. The screwdriver went forward a bare fraction of an inch. "I know all about that, Abner," he said, and hit the screwdriver again.

"Yeah?" I said. "Tell me about it, then."

He shrugged, hit the screwdriver again, pushed down on it. The vault door creaked slightly, but didn't appear to give at all. "Well," he said, "you know—it's a *dead* smell."

"You're fulla shit."

"No. It's a *dead* smell, Abner. I've smelled it before." He took the screwdriver out from beneath the vault door, nodded at the candle I was holding. "Hold that up a little higher, okay? I wanta check these hinges." I held the candle up. He fingered the vault door's hinges for a few moments, his tongue working on his lower lip as he did so. Finally, he announced, "Know what, Abner, I think these are capped screws here, and if I can get the caps off—" He shoved the screwdriver under one of the big, rounded metal caps on the door's top hinge. The cap popped off and fell to the floor. "Good," Sam said. Then, a moment later, "Shit!"

"What's the matter, Sam?" I asked.

"It's a fucking Phillips head."

"The screw, you mean."

He glanced at me, grimaced. "No, skillet-brains,

I mean Joe Hammet's head. Of course I mean the screw.''

"Oh.''

"So give me the Phillips head, damnit!''

"The Phillips head?''

"Abner, I'll take it from you. I really will.''

I reluctantly gave him the Phillips head screwdriver I had in my jacket pocket. He took it, began working at the top hinge with it. I said, "You forgot about the formaldehyde smell, Sam.''

"No, I didn't.''

"Sure you did. You don't smell anything else. Just the formaldehyde.''

"Big deal.'' He smiled, held a screw up for me to see. "There's the first one,'' he said.

"Uh-huh,'' I said.

CHAPTER NINE

I was smart enough to stay away from Art's apartment. I went instead to Serena Hitchcock's. She wasn't home, so I went to a hotel called The Cadillac on East 11th Street, registered. And left immediately. I had stupidly registered under my real name.

I went to another hotel, The Belmore on East 36th Street. I tried to register under the name Jack McKetchum, who was my baseball coach at Walter Pierpont High, in Bangor. I couldn't do it. The desk man wanted ID, and I had none for Jack McKetchum, so I made some weak excuse and left. That was when I began to feel desperate. My cash reserve was pretty low and I wasn't sure I wanted to take a chance and go to my bank. I probably should have started feeling desperate long before, and maybe I had. Maybe needing to find shelter in Manhattan in February and having a lot of trouble doing it, reminded me that I'd been desperate for a few days. But I doubt it. I'm adaptable. We're all adaptable.

I went to the building on East 95th Street, where Phyllis had taken me to meet her parents. The building was boarded up, so I found a rusty tire iron in the alley beside it, pried off the boards on the front door, and went in.

I had supposed that the building would be empty. It wasn't. Some people had found their way in; I could hear them as I stood at the front of the long hallway. Some men. Some women. A lot of guttural noises and slurred talking.

It was dark there, except for late afternoon light filtering through open spaces between the slabs of plywood on the windows.

When my eyes had adjusted to the dim light, I went up the metal stairway at the back of the building.

I got to the second floor. I heard the same low, gutteral noises that I'd heard on the first floor, but they were louder now. I went to the third floor, the fourth. I found silence there.

I went to the fifth floor, to Apartment 506, pushed the door open, and went in.

It was cold in the apartment. I could hear small animals running about in the walls, and the vague smell of urine was in the air. In the front room, the ancient, overstuffed, red couch stood in the center of the floor and the rose-colored rocker against the wall, where it had been when Lorraine Pellaprat was using it.

In the bedroom was a black iron bed with a mattress, box spring, and pillow, and in the kitchen an old Kelvinator refrigerator kept company with a Burnwell stove. Neither of the appliances worked.

I went back into the living room. "Hello?" I called. Nothing. "Hello. Mr. Pellaprat?" Still nothing.

Exhaustion caught up with me then. I sat on the red, overstuffed couch, felt my eyes close, forced them open, stood, sat again. I whispered, "Hello, is anyone here? Mrs. Pellaprat? Mr. Pellaprat?"

I woke after dark. I itched badly, especially inside my elbows, around my groin, in my hair, under my chin. I guessed that the red couch had some kind of lice living in it, but when I searched myself I found nothing, and after a while the itch went away.

It was very cold in the apartment now, and dark, though not pitch dark. Two windows at the back of the living room faced downtown Manhattan, which was casting a very soft, bluish-yellow light into the room, enough to see by. I could make out the rocking chair and the doorway to the bedroom. The door was open. From several stories below, I thought, I could hear the faint noises of people having a drunken good time. I wondered briefly why they chose to live only on floors one through three, why they hadn't gone higher, and I guessed that it was probably warmer on the lower floors, and safer, too, in the event of a fire. These were reasonable ideas, and I think that I believed them. But I was wrong.

I did not like the noises of people having a drunken

good time below, and I did not like the bluish-yellow
glow in the room, the darkened doorway, the bird-
print wallpaper. I was getting very nervous. I was
getting spooked.

I told myself that I was hungry. I remembered
passing a diner on Fifth Avenue near East 92nd
Street and I thought that I could go there, eat, and
come back within an hour. I'd call Serena Hitchcock
while I was out, and perhaps, I thought—feeling
cocky—I'd even give Detective Whelan a call, too,
just to assess my situation.

I got up from the couch and stretched, to try and
chase my fear away. It didn't work. I heard again the
sounds of little animals running about in the walls.
And something else. A small, gurgling noise, close
to a cooing noise. I thought it was a pigeon.

I started to itch again. I attributed it to nervousness,
to fear, to desperation, because I was feeling all of
those things at the same time. Who wouldn't, under
the circumstances?

I scratched. My chin, my groin, the inside of my
elbows, and as I scratched, the soft, gurgling noises
grew louder and I guessed that they were coming
from the bedroom. I took a couple of cautious steps
toward the bedroom, still scratching.

When I was halfway there, across the front room,
the light changed. It grew brighter, as if several
low-wattage bulbs had been turned on. I took a quick
glance around and saw that it was true. Two bulbs in
a grimy ceiling fixture were burning. They had changed
the soft, bluish-yellow glow to a gritty orange.

A low, confused grunt came out of me. I saw a woman appear in the bedroom doorway. She was carrying a baby.

"I'm sorry," I said. "I'm sorry, I didn't know."

She smiled. She was a very pleasant-looking woman in her late twenties, dark-haired, with large, friendly brown eyes. Her simple, off-white house dress was opened to allow her baby to nurse, and the baby was cooing delightedly as it suckled.

She turned then, glanced around at me, smiled again, and went back into the bedroom.

I went to the doorway, looked in. She was in a far corner of the room, seated on a low wooden stool, with her left side against the wall, her feet and knees together, her arms crossed. She did not have her baby. She had the unmistakable patina of sadness about her.

I thought, *This is the woman in the garden. Good Christ, she's doomed to play out the loss of her child again, and again, and again.*

But I was wrong.

I have learned this, too: I have learned that we are not *doomed* to anything. I have learned that we move, and that we change.

Again I said to the woman, "I'm sorry. I didn't know," and I stepped back into the living room. I do not like watching the grief of anyone. She came to the doorway. She had her baby again. She was nursing it; she was smiling; her baby was cooing delightedly, a nipple in its mouth. That mouth was its only feature. It had a face like a skin of tapioca pudding, and tiny, pink hands that kneaded at its mother's breast, as a kitten does.

I backed away, toward the front door, ten feet across the room. "I am so sorry," I said. The woman's very pleasant smile grew a little broader, even more pleasant, and I realized that she was telling me I had no reason to be sorry, that she had a kind of happiness, after all. But I said again, "I'm so sorry," because I *was* sorry, because I supposed that I had interrupted something eternal and inviolate.

I still itched abominably, but I tried to ignore it as I backed toward the front door. I reached behind myself and touched the doorknob, grabbed it, turned it, pulled the door open. I watched the woman go back into her room. Then I stepped out, into the hallway, and closed the door softly behind me.

To my left, down the hallway toward the stairs, a drunken, middle-aged man with an unruly mop of grayish-brown hair was lurching toward me, snorting and cursing and belching all at the same time. He hit the far wall, glanced off it, like a lopsided cue ball, kept coming at me.

He was saying this:

"You—" snort, belch—"mis-er-able bastard, you mis-er-able bastard—" snort, belch—"that's my *mo*ther's room, you stay *out* of my *mo*ther's—" snort, belch—"room, mis-er-able bastard, mis-er-able bastard—" And he fell at my feet, face-down, with one

hand around my left ankle. He continued snorting a
while, and belching, though in a muted way. Then he
fell silent. I turned him over. It was an act of kindness.
I thought if he vomited he would suffocate in it. I
propped him up on his right side, and after a minute
or two he started gurgling again. Little, cooing noises
came from his throat. I noticed he had a cut on his
nose, that one eye had been blackened recently.

His eyes fluttered open. "Whatchoo doin' here?"
he managed. "Whatchoo doin' in my mother's
room?"

I sat him up, propped him against the wall near the
door to Apartment 506. "I didn't know," I said.

He coughed. The smell of a half-digested whiskey
and wine mix wafted over me. He said, "You got—
you got a hundred rooms you can stay in here; why
you . . . gotta stay in my mother's room?"

"I didn't know it was your mother's room."

He belched.

"And I didn't mean to disturb her," I said.

Another belch.

"I'm sorry if I disturbed her."

He belched once again. A rolling triple belch.
Then he passed out. I grabbed him under the arms,
took him into Apartment 506, put him on the couch
with his hands folded on his stomach and his head to
the right, toward the center of the room. Another act
of kindness.

He was her son.

And I had brought him to her.

I saw her appear in the bedroom doorway, the

baby at her breast. I watched her take two hesitant steps into the room.

And I watched her smile fade when she saw what I had brought her.

And I knew at once that I had done something terribly wrong.

I shook my head. I said, yet again, "I'm sorry; I'm so sorry." I don't believe that she heard me. She let go of the faceless infant she was holding to her breast, and for the barest fraction of a second it clung by the mouth to her nipple. Then it thudded to the floor, soaked in, like water, as Phyllis had, at Art's apartment. And was gone.

The woman did not take her eyes off the man I had put on the couch. She went to the platform rocker, sat in it, folded her arms at her belly, put her knees and her feet together.

That patina of grief was heavy around her now, as if the air itself had become discolored by it.

I watched her a long time. The man did not wake. She did not weep. I do not believe that she could weep. I don't know. It's possible that they are both still there—he on the couch, she in the platform rocker nearby, while small animals run about in the walls and drunks have a good time on the floors below.

I had done this: I had stolen her happiness from her, small as it was.

CHAPTER TEN

I took a bus to Madeline's house on East 85th Street. I needed answers desperately, and I thought she could provide them.

Her house was dark, except for one light visible from the street, the lamp in her parlor, and when I knocked, I heard a distant, "Come in, Mr. Cray."

I went in.

I stopped just inside the entrance to the parlor and saw her in her Morris chair. She had her back turned to me; she was facing a window.

"Madeline?" I said.

"Hello." It was a soft and trembling whisper.

I came forward a few steps and saw her reflection in the window, on a background of darkness. She was seated with her feet flat on the floor and her knees apart slightly. Her hands were on the arms of the chair, and her head was back. She was dressed in something dark, something black, and though I couldn't see her face clearly, I sensed that she'd been crying.

"I need to talk to you, Madeline."

"Talk, then."

I noticed, again as a reflection from the window, that she had something on her lap, and I stepped closer to see what it was. It was Gerald's softball. She was caressing it with her left hand.

I began, "Madeline, I need your help—"

And she cut in, "I can't help you." I heard anger in her voice, and resignation.

I said again, with emphasis now, "I need your help."

"I don't even *want* to help you, Mr. Cray." She looked down at Gerald's softball. "Even if I could. And I can't."

"Madeline, I'm confused. I thought you—"

"Thought what? Thought I was some kind of guru, a spiritual Mr. Fixit?!"

"Sorry."

"I'm just a lonely, middle-aged woman, and I don't give a *damn* about you and your problems. That's the way it is, Mr. Cray, and if you don't like it, you can go piss up a rope." There was a brief pause; I heard a grisly, little chuckle come from her, and then she continued, "But I'll tell you this, Mr. Cray— I've figured one thing out sitting here, watching the daylight pass me by. I've figured one thing out. If you can't lick 'em, join 'em."

"My God, that's no answer—"

"Oh, blow it out your ass!" And I heard yet another grisly chuckle; I was seeing a side of her I had never expected to see. *"You* know what it's all about; at least you *think* that you do. And I do, too. So tell me—why not? Why not? What *difference* does it make anyway?"

"I don't understand," I said. "If you can see them, and hear them, and touch them—"

"I'm not *one* of them, Mr. Cray. I *need* to be one of them, you understand, to be *with* them; it's very simple, to be *with* Gerald, I need to be *one* of *them.* You can understand that, I'm sure. You're not a moron. The same thing applies to to you and Phyllis Pellaprat—I'm sure you've figured that out by now."

I said nothing. She went on, "Scares you, does it? Sure it scares you."

"I haven't thought about it—"

"Yeah, and the pope's not Catholic." Another chuckle. "Say that Phyllis was a fish, Mr. Cray. Say she lived in the Atlantic Ocean and you had this same, great overpowering need for her. Say that. Do you think you'd be content merely to put on your little swimming trunks and go frolic in the surf with her for a while? Of course not. You'd become a fish, if you could."

"That's absurd."

"So? I have a right to be absurd. I'm grieving. I need to be absurd."

"I'm going to find her, Madeline."

"Of course you are, but as I told you before, you may not like what you find."

I sighed. "Where's your son?" I asked.

She looked around at me suddenly from the chair, and I saw that her face was red and puffy from weeping. But she was no longer weeping. She had a look of intense, stiff resignation about her; her eyes were wide. She whispered at me, her voice a tight, high hiss: "Gerald is *dead*, Mr. Cray, My son is *dead!*"

At the Hammet Mausoleum, Halloween, 1965

"It'll knock you right over, Sam," I said as he strained to free the screw from the hinge.

"So I'll hold my nose." He got the screw out, it was the second one of three in the top hinge. He put the screw in his pocket.

I shook my head. "You're gonna puke your guts out, I know it." He started working at the third screw. "I did."

He looked oddly at me. "Yeah. When?"

"When my little cousin drowned. You remember. She was laid out in an open casket and when I went past her I got this little whiff of formaldehyde. I mean, if it was from a frog in a jar in biology or something, it would have been different. But it wasn't. It was someone I knew."

"So you puked your guts out?" He guffawed.

I shook my head. "No. Just a little. A little bile or whatever."

He got the third screw out, started on the bottom hinge. "Well, I smelled it before, too," he said as he worked at the hinge. "You remember, that woman that got shot by her husband. She smelled of it a little. Course we didn't look long 'cuz we heard someone comin'—''

"You're lyin', aren't you, Sam?"

He popped the cover off the top screw on the bottom hinge. He said nothing.

"Aren'tcha?" I coaxed.

"Course not," He said.

"You get a little whistle in your voice when you lie, Sam, did you know that?"

"That's bullshit." He twisted the screwdriver hard counterclockwise. "Damn it to hell!" he muttered.

"Want me to try it?" I asked.

"No. Shit, I can get it."

"You woulda told me before if you'd really done something like that, Sam."

"Okay, okay," he said. He smiled. "Got it," he said, and held up the first screw to the bottom hinge.

"Just tell me if you're lying or not, Sam. What's the big deal? So you lied."

"So I lied." He was clearly angry now. "So I fuckin' lied. You never lied?"

I decided to change the subject. "How we gonna get it outa there, Sam?"

"What? The casket?"

"Sure. It's heavier than shit, you know. I was a pallbearer once—"

"We'll slide it out."

I shrugged. "Maybe, maybe not."

"Chickenshit!"

"Yeah, I am, Sam."

"You'll grow up to be an insurance salesman or something."

"No, Sam. A photographer."

"Well, then, open your *eyes*." He started on the second screw.

CHAPTER ELEVEN

I remember going to a seance when I was twenty-one or twenty-two and sure that I was pretty good at all those things that required a special kind of "sensitivity" (I wrote poetry, got it on with a succession of older women—who were supposed to enjoy young, sensitive men—did a lot of walking at night on dark, country roads, wept, longed for insanity; looking back on all of it now, I think that I must have been pretty much of a bore), and at this seance there were several very attractive teen-age girls, two middle-aged women—one a poet with three names, the other the wife of a well-known Bangor businessman—and my brother, Ike, who has since gone off to Yakima, Washington, where he works as a logger.

The poet with three names—names I cannot for the life of me remember, so we shall call her Pat—had set up the seance. She was in her early forties, a tad chunky, with short, black hair, moist lips, and an almost perfect nose. She spoke well, with the barest trace of a Boston accent. She must have cultivated it, because she told me that she'd been born and raised in Brooklyn. She was, I would much later come to realize, the quintessential "older woman," at least for me—not quite "appealing," but interesting, intelligent, sensitive, of course, and completely unattainable. Which is precisely why I'd accepted her invitation to the seance.

We seated ourselves at a big, round, wooden table. Introductions were made; I knew most of the people there, except for one of the teen-age girls, whose name was Loretta, and who, I was told, "writes poetry, too," and was just then beginning to acquire the kind of earnest, intense sensitivity that I had acquired several years before and which had become my trademark.

At my request, the lights were dimmed, and candles brought in on three silver candle holders. We joined hands. Pat was to my right, and the sensitive teen-ager, Loretta, to my left. It was an arrangement I very much appreciated, and on which I planned to capitalize completely.

I said, "We must all be very, very quiet now," exactly as if I knew what I was doing. I felt Loretta's hand tighten. She was fifteen, maybe sixteen, no older, and pretty. Her hand was soft, very warm. Pat's hand was stiff and cool.

I went on, "I feel the presence of several destructive spirits." A pause. "We have no place here for you," I continued. Loretta's hand tightened further. Pat said, "Perhaps this isn't something we should be fooling around with, Abner." I smiled a small, secretive smile. She looked very concerned. I liked that. I was enjoying myself. What great entertainment the dead were.

Night on East 84th Street. 8:30. Someone who didn't care much if I knew he was there was walking a couple of yards behind me.

I glanced back. He was shorter than I am by at least half a foot, and thin, and very nervous. And he was carrying a good-sized blade, which he was holding point-down. "I have a gun," I said.

"Yeah? And I got *her*pes!" he said, chuckling.

I quickened my pace, glanced back again, very briefly; I saw that he had quickened his pace, too. "Gimme a break!" I said, and was surprised at how *annoyed* I sounded, as if he were no more than a Jehovah's Witness trying to give me religion, or an Amway salesman, or someone passing out invitations to a massage parlor. "Because I really do not have the time to mess with you!" I went on.

He said nothing; I picked up my pace so I was moving at close to a run.

We were near the corner of East 85th Street and Third Avenue, and there were a few other people around—across East 85th Street, a hooker was strolling;

near her were a couple of young white guys wearing baseball caps, jeans, and plaid jackets.

The man just behind me said, "You come to an alley, you just go in, okay?"

"No," I said. "I don't think so."

Half a block away there was a bar called Smitty's. If I'd had a choice, I wouldn't have gone anywhere near it, but I ran for it now, fully expecting that because I was quite a bit taller and probably a lot healthier than the man behind me, I'd quickly outdistance him.

I was right. I got to *Smitty's* several seconds ahead of him and pushed my way through a crowd of six or seven people just outside the door, and then I was inside.

It was not what I would have hoped for.

"Get the fuck outa here!" one of the patrons said. He was a very large black man with a round, smooth face and big, expressive eyes: "You get the fuck outa here, *now!*" Several of the other patrons—a mix of male and female—chorused him.

I coughed. The air was gray with what I supposed was cigarette smoke, and it bothered me. I pleaded, "There's a man following me. A man with a knife!"

The big man laughed. "He ain't followin' you no more, honky!"

And I heard, just behind me: "You is really a dumb ass, ain'tchoo?!"

I nodded, felt my knees begin to quiver, said, "Yes, I am."

"Whatchoo doin' down here anyway?"

"Looking for someone," I answered, "looking for a woman." And there was general, easy laughter in the room.

The man behind me said, "Yeah, well, ain't we all," paused, went on, "See that phone over there?"

I looked to my left, my right; I saw a phone booth against the wall to the left of the bar; the bartender was looking at me, something close to disgust on his face. "I see the phone," I said.

"Good. You go on over there, put your dime in, and phone the cops. Go ahead."

"No. I don't think I want to do that."

"But I *want* you to do it," said the man behind me, and I felt the point of his knife against my lower spine.

I said, "Could you tell me why?"

"Cuz I'm *fair*," he answered.

I walked the length of the bar, felt several dozen pairs of eyes on me, heard laughter, heard someone—the bartender, I think—cursing under his breath. Several people pushed half-heartedly at me, taking me by surprise—I tilted away from them, nearly fell, which elicited quick laughter. I stopped in front of the phone booth, looked at the bartender, who was looking at me, and said, "You're going to allow this?"

He looked down at the bar, swiped at it with a white cloth, and shook his head in disbelief. I stepped into the phone booth, searched my pockets, and came up with several quarters, a few pennies, but no dimes. I looked at the man with the knife. It was the first time I'd been able to see his face well. He was in his early twenties, perhaps his late teens, with a broad, flat nose, full lips, and high cheekbones. He wore his hair very short, and his Adam's apple bobbed when he talked. I asked him if he had a dime.

"I ain't got no dime," he said, and he sounded confused. He looked around, at the bartender, at the big man, at the other people near the bar, "Hey, any you gotta dime?"

The big man shook his head. "I ain't got no dime," he said, shrugged, went on, "We ain't none of us got no *dimes* at all?" And he grinned. "But you can use a quarter—the phone company'll let you use a quarter, and if you ask, they'll send you the difference in the mail." Another grin; his teeth were large, white, shiny. "Why don'tchoo use a quarter?"

I nodded. "Yes," I said. "Okay," and took the receiver off the hook, held it to my ear, put a quarter in. Nothing. I looked at the man with the knife, nodded at the phone. "I don't think it works."

He said, "It don't work?" Another grin. "I thought it worked." His grin faded. He shrugged. "Guess you can't call the police, then. Guess you gonna have to come outa there—come on outa there."

I stepped out of the phone booth; he backed away from me. His knife was pointing at the floor. He held it up, near his face, so the blade was between his eyes, pointing up: "Hey, man, you wanta *see* somethin'?"

I took my wallet out. "No." I offered him the wallet. My hand was quivering. He looked at the wallet as if confused, "I don't want your fuckin' money; I don't want to buy nothin'; I ain't in need of buyin' nothin'. Hey—" He looked around, at the bartender, at the big man. "Hey, any you in needa buyin' somethin'?" The bartender shook his head; the big man shook his head; all of them—about twenty of them—shook their heads: "No," they said, nearly in unison, "we ain't in need a buyin' nothin'."

I noticed that nobody at the bar had a drink, that all the bottles on display were empty.

The man with the knife looked back; he grinned, said again—the knife still pointing upward, midway between his eyes—"You wanta *see* something?" and he pushed the knife hard into his forehead so it was buried to the hilt, and then twisted it, still grinning, right, left, and pulled it out. It was clean. He said, "Never could do that before; can do it now—neat, huh?"

"Jesus," I breathed.

"Hurts a little, hurts just a little; little twinge, still tied in they tell me, still tied in, can't help the hurt, still tied in, but it's kind of a talent, you know, kind of a wild talent, putting the knife in, pulling it out, still hurts, still hurts, a little twinge, not bad, I like it," and he did it once again, his grin broader now, an almost sexual grin, and I watched, open-mouthed, and the bartender watched, and the big man watched; all of them watched. And when he was done, there was applause in the room, a few cheers, and the big man got off his stool, came over and announced that the thing the man with the knife had done was "kid's stuff," that he was going to do something "even better, wait and see," and he took the knife from the young man (who scowled), pulled his own shirt up, and made a very deep incision in his belly, a square incision six inches wide, reached in and withdrew several feet of gut, which he held up for all to see. "How about *that!*" he said proudly, "How about *that!*" And a woman came over. She was in her twenties, with long, well-coiffed hair, and a hard, much-used look about her: "Gimme that!" she said, and the big man stuffed his intestines back, handed her the knife, tucked his shirt in. She grinned, gouged an eyeball out, popped it into her mouth—

"Oh, for Christ's sake!" I breathed.

But they weren't listening to me. The woman got louder applause than the big man, a few more cheers, so she did the same thing with the other eyeball. And I heard, above the cheers and the applause:

"Aaaaahhhhhhhhnnnnneeerrr?!"

I stopped breathing for a moment, and looked frantically around the room. There were several women there, ten at least, most of them Phyllis' age or close to it, and because of the haze and the darkness there, and the background noise, I had trouble locating the source of the voice.

But I did locate it. After a few moments.

She was on the opposite side of the room, in a

doorway, under a sign that read LADIES/GENTS. She was naked, and her face was obscured by darkness and smoke; she had her arms extended. I started for her. She stepped back. I yelled, ''Phyllis, please, wait—'' and ran toward her. She stepped back again. And was gone.

CHAPTER TWELVE

I met a man on East 82nd Street who was gay and wanted me to spend the night with him. His name was Jerry Swan, *Dr*. Jerry Swan—pediatrician—and he said that he maintained a loft apartment in a former electrical parts warehouse near Second Avenue. I offered him fifty dollars to let me spend the night in the apartment, *sans* sex, and he accepted, certain, I think, that he'd be able to swing me around and have some fun.

I was feeling very bad. I was beginning to doubt where I was exactly, literally in what world I was, and I trusted no one. Which meant that I trusted everyone, of course. Or had no choice but to trust everyone. Even Dr. Jerry Swan, gay pediatrician.

We were going to walk to his apartment. He explained, on the way, that he carried a gun. "You

come here without a gun, you're a goddamned fool!''
he said. I conceded, very willingly, that I was a fool.
"What *are* you doing down here, anyway?'' he went
on.

"I'm looking for someone,'' I answered.

"Oh? Who?''

"A woman.''

"Too bad.'' He grinned. "Maybe I know her.
Maybe I can help.''

"No. I don't think so. She's a black woman. Her
name's Phyllis.''

He shook his head. "No. Don't think I know any
black women named Phyllis. Sorry. Kind of an odd
name for a black woman, though, don't you think?''

"It's her name,'' I said.

"And she lives around here?''

"I've seen her around here. I saw her at Smitty's.''

He chortled. "Hah, you go to that place and you're
a goddamned fool. Why'd you go in there?''

"I was being chased by a man with a knife,'' I
answered.

He nodded sagely. He was blonde, though his hair
was thinning dramatically, lean, and he walked
gracefully, not at all effeminately; his stride betrayed
a certain power. "Yes, sir,'' he said, "we do get lots
of people chasing other people with knives. Unfor-
tunate, but true. Why was he chasing you?''

I thought a moment. "Out of habit, I think.''

"And you say he chased you into Smitty's?''

"Yes.''

"Bad place, Smitty's.''

"Yes, I found out."

"You go in there, you're a goddamned fool."

I was getting a little nervous. We made a turn onto East 83rd Street, headed toward Second Avenue. "Tell me who you are," I said.

"I told you that," he said.

"And if I don't believe you?"

"Your beliefs are no concern of mine, my friend." He nodded to indicate the end of the street. I looked. There was a large, windowless brick building there. "My place," He said. "I've lived in it for quite some time now. Thirty years now."

"Thirty years?" I was incredulous. He didn't look to be much past forty.

"Thirty years. Maybe thirty-five. I don't know; you lose track. You mark time; you lose track."

I stopped walking. He went on a few yards, stopped, looked back. "And you want to know what I *don't* miss at all? I don't miss those goddamned little kids pissing all over me."

"Good Christ!" I whispered.

He turned, started walking again. "Don't miss little kids pissing all over me one tiny bit," he ranted, "one tiny bit, not one tiny bit, no; you coming there, you! You coming? You're welcome; show you a good time; you're welcome at my house—" Which was the last I saw of him because I turned and walked quickly away.

I met an older man dressed in a brown turtle-neck sweater and gray slacks on East 85th Street. He called himself Mr. Winchell and he was walking a small dog. He said the dog's name was Peaches: "After my wife," he said. "Her name was Peaches."

I told him that I was looking for a place to eat.

He asked, "What kind of place?"

"Any place," I answered. We were walking together toward Second Avenue, Peaches trailing behind on a leash. "Anyplace at all," I went on.

"Do you like Chinese?"

"Not particularly."

"German? French?"

"It doesn't matter."

"Irish, then? Stewed potatoes, corn bread?"

"Anything."

"We're very big on eating." His voice was getting louder. "We're so damned *big* on eating; we *love* to eat: we eat Chinese; we eat French; we eat Irish, English, too; we *love* to eat—Italian, Spanish, it's all the same to us—right Peaches?" He yanked hard on the leash; Peaches whimpered. "We do surely love to eat; we're very *big* on eating!" He was shouting now, and beginning to gesticulate wildly. It wasn't doing Peaches any good; he was being yanked this way and that as if he amounted to nothing at all. The man ranted on, "We eat Chinese; we eat French; we eat Japanese—it doesn't matter to us!" Peaches was now all but flying through the air and squealing in pain at the same time. "Christ," I said, "you're hurting that animal!" But he didn't hear me. I grabbed hold of his arm. It did no good. Wherever his arm went, I went—I was thrown, like Peaches, forward, back, forward again, up several inches, forward.

So I let go of him.

And watched him move off toward Second Avenue that way, yanking his little dog around and ranting about eating Chinese and eating Japanese and eating Irish.

I think that I laughed at him.

I heard "Aaaabnnneerrr!" I turned to my right, looked down a little alley there. I saw Phyllis at the end of the alley, her face obscured, as if she were wearing a kind of yellow veil—and I called to her, "Phyllis, wait for me, please!"

But she didn't.

Not then.

Serena Hitchcock buzzed me up, but would not let me into her apartment.

"I'm not going to let you in, Abner," she said. She had opened her door only a few inches; I could see that she was dressed in a blue robe, and I guessed that I had interrupted her in a bath, or in lovemaking. "I don't even want to talk to you; you make me nervous."

"I know that, Serena. I'm sorry."

"And you don't smell very good. Where have you been?"

I sniffed; I smelled nothing. I supposed that if I did smell bad, I had gotten used to it. I grinned boyishly; I hoped it was charming. "I don't know where I've been, Serena. I need to talk to someone. Anyone. And I thought of you."

"I'm flattered, Abner." She clearly wasn't. "But I am afraid that I have company."

"Oh, I'm sorry. Forgive me."

"Yes. And so you'll have to go away."

I shook my head. "I have no place to go, Serena."

She grimaced. A man's face appeared above her; it was craggy, with a full, dark gray beard, and intelligent blue eyes. He smiled. "Hello," he said. "Do you want something?"

"I, uh—" I began, and faltered.

"Money?" he said. "Is that what you're after?"

"No," I said. "I have money."

"Good," he said, "so do we." And he pulled Serena back and closed the door.

At the Hammet Mausoleum, Haloween, 1965

Sam stopped working at the last screw on the top hinge and nodded at the plastic bag just outside the circle of candles. "Wanta get me a Mallo Cup there, Abner?"

I went over to the bag, peered inside, saw little, because of the darkness, stuck my hand in. I shrugged. "It's empty, Sam."

"The shit it is. I put a half-dozen Mallo Cups in there and I know I didn't eat all of 'em."

I checked the bag again. "You must have, Sam, because the bag is empty."

"Damnit to hell!"

"They'll just rot your teeth out anyway, Sam."

"Yeah, yeah, you sound like my mother, Abner." He began working at the last screw again. He'd been working at it for some time, five minutes, at least.

"Probably rusted, huh, Sam?" I suggested.

"Got it," he said.

"You got it?" I was surprised, apprehensive.

He held the screw up in his fingers. "Got it!" he said again, as if declaring some great victory. He stuck the screw in his pocket, studied the hinges, and the edge of the vault door for a while. Finally, he cursed.

I said, "What's the matter, Sam?" and went over to him.

"This is a fucking waste of time," he said.

"What's a waste of time, Sam?"

"It's not gonna come open. No way, nohow." He nodded at the edge of the vault door, where it joined with the mausoleum wall. "I gotta pry it open somehow, Abner, and I couldn't get even a *pussy* hair in there."

"Yeah," I said, pleased.

"So let's go," he said, and put the tip of the screwdriver to the opening between the vault door and the wall.

"Yeah," I said again, and started for the area where Flora's skull was, so I could begin cleaning the place up. I heard a metallic popping sound behind me, then I heard Sam yell, "I got it, goddamnit! I got it!"

I turned, looked. The vault door was hanging open from its left hand edge, and one end of Joe Hammet's silver casket was visible. "Put the door back, Sam," I pleaded. "Why don'tcha just put the door back and we'll clean the place up and get outa here, okay?"

He didn't answer. He reached into the vault, got a hand-hold on the coffin, pulled. I heard a brief scraping sound, then he called to me, "Shit, Abner—you gonna help me with this or what?"

I said nothing. I took a couple of steps toward him, stopped, saw that he'd gotten the casket several inches out of the vault. He tugged at it again. It moved a few more inches. He shouted, "For Christ's sake, Abner—"

"Okay," I said sullenly. "Okay." And I went to the other side of the coffin, reached, got hold of the handle.

"On three," Sam said.

"Yeah," I said.

"One-two-three-tug!"

We tugged together. Hard. The casket moved nearly a foot out of the vault.

"On three," Sam said again.

"On three," I said, and realized that I was getting into the spirit of things.

"One-two-" He paused, took a breath. "Three." We tugged. Harder this time. We got the casket at least three more feet out of the vault. Far enough, in fact, that it would have been off-balance and fallen to the floor, had the ceiling of the vault not been only a few inches from the top of the casket.

"Again," Sam said.

"Again," I said.

"One," he said, "Two, and—"a pause; a breath—
"three!" We tugged. The casket all but sailed out of
that vault. It hit the cement floor with a low, but very
powerful whumping sound, like two cars hitting
each other at slow speed, and seemed to go on shud-
dering from the impact for at least a minute. Sam and
I stayed quiet while this was happening. I think we
both entertained the idea that old Joe Hammet was
shaking himself awake.

And, at last, Sam said, "Criminey!"

"Yeah!" I said.

We knelt over the casket, then, in unison, as if we
had come to pray at it. We fingered it; it was made of
metal, and it felt like metal, though it was very cold.
Sam said, nodding to indicate the perimeter of the
casket, "It's screwed together, Abner. It's screwed
together."

"Unscrew it," I said.

"Yeah." And he started to work at what looked
like half a hundred screws. A little, lopsided smile
appeared on his lips as he started the work, and
as he progressed with it, that smile increased, got as
broad as the smile of a clown, until, when the last
screw came out, he was literally grinning from ear to
ear.

So was I.

He said, "The grand opening, Abner!"

"This is it!" I said.

And together we lifted the lid on Joe Hammet's
coffin.

We did not look in until we'd put the lid down, in

front of the coffin, near Flora's skull. We stood facing each other, eyes locked, for a few moments; then we lowered our heads and looked in.

Sam said, "So what?"

I said nothing.

"So what, Abner? So what? So we got a dead man here."

Still I said nothing.

"Might as well be looking at *hamburger*."

"Yeah," I said.

"Might as well be looking at a piece of chicken, right, Abner? A piece of white meat."

"Yeah."

"Meat that stinks, too, right, Abner?"

I nodded. "Yeah."

"White meat chicken with *hair*, besides."

"Yeah," I said. "White meat chicken all dressed up."

"Tennessee Tuxedo."

"Let's put him back, okay, Sam?"

"Yeah."

"Poor old guy," I said.

"Yeah," Sam said.

We got the coffin lid and put it back. We lifted the coffin, amidst lots of quiet groaning and cursing, and stuck it back in the vault. We put the door on, screwed the screws in tight, put the caps in place; then we gathered up Flora's skull, and the candles, and the wrappers that the Mallo Cups came in. And we left the mausoleum.

Just outside—it had stopped raining and some stars

were visible—Sam said, "Did he look like he was smiling, Abner?"

"Yeah, I guess," I said. "But maybe they all do. Maybe they can't help it."

"Maybe," he said.

"Like maybe their muscles freeze," I said. "So they just keep on smiling forever and ever."

"Could be," he said.

" 'Cuz what they got to smile about, Sam?"

"What have any of us got to smile about?" Sam said.

"Being happy," I said.

"Yeah," Sam said. "Being happy."

And we went to our homes.

CHAPTER THIRTEEN

I was asked no questions at a hotel called The Emerson, on East 115th. The counter man—short, frail, black, dressed in a ragged, white, button-down shirt and blue, rayon pants—looked very properly bored. He took a week's rent in advance, gave me a key to Room 432, told me not to vomit on the bed—"Or I throw you out, okay?" I said okay, and went up four flights of crumbling cement fire stairs to my room.

I had managed to catch a bite to eat at a diner on East 109th. Not a big meal—I ate only because I knew I should. Half a grilled cheese sandwich, a full cup of coffee.

Room 432 of the Emerson Hotel is small, and nasty. It's painted blue and gold; the bottom half is

blue, the top half gold. The paint is nearly as old as
the hotel, probably. When traffic is heavy on East
115th Street, the building vibrates sympathetically
and the paint flecks off here and there, especially on
the wall that faces the street, where there is some
kind of moisture problem.

The floor has a large, threadbare, red oriental rug
on it—from Woolworth's, I imagine, circa 1960—
and there is a wrought-iron, floor-standing lamp, no
shade, alongside a green, one-drawer writing desk
near the door. The bed is wrought-iron as well, the
mattress lumpy and soft. A Gideon Bible rests on a
small, dark wood nightstand close by.

My first night in this room, I woke early, at about
2:00, and found Phyllis standing naked beside the
bed. And when I reached for her, she put one leg
over me, straddled me, kissed me.

And whispered, "We had some good times, didn't
we, Abner?"

I whispered back, "We did, Phyllis."

"Lots and lots and lots of good times." She still
was whispering. "Lots and lots of good times." The
yellowish glare from street lamps on East 115th Street
was illuminating her left side, and I ran my fingers
across her cold cheek, down her shoulder, her breast,
her hip.

I felt her shiver under my fingers, not as if in
pleasure, but as if in pain. I said, "I'm sorry," my
voice low and quivering, and I realized that somewhere
deep inside me fear was trying hard to get out.

She straightened so the glare of the streetlamps shone nicely on her torso. she put her hands behind her head; raised her head; her mouth hung slightly open.

And the light on her brightened, as if the sun had risen and its light was on her, not the glare of the street lamps.

She slid off me, off the bed, up onto the sill, and into that light, out, over the edge of the window.

And when I went to the window, I saw the glare of street lamps on streets wet from a quick rain, a taxi making its way west, some people here and there. And I saw Art, too; he looked briefly up at me, just long enough that I could see the overwhelming fear on him. And then the people around him—the casually dressed woman, the small boy, the young black man, and several others now, too—hustled him off, around a corner, and he was gone.

I stood at that window for some time. I watched the streets lighten as the sun rose. And I screamed, very loud and very long. Until, at last, the counter man pounded on the door and yelled something about keeping the noise down, that if I belonged in Bellevue, maybe that's where I should put myself.

It was the first time in my life—I believe—that I had done something completely spontaneous, something uncontrollable, and it felt incredibly good, as good as sex. So I did it again. And the counter man pounded louder and stronger. And after a few moments, I fell silent.

I opened the door. The counter man said, ''What're you—outa your fuckin' head?''

''I'm sorry,'' I told him.

''You want a fix, you go get one; just don't bring the man down on my hotel, okay?''

I nodded. ''Yes. I'm sorry.''

''That's truer than you know,'' he said, turned, and went back downstairs.

CHAPTER FOURTEEN

Several nights later, I made my way into a small park on Second Avenue, near East 77th Street. It was 10:00 or 10:30, and there were only a few people there—a couple of old men, a bag lady feeding the pigeons crowding around her, two young guys, one of them asking the occasional passerby if he wanted any dope. It was a typical New York City park scene, and I took a little solace from it, because it was so comfortably mundane.

I put myself on a bench near the edge of the park, stuck my hands into my coat pockets, and lowered my head. Almost at once, I felt someone sit down beside me. I kept my head lowered; out of the corner of my eye, I could see the person beside me. It was a woman, and she was dressed as Phyllis used to dress, in fake, white mink and green silk and high, white boots.

But I was frightened and did not want to look at her.

One of the guys selling dope came over. I looked up at him. He smiled, his mouth full of gray and rotted teeth. "Hey, you looking to get high, man?" he asked.

I shook my head.

"How about the lady?"

Again I shook my head.

"It's good stuff."

"No. Thank you, no," I said.

He shrugged. "Okay," he said, and walked off.

I looked at the woman sitting next to me. She was a white woman, in her mid-forties, I guessed.

"Hi," she said.

I said, "Hi."

"Round the world, fifty dollars; straight fuck, twenty-five."

"No, thank you."

She hesitated. "A few quick feels, right here—ten bucks; that's pretty good."

"No, I don't think so."

She stood. "You smell anyway," she said.

"Shit," I said. And she went away.

I sat alone on that bench for quite some time. I heard the noise of traffic decrease; I felt cold, late evening air come in, and I became aware that the park itself was emptying. And then a cop came over.

"Got some ID?" he asked.

"Yes," I told him.

"Uh-huh. You want to look at me when I'm talking to you?!"

I looked at him. He was a very typical New York cop—stocky, with short, black hair, a square face, and a distinct no-nonsense, I-don't-like-this-job-any-more-than-you-like-me attitude. "You want to show it to me, then?"

I got my wallet out, handed him my driver's license and a Visa Card. He studied them both a good long time and finally handed them back. "What are you doing here, Mr. Cray?"

"Sitting," I answered.

"I can see that."

"Resting. I'm tired."

"You have no home?"

"Yes. But I like it here. Am I doing anyone any harm?"

"You want to stand up, please, Mr. Cray?"

"Why?"

"Because I asked you to."

"I don't count that as reason enough."

"Stand up, please."

I stood.

"Raise your arms, please."

I raised my arms. He frisked me. "Okay, you can sit down."

He nodded to his left, toward East 78th Street. "I'm going to walk down the block there, Mr. Cray. I'm going to go over to Second Avenue, to East 79th; then I'm coming back here. I walk fast. I'll be back in fifteen minutes. And if I find you here, we'll go through this little routine all over again, only I won't come up empty-handed. You understand what I'm saying to you?"

I nodded. "Yes, I understand."

"Good boy. We like to keep our city clean, Mr. Cray." And he walked off. I waited ten minutes, then got up and started out of the park. I passed him on the way out. He nodded at me, and I nodded back. And I saw Art DeGraff across the street, at the corner of East 78th and Second Avenue. I stopped walking.

"Keep a move on," the cop said behind me.

I glanced back at him, then at Art again, who was crossing the street now. He had apparently been waiting for the light to change.

The cop said, "Keep on moving, Mr. Cray, or you and I will have another go-round."

I walked. I did not believe that Art had seen me; he was in the glare of a street lamp, and I was in relative darkness. His back was to me now, at any rate; and he was walking at a casual pace, as if he had nowhere in particular to go.

I was a good half-block away. I started to call out. "Art—" I said, and stopped. And I saw what I had not seen seconds earlier. I saw the people around him. To his right, the young woman in a gray pleated skirt and red-checkered blouse. Beside her, a child, perhaps four years old, who had ragged, blonde hair and was wearing blue overalls and a white short-sleeved shirt. The young black man, cigarette in hand, was there, to his left. And there were people in front of Art, too, though I could see little more than their heads bobbing.

"Art! I called, because I suddenly, and strangely, felt protective of him, as if what he had done to Phyllis, and to Stacy, didn't matter any more, as if the people near him meant him harm, and I wanted to help him, though it was a feeling that lasted only long enough for me to yell to him. I got no answer, and he continued walking. The woman looked around, though, very briefly. The little group was passing a well-lighted storefront, so I had a good view of her. She had short, dark hair, dead gray eyes, round cheeks—the sort of woman one sees on detergent commercials—and she had a little smile on her lips. A kind of Mona Lisa smile. *We're taking care of him now!* it said.

I watched them until they disappeared around a corner, down East 79th Street, I guessed.

And then the streets began filling up.

CHAPTER FIFTEEN

People in coats and hats, people carrying umbrellas, carrying briefcases, carrying babies on their backs, and people lugging groceries home; people arm-in-arm; people in polo shirts, in hand-me-down dresses, in gray suits; people laughing, sweating; people carrying tennis rackets, showing off new shoes, coaxing youngsters to come along; people looking in shop windows.

Old people who had trouble walking, old people jogging, old couples smiling affectionately at one another, as lovers do.

Teenage couples with their hands on each other's rear ends; boys on street corners learning about lust.

It was daytime.

And Manhattan's streets were crowded, as they always are then.

But it was not daytime. It was a little after 2:00 A.M.; it was 2:15, and a waning gibbous moon should have been setting behind me.

I heard then, from just to my right, "Hello, Abner." I recognized the voice. It was Phyllis' voice. And when I turned, I saw that she was standing beside me, dressed as she always dressed, in fake, white mink and green silk and stacked heel, white boots.

And she was whole. She was as beautiful as I remembered, just as beautiful as I remembered she was.

And she said to me, a soft, pleased smile playing on her lips, her gaze on the crowded streets, "This is *our* city, Abner!"

That was four months ago.

She used to come here, to Apartment 432 of the Emerson Hotel, now and then. I used to hear the clop-clop of her boots on the bare wood floor in the hallway, and I used to listen to the clop-clop get louder as she got closer, and I heard her gentle knock on the door. I listened; I waited. And after a while, she called softly to me, "Abner, please, I love you."

But I stayed away. I sat on the edge of my bed and I stared at the door until she went off. She never stayed long. A minute, no longer. Maybe less. Maybe far less. Perhaps just a second or two.

She has not come here for quite some time, and I miss her.

*   *   *

It is daylight, as it was that morning. The daylight comes and goes—the dead have lots of daylight, apparently, lots and lots of daylight. They have a kind of eternal Land of the Midnight Sun, you might say, which I suppose is very nice for them.

But it scares the hell out of me—it would scare the hell out of anyone, I think.

"This is *our* city, Abner," she said, that last time I saw her.

And I remember I said to myself, *This is wonderful: we'll get a little place, two rooms, three rooms somewhere, a place with a view; we'll go shopping for furniture; we'll find a little deli that sells only the best meats and the best cheeses.*

"This is *our* city, Abner," she said.

People in coats and hats, people carrying umbrellas, carrying briefcases, carrying babies on their backs and people lugging groceries home; people arm-in-arm; people in polo shirts, in hand-me-down dresses, in gray suits; people laughing, sweating; people carrying tennis rackets, showing off new shoes, coaxing youngsters to come along.

All like colorful paintings on a cement wall.

"Oh, Abner," she said that last time we were together, "you cannot see this as we do."

Which was true.

But I said, anyway, "I love you, Phyllis. I want to stay here with you."

"You can," she said.

And that is when I ran from her to where I am now.

Because fear had finally caught up with me.

BOOK FOUR

This land is your land,
   This land is my land,
   From California,
      To the New York Island . . .©
         —Woody Guthrie

CHAPTER ONE

Go to the door, peer through the little security peephole; what do you see? Someone peering back. Someone coming through, sliding through the little security peephole like water, or air—and you think, *What a trick this is*. It's no trick. It's just a matter of seeing. All just a matter of how you look at it.

We put them in the ground, and we do not see that they are smiling.

I have a problem. I look out the window and I don't see much. I see the brick wall of an apartment building next door. It's vacant—most of the buildings on this block are, except for this building, the Emerson Hotel.

And I know that Manhattan is beyond that window, beyond that brick wall. That the World Trade Center is there, the RCA Building, Harlem, the Garment District, Fifth Avenue—all the landmarks, the streets, and the buildings that the living have set up for themselves to move around in. To live in. I know it's all there. But I don't know *whose* it is, you see.

I've gone back to several places since coming here. I've gone to Madeline's house again. It was empty. I peered in through the front windows, went around to the rear, got in through a cellar entrance, and went upstairs. There were a few pieces of furniture remaining, the rococo settee, a floor lamp. And I found Gerald's softball, too. I brought it back with me, in fact, and have it on the green desk near the door.

I have gone to the little cemetery in Brooklyn as well. The place where Phyllis was put. I went back there quite recently, not more than a week or so ago. I don't know what I was expecting to find. I found nothing. Only that ugly green plaque, which was covered by a page from *The Wall Street Journal* blown in from the street. I wept again, but it didn't feel quite the same. So I came back here. I kept my head down and came back here. I was afraid of what I might see, so I kept my head down.

I'm going out again.

Tomorrow I'm going out. I'm going to a restaurant; I'm going shopping for a new pair of shoes. Then I'm going to go to that little cemetery again, and I'm going to stay there a while. That's all I really want of Phyllis, I think—that ugly green plaque, and the sure knowledge that she's several feet beneath it, quite a bit less tidy than I remember her, a little bit less pleasant to the touch than I remember her.

But so predictable, and so secure.

I'm going out, and I'm going to see whose city this is, exactly. Whether it's ours, or whether it's theirs. And I'm going to find out if it really matters, if it really makes a difference.

Stick around.

I'll let you know.

THE END